WICKED FATE

REJECTED FATE TRILOGY
BOOK 3

JEN L. GREY

CHAPTER ONE

The ground shook underneath my feet, or at least, it felt like it did. The first time I'd trusted a vampire, and *this* happened.

Betrayal.

An actual knife to the back would have been preferable to the sting that ached throughout my body and soul.

It reminded me of how I'd felt the day that Reid rejected me.

I scanned the area, noticing that Cassi, Ryker, Briar, Kendric, Xander, and Gage shared varying expressions of disgust, and then glared at Raven as the words she'd spoken moments ago repeated in my head—*I can explain.*

If I weren't so shocked, I'd have been laughing at her audacity.

She'd better explain why vampires had slaughtered Ryker's and my packs besides causing countless other deaths.

No.

Fuck that. That wasn't strong enough.

Hell no.

There wasn't *any* explanation that could justify their actions.

My attention was diverted to the dead vampire that had just been uncloaked at our feet. The Blackwood witch, Cassi, was still leaning over him. This was the first time we'd seen who the enemy attacking us was, and the irony wasn't lost on me that he was the only thing between us and Raven.

The scab on my heart ripped wide open, and the grief I'd been trying to avoid coursed through me. My blood began to boil, and the warmth I'd been feeling from the invisible barrier within me seemed to vanish, leaving me even more raw.

Ryker edged closer to my side, his hand grazing my fur. The familiar buzz sprang to life between us, easing a little of the anger and grief. Even so, neither of us could tear our gaze away from the threat in front of us.

Raven's long, dark hair framed her face and hit her shoulders, emphasizing her pale skin in the twilight. She looked ghostly instead of vampire pale, which seemed fitting because these vampires had found a way to cloak themselves and hide in the shadows like ghosts.

Tugging on his dark locs, Kendric narrowed his milky brown eyes. "Explain what, Raven? That you've known about the attacks and have been lying to us this whole time?"

Her cognac eyes widened, and her crimson lips parted, but no sound came out.

She *had* known this entire time. Though I understood this, the logic didn't make sense to my brain. She'd been attacked, like us. She'd been injured. She'd bled alongside us, and the vampires had shown up at the Shae pack lands and saved us from the attackers.

"We thought you were one of us." Gage's shaggy, dirty-blond hair fell into his darker-than-normal sparkling blue eyes. "Was it all a game to you? Messing with us and my boy's heart?"

"I wasn't...it's not what you think," Raven stammered.

Ryker's fists clenched tight enough that his knuckles blanched. The golden flecks in his eyes vanished as the sheen that showed the witch's magic taking hold glimmered, and the buzz of our connection ebbed. He gritted out, "Then tell us what it is."

Raven hesitated, searching our faces for something I suspected she would never find here—understanding or forgiveness. Her attention landed on Kendric, no doubt hoping their romantic relationship would push him to protect her.

She should've known better.

After everything we'd been through, did she really think any of us would be on her side?

Frankly, her silence was answer enough.

Her shoulders finally sagged. "I protected you all too." Her voice was strained, almost broken.

A bitter laugh escaped me, sharp and humorless. It channeled all my rage and hurt and felt like sandpaper against my throat and, of course, sounded like I was coughing up a hairball in wolf form.

Briar's head whipped around, her light-copper hair swinging and her jade-green eyes widening as they met mine. Her brows furrowed like she was seeing me for the first time.

I must have come across as unhinged, which made me laugh harder. My ribs shook hard, and the laughter had my injuries on my back legs and sides throbbing so hard it soon stole my breath. Worse, my fur felt weighted down with congealing blood, but at least that meant I was healing. The strange, warm presence inside me that I'd been experiencing ever since my parents' deaths pulsed through my body in time with the vibrations of the invisible barrier around us.

Lifting a hand in my direction, Xander shook his head, his tan skin flushed with anger. "I'm in agreement with her, and I don't even need to pack-link to know how she feels. You expect us to say *thank you*? You knew who killed our pack and kept it from us."

A deep snarl came from the left, where Bruce stood over Reid's frail body. His sharp green eyes were full of fury, and drops of blood dotted his salt-and-pepper head. "Don't forget how she and the vampires showed up to *protect* my pack after they slaughtered half of them."

I took a shaky breath, filling my nose and lungs with the stench of copper, and looked at all the wolf shifter bodies that lay dead at my feet.

The thirty-year-old shifter from the Blackwood pack kept her hands pressed against Reid's neck, trying to stop the bleeding like Cassi had instructed. Her face had turned an ashy shade. At least thirty dead bodies littered the ground, and there would have been a lot more if the magical barrier separating us from the shadows—er, vampires— hadn't been created.

We now knew who our *real* enemy was.

Vomit burned the back of my throat as I realized how many lives had been taken because we'd included the vampires in our plans. A heavy rock seemed to sink into my stomach, which churned even harder.

The dead bodies of at least twenty Blackwood pack members lay spread around the clearing, with a few more dragged partially into the woods. Each one had their throat ripped out the way a wolf would do it. However, wounds from vampire claws were very similar to those made by wolves' teeth, so that made sense.

The only lingering question was... how in the *hell* had they managed to smell like wolf shifters?

Five more wolves were in poor condition, with deep scratches down their chests and arms, though Reid's injuries were the worst of the ones still alive.

When my gaze landed on Perry, my heart squeezed. He and my father had always been friends. Tears burned my eyes, and my wolf snarled.

She didn't want to look weak, especially in front of our enemy.

A rush of footsteps sounded in the distance, and the warm magic thrumming against my skin ebbed as if the barrier had vanished.

Someone's coming, I linked with Briar. *And the barrier has come down.*

Once again, her head snapped in my direction, and she tilted it as if she were examining me. Still, she said, "The vampires may be returning."

"There's no reason to think they're here now, especially with the barrier up." Ryker exhaled loudly. "Let's not get everyone riled up." He locked eyes with me.

Shit. They couldn't hear it.

Gesturing to me, Briar rolled her shoulders back. "Don't lecture me. Ember just informed me that the barrier is down and footsteps are rushing our way."

The taller of the other men shook his bald head and held both hands up. "I don't hear them yet, but it'll be more of our pack. They're bringing a few stretchers to carry the injured and the dead back to the neighborhood. We need to gather together in case the vampires attack again."

Relief washed over me, easing my tension but causing the pain from my wounds to ache more pronouncedly as my adrenaline subsided.

Ryker bit his bottom lip and looked at me, his chestnut-brown hair slightly darker from sweat and the darkening sky. "Are you sure about the barrier?" A muscle in his jaw twitched.

Before I could respond, Cassi stood up and gasped. Her golden-brown eyes sparked, and her long black hair swooped behind her like a cloak. Faint swirls of iridescent mist surrounded her, indicating she was using magic. "She's right! The barrier is gone. I can't feel the otherworldly magic anymore."

Kendric snarled and walked toward Raven. "When are they coming back?"

She jerked back faintly, showing barely any movement unless her reactions were watched closely. "I-I'm not sure. If they've retreated, they'll need to regroup. They don't under-stand what's going on with this barrier either or why it keeps protecting us."

"*Us?*" Ryker bared his teeth. "There is no *us*, blood-sucker. Say it again and see what happens."

"Okay, please say it again." Gage clasped his hands together like he was begging. "I want to see you get your throat ripped out."

The footsteps were upon us, and the Blackwood pack would be here minutes later. We didn't have time for a fight.

"As much as I would love to take revenge, we need to be strategic." Kendric pivoted toward Ryker and me.

My heartbeat quickened. Maybe Gage, Kendric, and Xander were over being mad at Ryker for keeping the secret that he had been spelled from them. We needed a united front.

Ryker looked ready to bark orders, but then Kendric said, "Ember, what do you want us to do?"

A sour taste filled my snout, and the warm hope in my chest deflated.

Gage and Xander gazed at me, not Ryker.

Ryker's nostrils flared, but he placed a hand on my neck, and the buzz hummed between us again.

He wasn't angry with me, thank Fate.

I wasn't sure what to do. Someone needed to give us direction, but I didn't want to betray Ryker by stepping up. At the end of the day, Ryker and Briar were the two most important people to me.

Pinching the bridge of her nose, Briar flinched. *How do you want to respond?*

Each second felt like an hour, and I knew I had to answer. *Ask Ryker what his thoughts are.*

Briar nodded and opened her mouth just as twenty people poured into the clearing, carrying ten stretchers.

Mavis Blackwood, Perry's fated mate, rushed to his side and fell to her knees. She placed a hand over his heart and reached for one of his hands, looking like she couldn't believe he was dead.

The woman I'd seen Reid speak to before our mating ceremony ran across the clearing to Reid. Tears streamed down her face as she squatted next to the woman who'd been keeping her hands pressed over his wounds. The woman lifted her hands, and the new girl replaced them with her own to continue the pressure. I hadn't noticed how pale Reid was until his ghastly appearance contrasted with the new woman's dark skin.

That had to be Reid's fated mate.

Two bulky men rushed over to Reid and laid their stretcher next to his body.

The dark-skinned woman turned to Cassi. "Please, help him." Desperation rang in her voice.

"I have, Sun." Cassi moved to her side. "I applied an herbal ointment that will manifest healing if we keep pressure applied. He needs constant pressure until he regains full consciousness."

"So he's going to be okay?" Mavis rasped from where she'd remained seated beside Perry. "I... I can't lose them both."

I whimpered, my insides twisting. I hated that I had doubted the Blackwoods and allowed Reid's rejection to taint my perceptions of all of them. I'd fallen for the illusion the vampires had created. Even though Reid and I hadn't been super close growing up, we used to respect and trust each other.

"None of us wants to lose Reid." Cassi pressed her lips into a firm line. "He'll make it."

Had she said that because she was certain or so we wouldn't spiral into more chaos?

"Is there anything we can do to help?" Briar clutched her shoulder, where she had a deep gash.

"Stay with us." Sun continued to press on Reid's wound as she studied Ryker's and my packs. "Though it pains me to ask right now, with enemies that can hide in thin air, we need to be together. Not separated."

Ryker growled. "I don't think that's a good idea."

"Well, we think it is," Kendric snapped. "So I'm staying with them unless you're going to alpha-will me to do something I don't agree with *again*."

"Same," Gage and then Xander chimed in, making it clear where they stood.

I wanted to shift back into human form and try to calm the rising tension, but being naked in front of Reid would no doubt make Ryker come unglued. Though he shouldn't feel threatened, I had at one time believed Reid was my fated mate and had been willing to complete the bond with him.

"I'm not thrilled about my request either, but we can protect each other. You have a small pack, and half of our pack is injured." Sun kept holding the now crimson cloth on Reid's neck as the two men gently placed him on the stretcher.

"Half your pack?" Briar squeaked. "But only about a quarter of them came here."

The Blackwoods had slightly over a hundred pack members, and about thirty of them had been here with Reid and Perry when we'd been attacked.

"You weren't the only ones under attack." Sun grimaced. "We were attacked in our homes. Do you think I wouldn't have raced here as soon as I realized Reid was in danger? I would've been here to fight beside him, but Mavis and I had to protect the rest of the pack."

The entire Blackwood pack had been attacked. And their strongest wolves had been here, separated from the ones remaining behind because they'd thought *we* might pose a threat.

"What do you think, Ember?" Gage pushed again.

This issue within Ryker's pack had to be resolved, but now wasn't the time or place to do it. However, I didn't want to lead Ryker's pack without his blessing. I lifted my head and bumped into his side, asking him to look away from his packmates and at me.

When our eyes connected, I hoped like hell he understood what I wanted—for him to state his opinion because I trusted him to put aside his personal feelings and make the right call.

The sheen vanished from his eyes, the golden flecks warm as he gave me a tight smile. "Even though it's the last thing in the world I'd want to do, Sun has a point. I agree with my pack. I think we should stay here and work together."

My chest expanded uncomfortably from how much I loved this man. I hated that it'd taken me so long to see him for what he truly was—remarkable underneath that hard exterior. I nodded my head and linked with Briar, *Please tell them I agree with Ryker's decision.*

I love the way you two work together, even in a situation like this. Briar's approval pushed through our bond, causing my chest to ache more. Then she turned her attention to Kendric, Gage, and Xavier. "She agrees with Ryker."

A quick breeze hit my face, and the overly sweet scent of vampire made me want to gag.

Raven.

"Fucking hell," Ryker snarled, and Kendric took off.

I spun around to see what the commotion was about...and stopped dead in my tracks.

CHAPTER TWO

I blinked, hoping like hell that Raven had cloaked herself and, if I just stared harder, I'd see some sort of shadowy iridescent presence there.

All I saw was a swirl of orange and yellow leaves by the huge, bare oak tree. No sheen, no glow.

Nothing.

The vampire bitch had escaped.

As the leaves settled back on the mulchy ground, her scent began to weaken as the wind from her vampire speed stilled.

"She ran." Briar's hands fisted at her sides, and her eyes glowed.

Kendric's long legs pounded the earth, propelling him forward in human form as he ran after the woman who'd not only broken his heart but likely caused lifelong emotional damage.

I charged after him. My legs throbbed, but the cool air eased some of the agony, and my adrenaline fueled me.

The warm, strange magic strengthened inside me, and

my pace quickened, helping me close the short distance between Kendric and me.

The snap of branches and curses behind me told me the others had taken off too—Ryker, Gage, Briar, and Xander. They were all in human form and just as injured as Kendric and me. However, their injuries were all upper body, while most of mine were on my legs, each step feeling as if I were being punched in the gut over and over again.

Wait up, Briar linked, her panic swirling through our link.

I can't, or she'll vanish.

Her frustration charged the bond, and I heard her tell Ryker what I'd said.

He growled, and his footsteps quickened. "Of course she fucking did."

Great, both of them were furious with me, but lately, that seemed par for the course, so I narrowed my focus on the trail Raven had left behind. If she got away, the answers she had would disappear with her.

I passed Kendric, who glanced down at me like he might try to grab me. I prepared to jump away, but then his lips pressed into a hard line, and he rasped, "Get her, but don't risk yourself."

Grateful that he hadn't tried to stop me, I pushed myself even harder, the warm magic spiraling through me and surrounding my wolf.

My sense of smell heightened, and my focus narrowed further. She'd zigzagged, slipping through the underbrush like a shadow, trying to cover her tracks, but I was locked in on her scent.

Trees blurred around me, and agony throbbed with every step. Still, I pushed harder, letting my anger fuel me.

Raven had used the chaos, the dead, and the dying to slip away like the coward she was.

All that talk about protecting us? Bullshit.

A low branch smacked my shoulder, but I ducked and kept going, paws flying over twisted roots. Her trail veered left, moving deeper into the woods where the now rising moon's light barely touched the ground. The scent grew stronger. She was close. I could feel it—hear the frantic rustling not far ahead.

This was it. I would catch her and finally get some damn answers for both Ryker and me.

Just as her scent thickened, faint murmurs from ahead reached me.

My legs slowed on their own, and I strained to hear over my own breaths and the thumping of my pulse. The overly sweet scent of not just Raven but several others carried toward me on the wind.

More vampires.

A twig snapped, and I froze, not wanting them to hear me. I edged into the growing shadows, holding my breath as the vampires' voices grew clearer and my pulse calmed.

"...the hell are you doing here?" a woman's sharp voice spat.

I'd recognize that voice anywhere—Lucinda. One of Vampire Queen Ambrosia's head guards.

My breath lodged in my throat. This must be where the vampires had disappeared to, and the last thing we needed was Ryker and the others showing up when we could easily be captured and killed.

Knowing this would make Briar and Ryker panic, I swallowed and linked with my sister, *Don't come any closer. Raven found the other vampires.*

Her panic surged through the bond like wildfire. *Are you safe?*

Yes, I'm staying still and listening. I needed to provide her some sort of assurance before Ryker decided to go rogue and "rescue" me. I'd no doubt hear all about how I was reckless and shouldn't have gone off on my own.

"I was outed," Raven answered tensely.

The words shouldn't have stung. Shouldn't have meant anything after what she'd done. But something about hearing her say it aloud... it hit deeper. Like a blade twisted into the wounds in my heart that I hadn't realized were still bleeding. I wished I could see her body language and face so her no doubt smug look would erase the awful gut-numbing torture, but I couldn't risk them detecting me.

"How were you *outed?*" Lucinda shot back.

I could imagine her wrinkling her nose and tossing her blonde hair over her shoulder.

Raven spat, "Because *you* didn't get all the dead vampires out of the clearing."

"So what? The bitch ran off after shooting at us. She's gotta be dead." Martin's condescending voice rose higher at the end, like the thought of my death made him joyful. At least he'd never hidden his disdain from us.

"You've been huddled out here the entire time, and no one informed you that she's still alive." Raven snorted. "She returned to the clearing and saw a shadow. The Blackwood witch was able to remove the cloaking in front of everyone there."

"*Simon,*" Bella croaked. "Why didn't you tell us?"

Simon.

No.

There had to be another vampire with that name—it couldn't be the one I'd helped escape from Ryker.

"Oh, I'm *sorry*." Simon gritted out. "But her life isn't nearly as important as them finding a way to block us from killing them despite being invisible. I'm pretty fucking sure that's more important right now."

I exhaled and hung my head. It most definitely was the same vampire. Ryker had said Simon had information we needed. If I could go back in time and not interfere, I would without hesitation. I'd been so wrong not to trust Ryker back then.

"We don't have time for this," Raven snapped. "They're close. I bought us what time I could, but it's over. We need to go—now."

A low snarl built in my chest, but I swallowed it down.

She knew we were on her trail. She'd claimed her involvement wasn't what it seemed, but here I was, hiding in the shadows and listening to the truth.

She was a fucking coward.

"Wait." A male vampire's voice cut through the air like a blade.

Every part of me stilled, and every muscle tensed.

"There's something near," the vampire muttered as leaves crunched a little closer than before. "Do you smell that?"

Shit.

With barely a twitch, I dropped lower, letting the mulch press into my belly. If they caught me, I'd be dead. They could run faster than I could, so my best option was to try to hide to the best of my ability and attack them by surprise.

My lungs screamed for air, but I didn't dare inhale. Not yet.

Another vampire grunted. "Yeah. I caught it too. It's... odd."

My pulse thundered in my ears. Maybe, miraculously, it

wasn't me they smelled. *Please tell me you five stopped.* The last thing I needed was for the vampires to be smelling them.

"It's something floral but unfamiliar," the first one said again. "It smells wrong. Like it doesn't belong."

My skin prickled with heat and cold all at once. I suspected I knew the scent they were referring to. My fur rose as if the comment alone had brought on the sensation of being watched.

Bella, the final of Queen Ambrosia's most trusted three guards, interjected, "That scent—it's the same one from when the barrier formed."

A beat of silence.

My lungs screamed, and my body felt heavy.

What's going on? Briar linked.

Just stay put. Don't come any closer. They smell something, but it's not me. I'll let you know if that changes.

"Yeah," the first vampire said slowly. "That's it. That strange vibration in the air. The scent comes with it, same as when it happened in the Shae pack territory."

"We need to leave." Martin's voice sounded urgent. "If the magic's building again—if it's coming back—"

"That's what I've been trying to tell you all," Raven hissed. "Now let's go."

Still no movement. None of the guards were listening to Raven.

"We can't risk attacking again until we gather more information." Lucinda's tone had turned ice cold. "Everyone, get in the vehicles and move out."

Now rushed footsteps retreated.

Car doors shut, and vehicles started. Still, it could be a trap. One I refused to be caught in.

Is everything okay? Briar linked. *Ryker is about to head toward you.*

Most, if not all, have left. I'm making sure none stayed behind before heading back. Tell him if he comes now, he could cause me to be attacked because they'd find me on the way to head him off. Even though I was playing dirty, knowing that was the best way to ensure he didn't come, it wasn't a lie. The tingling sensation of being watched increased, but its source was behind me, not in front of me.

I slowly turned my head, making sure I made no sound, and waited, not confident that I was truly alone.

My chest finally rose, shallow, sharp. Air scraped into my lungs, filling them, while my legs protested the tension and my injured muscles pulled tight like a bowstring too long drawn.

The vampire scents faded, and there were no sounds of footsteps or vehicles to indicate they were still near.

The strange, haunting floral scent that didn't seem of this world drifted to me. It was the same scent I'd smelled the night that Simon had escaped.

That prickling, charged awareness of being watched deepened and sank its teeth into my spine.

For some reason, I didn't feel threatened. The presence pulled at me like something strangely familiar.

We're going to head your way, Ember, Briar connected. Her worry and fear added to my own and made me feel as if I were being strangled. *This is taking way too long.*

The warm magic inside me flickered like a warning. Somehow, I understood that the essence didn't want them to interfere, but my wolf edged forward. I took a deep breath and agreed with her. If Briar or Ryker were in my place, I'd be going out of my mind. I couldn't ask them to back off again.

The vampires are gone, but something else is here. Tell Ryker I smell the same scent and have the same feeling of being watched like that night in the park, but this time it's stronger.

Ryker's deep howl ripped through the trees, echoing with a desperation that wrapped around my rib cage and squeezed.

My wolf whimpered, wanting to run to him but knowing that we couldn't risk turning our back on this threat.

I slowly climbed out of the brush, scanning the area for the reason I was feeling this way. My injuries ached as my muscles stretched. I'd just stepped cautiously between two sizable oak trees when leaves rustled right behind me in the spot I'd just moved from seconds ago.

My heart leaped into my throat as I spun around and found *something* there.

No. Not something.

Someone?

But how? Nothing had been around, or I wouldn't have come out.

His presence blurred and warped as if the forest had exhaled and created him from its shadows.

My breath hitched.

He wasn't a vampire, a shifter, or a witch. I didn't know what he was, but he stood as still as stone, tall and lean, with power radiating off him like heat waves. Not cold like the vampires. Not musky like shifters. Not of Earth like witches.

Something powerful and otherworldly.

His hair, a long, dark auburn, rippled as if wind had curled around only him. His skin was a shimmering golden brown, and his eyes were similar to liquid gold, burning just beneath the surface. The strangest thing of all was that his ears were sharply pointed.

He didn't speak or move. He tilted his head and stared at me like he could see inside me.

I swallowed, but my throat was dry. The scent—like roses and lilacs mixed with storm-soaked earth—flooded my senses. It clung to him like a second skin.

My legs tensed, every instinct torn between fight and flight. I was both fascinated and terrified. But fascination seemed to be winning out. There was something about him that resonated with me.

My warm new magic changed its cadence to match the rhythm of power that seemed to emanate from him.

His golden eyes turned more molten, like he was seeing everything within me.

My pain.

My power.

My past.

My soul.

And the part of me that wasn't just wolf.

I couldn't breathe. Not from fear but from *recognition* that I didn't understand.

What the hell was wrong with me?

Ryker's frantic paws beat the ground, and Briar's, Gage's, Kendric's, and Xander's frantic footsteps raced toward me. They were desperate to reach me. Ryker, so much so that he'd clearly shifted into animal form.

The energy between the stranger and me thrummed, and my wolf growled in fear and anger. She didn't like what my new magic was doing as it spiraled through me, making me dizzy.

He took a single step forward, and I stayed frozen, transfixed.

Ryker's panting breaths came closer. He'd be here any second, and my wolf stirred restlessly, wanting to get away from this man. Yet my feet refused to budge as our eyes remained locked together.

The strange man tapped his nose.

Barreling into the clearing, Ryker snarled.

I whipped my head toward Ryker, intending to communicate that he shouldn't hurt this man. I moved between him and the strange man, wanting to protect them both.

But when I glanced behind me to make sure he wouldn't hurt Ryker, the strange man wasn't there.

CHAPTER THREE

He'd vanished into thin air.

My head spun. How was that possible? There had been no rustle of retreating footsteps, no blur of movement, nor even a flicker of shadow to prove he'd been there at all.

Just… emptiness.

The otherworldly floral scent had already begun to disperse.

Almost like I'd imagined it.

My heart thudded against my ribs, and I took a step, damn near tripping over Ryker's huge wolfish form. He leaned forward, steadying me, and growled, deep and threatening.

I scanned the area, desperate to find some trace. A bent twig. A footprint. Anything.

But the earth was undisturbed, and not even the mulch had shifted.

What the hell? My pulse roared in my ears as if my sanity was being tested. None of this made sense. Even with the witches, I was able to see a trace of them.

As soon as my feet steadied, Ryker charged in the direction I'd been staring at. His claws dug into the mulch as he sniffed, searching for the enemy.

I wanted to tell him that the man was gone, but I couldn't, not with us both in wolf form. I swallowed hard at the possibility that I could actually be losing my mind.

Ryker's fur stood on end as he continued trying to pick up the scent of what had bothered me so much. But he walked in circles, trying to locate it. His head tilted as he glanced at me, the gold in his eyes warming like he was pack-linking with the others.

Their footsteps were now upon us, and they stormed into the small opening. Gage, Kendric, and Xander each held a gun while Briar ran directly to me.

"Ember, what's going on?" she asked, her voice full of concern and tenderness. She touched my shoulder lightly.

I... I blinked a few times, still trying to come to terms with what I'd seen. *I saw someone strange, and then he just vanished,* I linked. I felt like I was twelve again, waking from a nightmare and not sure what was real. But this hadn't been a dream. My magic still buzzed beneath my skin, sharp and unsettled.

Briar told the others what I'd said, and I wanted to avert my gaze downward. However, I couldn't be seen as weaker than I already seemed to be.

"Vanished how?" Kendric narrowed his eyes. "Like shadows again? Why would the vampires need to continue to cloak themselves?"

I don't think it was a cloaked vampire. I shook my head, trying like hell to get my nervous energy out. *He didn't smell like a vampire or a wolf shifter, and his presence didn't feel like theirs. He was... different in every way, even in appearance.*

Once again, Briar recited my words.

Gage lowered his weapon but didn't holster it, his voice rough. "Different how? Because right now, you aren't making much sense."

My warm magic cooled like the strange man's absence allowed it to calm once again, so I shook, trying to rid myself of the cold creeping into my bones. *I know this is weird, but his skin was more gold than brown or tan, and he had pointy ears. It was as if he materialized and vanished into thin air.*

As Briar informed everyone, Ryker huffed and looked toward the woods again. He then glanced back at me, and I could see the concern in his eyes.

I swear I'm not losing it. But even the words in my mind came out a little too sharp and a little too desperate, revealing my own fear.

Briar petted my head and linked, *We know you're not. But we're all raw and vulnerable right now.* Then she began talking out loud to the other four. "The vampires were close and scared, so maybe they have their witch messing with you right now like a lingering aftereffect to sow doubt among everyone here."

Some of the weight on my shoulders lifted. That explanation made sense, which meant that the vampires wanted me and the others to believe I was going crazy. *You think she cast a spell on me?*

She nodded. *Maybe.*

"You got a point," Kendric muttered, rubbing the back of his neck. "If this is the same kind of magic Queen Ambrosia's witch used, maybe she can also mess with our minds."

Ryker bared his teeth and paced a few feet in front of me, muscles so tight they quivered beneath his thick black coat.

I ached to press against his side, but I wasn't sure if he'd want me to, considering the way he was reacting to my potentially manipulated mind. He probably saw me as weak.

Hell, maybe I was. The most likely solution was that my mind *was* manipulable, which wasn't a good attribute for an alpha.

Ryker stopped pacing and looked at me. Something in his expression sent a spike of guilt and something uglier through my chest.

Doubt.

Of me. Of us. Or maybe even my sanity at this point.

He moved closer, and for one breathless second, I thought he might nudge me or offer some kind of comfort. Instead, he turned and jerked his head in the direction we'd come from.

Right. Message received. He had to hate how much time we'd wasted when there were injured wolves that needed protecting and dead that needed burying.

"Ryker's saying we need to head back. I hate to agree with him, but there are only six of us out here, with no sign of Raven. We'll be safer with more shifters around." Gage wrinkled his nose. "Whatever *it* was, it's gone. And we've got wounded who *aren't* disappearing into thin air."

Even though Gage hadn't meant it as an insult or sneer, his words were the equivalent of a gut punch. I'd caused us to waste additional time that was precious when the Blackwoods needed and deserved everyone's help. I needed to go back there and make up for all the horrible things I'd thought and believed about them. Still, there were questions I needed answered from them when the time was right.

"This time, no one should run off for any reason." Kendric turned in my direction and continued, "That way, if she does see the man again or vampires pop up, we'll all be together."

Xander rolled his shoulders, keeping the gun gripped in his hand. "Agreed. Ryker wants Ember in the center of the group. We can't be sure she's not still a target."

I snarled at the implied insult. I wasn't a damn damsel that needed surrounding, but Briar moved so that I had to look at her face.

"Humor us, please." Briar squatted so she was face level with me and gave me her classic puppy-dog look, her eyes glassy. "You don't know how hard it was for us to stand back when there were so many damn vampires around you. Imagine if it were me and I'd asked you to stay back like you did us."

A cold knot formed in my stomach, and a little bit of pride swelled in my chest. Briar rarely acted like a leader and was quick to obey as long as she agreed with us, but when she needed to get her way, she knew how to work me. I exhaled and nodded my head. *Fine. I'll stay in the center. This one time.*

The corners of her mouth tipped upward, but she fought the smile. "She agreed."

Head dropping, Ryker let out a breath like he was relieved.

No doubt, he expected me to fight against them more than that, but how could I when Briar put things in perspective for me?

Gage took the lead with his shoulders squared. Kendric and Xander flanked my sides, their eyes constantly scanning for a threat that we couldn't see or hear. Briar drifted a step behind me, close enough that her breath brushed my shoulder.

And Ryker stalked right behind me, which made me want to slow down so I could feel him at my side.

I both hated and loved the way his presence pulled at something buried deep in my chest. It felt even stronger now, like my ribs ached from my soul pressing against them, trying to break free to connect with him.

If Reid Blackwood hadn't been my fated mate, there would've been no doubt that Ryker Grimstone was Fate's pick for me. But that wasn't how fated-mate bonds worked. Even if your fated mate rejected you, you didn't get a second fated. People either lived out their lives alone or with a chosen mate who would never truly measure up to what Fate had in store for them.

Maybe the vampires' witch had been messing with Ryker and me all along, if she could make me feel and see things that weren't real.

The silence stretched as we moved quietly through the woods. My muscles twitched with every step, my aching wounds reminding me I was injured as well. Guilt sat like a lead weight in my stomach, gnawing at me.

A tingle ran down my spine... the same sensation all over again. Like I was being watched.

I couldn't stop myself from glancing around and sniffing, hoping and fearing that the strange man would appear. Fear, because what if they didn't see him? But also hope... because what if they did?

Ryker's footsteps halted, and I glanced over my shoulder to see him studying the area more intently, like he was searching for the same thing as I was.

The sounds of footsteps and something being dragged hit my ears, followed by the scent of blood. We were almost back to the clearing where our group had been attacked.

Soft murmurs and whimpers echoed through the trees, followed by a single, broken howl.

One that screamed of death and heartbreak.

We stepped through the tree line, and everything slammed into me at once.

Bodies had been lined up with careful hands—some still breathing, others not. Blackwood pack members hovered nearby, their faces masks of grief and exhaustion. Someone sobbed softly, the sound muffled, like they were trying and failing to hold it in.

"Where are Reid and Perry?" Briar asked.

My heart dropped. Had Reid died as well?

A young man with reddish-brown curls and a limp jogged toward us. His jacket was half zipped, blood staining the collar and one sleeve. Recognition tugged at the edge of my memory—Jaren, one of the younger Blackwood guards who'd trained under Reid.

He stopped, chest heaving. "I've been looking for you two everywhere." He pointed at Briar and me.

Ryker's growl rumbled low beside me as he brushed against my side, the jolt between us springing to life once again.

Jaren held up both hands. "Whoa. I'm not here to fight; I just came to relay a message. Sun moved Reid to their home for healing, and he wants Ember to come by the house so they can talk."

My head jerked back. Sure, Sun had thought it would be safest and wisest for all of us to stick together, and I agreed. But going into the house of my fated mate, who'd completed the bond with another woman, took things to a whole different level.

Hunkering down, Ryker snarled, drool oozing from his teeth and rage shaking his entire body.

"Whoa." Jaren hobbled back a few steps. "Don't kill the messenger. But he said there's something important that he needs to explain to you."

If he thought that would make Ryker more comfortable with the request, he was dead wrong.

Tell Ryker he can come with me, I linked to Briar. Not being able to communicate directly was getting old. I needed to shift back to human form.

Instead of regurgitating my words, Briar shook her head. "It won't be just Ryker joining you, *all* of us will."

"Yeah, I'm in agreement with that." Gage nodded like it was a done deal. "After what we just learned, I'm all about us getting information together." He cut his eyes at Ryker, letting his sense of hurt and betrayal be known.

"I'm good with that." Xander gestured in the direction of the pack neighborhood. "Let's go."

We all took off, and I linked with Briar, *I'm going to go shift back real fast. My clothes are nearby.*

She nodded and told the others.

When I split off, Ryker did the same, and I had no doubt he was shifting as well.

As my body contorted and bones cracked, my wounds ached, but I could also feel them closing up. Back on two legs, I slipped on the black shirt and pants. Within seconds, I headed back out to Briar, Xander, Kendric, and Gage.

Kendric still held a gun in case an enemy appeared. His face was twisted, and I knew the expression well —heartbreak.

Gage and Xander watched two separate directions, each tense and pale. Even though we'd all been hurt by Raven's betrayal, our pain was nothing compared to Kendric's.

Heading straight to Briar, I examined the scratch marks

on her shoulder. Though she hadn't complained, I hated that she was injured. I kept failing to protect her.

Ryker emerged, his shirt torn, but since we'd shifted, like mine, his wounds had healed. His eyes met mine, but he seemed cold and distant.

"We'd better go see what *Reid* urgently needs to tell you." Ryker's nose wrinkled, making his feelings clear.

I just turned and led the group toward the Blackwoods' town. We slipped through the woods in tense silence, our group tighter than before, not one of us straying more than a step from the others.

The Blackwood neighborhood came into view—rows of tan, two-story homes built from the same sturdy materials, identical in layout, structure, and spacing. Every house had the same wraparound porch, the same white-painted trim, the same gabled roof. Cookie-cutter homes, designed for pack functionality and order. Nothing fancy. Nothing unnecessary. Just practical.

We walked past at least a dozen dead bodies surrounded by pack members crying and tending to the ones they loved. Images of my parents and our pack flashed into my mind, and I guessed that Ryker and the others were feeling the same way.

Ryker stayed by my side, just an inch away. With him on one side and Briar on the other, some of my worry eased.

Reid's house was the last one on the corner, three rows in, and close to the west edge of the territory, the woods curving behind it, with a wide backyard for training and a reinforced fence.

When we reached the porch, Ryker's breathing became labored and rapid. I tried to ignore his anger because there was no reason for it. Reid had mated with someone else;

there was no coming back from that. Ryker had nothing to fear.

Our footsteps creaked on the painted wood, and Ryker stalked at my side, his jaw tight and hands fisted. He hadn't said a word since we'd shifted to human form, but the weight of his silence pressed against me harder than his words ever could.

I lifted my hand to knock, but the door opened before I could.

Sun.

Her eyes snapped fire, and her braid looked frizzed and wild, like she hadn't slept in days. Her body blocked the doorway like a wall. "What the hell are you doing here?"

I froze, breath catching. The others stilled behind me, but no one moved forward.

"Jaren said Reid wanted me to come by so we could talk." I didn't understand why this was taking her by surprise. Surely Reid would've told her.

Sun's lips thinned, and something flashed in her eyes. Not shock exactly. Not quite anger either. But something close to... unease.

"He's not in any state to talk. Cassi sedated him."

I blinked. "But—"

She stepped forward, expression hardening. "He's not lucid, Ember. Not right now. You showing up like this after everything... it's not what he needs."

Ryker's growl rumbled low beside me, his energy pulsing hotter by the second. My hand brushed his clenched fist. He didn't look at Sun—his gaze stayed locked on me, burning with something too raw to name.

The two of them made me feel as if I'd done something wrong by coming here. Fuck that. "I didn't ask to come here.

Reid sent for me. If you've got a problem with that, take it up with him."

Sun flinched but covered it quickly. "Maybe he *did* send for you. Maybe he *thinks* he needs to talk. But he's severely injured, so I'm making the call right now."

Her eyes flicked toward Ryker like she wanted to say something more—something aimed directly at him—but whatever it was, she bit it back.

The silence was deafening.

Briar took a small step forward. "We'll come back later. When he's stronger."

Sun didn't reply. She just crossed her arms and stood in the doorway, daring me to try again.

"Let's go," Ryker gritted out. He turned sharply and stepped off the porch before anyone else could react.

"Wait," Cassi called from somewhere behind us.

I looked over my shoulder and saw her beyond the hedgerow, her long auburn hair tousled and wild like she'd run here. Her face was pale, her eyes wide.

"I need to talk to you," she said, voice trembling. "I did something horrible."

CHAPTER FOUR

My heart began to pound even harder than it already had been from the last thirty seconds of bullshit. Ryker's entire body turned rigid, reminding me more of a vampire than a shifter.

Still, I could feel Sun's eyes homed in on me. "It'll have to wait," she spat. "Reid is injured and clearly not thinking straight right now."

"That's the thing. He is." Cassi winced. "That's why we have to talk *now*. It's important."

Despite the desperate plea in Cassi's voice, Sun didn't turn her head. "Fine. Once *they* leave."

Cassi cleared her throat and jerked her head to the side slightly. "Ember and Ryker should be part of this conversation. Reid is your alpha, and he *did* request them to come here."

Gage snorted, and Sun's head finally jerked toward the witch.

A vein pulsed in Sun's neck. "He's severely injured; his father died, and nearly half our pack just got slaughtered. He needs to rest before having discussions with anyone outside our pack or make any decisions, especially regarding *her*."

I opened my mouth to say something when Briar spoke from her spot directly behind me. "I know you feel that you're making the right call, but believe me when I tell you that if you disrespect his wishes, it *will* create a wedge between you."

Glancing over my shoulder, I noted that Briar's face was lined with concern, but her sharp, jade-green eyes were set in determination. Frustration bit through the bond.

No doubt she was thinking about when I'd almost forced her to leave our allies with me against her will. My plan had been to run away solely to protect the two of us while leaving the rest of the packs and shifters here to continue to be murdered. That lesson would always stick with me.

Sun's lips parted like she wanted to argue, but then she clamped them shut. Her jaw clenched for one long, stretched-out moment.

When I expected her to march into the house and slam the front door, she pivoted on her heel. "Fine," she bit out. "But not for long."

Without another word, she entered the house, her feet squeaking against the hardwood floor. She stood at the door, waiting for each of us to enter.

Ryker gritted his teeth so hard his jaw cracked.

My wolf both whimpered and growled, the strange combination sounding foreign in my head. She was as conflicted as my human side. If Reid wanted to talk, I wasn't in a position to decline. I had my own questions about the night my pack had been murdered and Reid's pack's presence there, but an almost equal-sized part of me didn't want to go in, given how upset and uncomfortable Ryker seemed.

Cassi hurried by at a run, like Sun might change her mind if she didn't act quickly.

I slid my hand into Ryker's, the jolt stirring to life as Gage, Xander, and Kendric climbed the stairs.

Everyone but Ryker, Sun, and I was clearly eager to get this conversation over and done with.

Ryker's fingers tightened, holding my hand in a death grip as we entered the house together.

The air inside the house hit differently—warm.

Too warm.

Like the heat had been cranked in a desperate attempt to burn away the chill of death that clung to everything outside. But it couldn't.

The faint scent of blood hung in the air from outside and from Reid. My stomach twisted, and my heart ached as I realized that, even inside the pack members' homes, death would haunt them.

The hallway stretched out in front of us, leading deeper into the house.

I'd only ever been inside Perry and Mavis's home, but the layout was identical—the same narrow corridor running toward the back, the same pale walls, and the same scuffed hardwood floor beneath our boots.

The farther we moved into the house, the more claustrophobic it felt.

Every breath came heavier, every step echoing louder as if we were intruding on something we shouldn't be part of.

My palm stayed locked in Ryker's, the jolt of our connection anchoring me, but it didn't seem to be helping him at all. He hadn't said a word, and I wasn't sure if restraint or resentment was boiling beneath his skin. Probably both.

Sun kept glancing over her shoulder, her shoulders stiff

and her jaw twitching. It was clear she didn't want any of us here—especially *me*.

One thing was certain.

No matter what this visit would cost, I needed to know what had actually happened that night when Reid and the Blackwood pack had come to our land. If they hadn't attacked us, and the vampires had been cloaked with a diluted wolf shifter scent, then how had they known to come?

We passed a bathroom and then a side room with navy-blue blankets.

Another turn, then Sun stopped in front of the last door on the left. She took in a ragged breath and opened it.

My pulse stuttered as she waved for us to follow and marched inside.

Ryker stood still, so I tugged on his hand. We couldn't speak without the others hearing, so I hoped he understood my intention—I wanted him to come with me, but I would go without him.

He huffed like he understood my message and then moved alongside me into the dimly lit room.

The curtains were drawn, and a single lamp glowed on the far dresser. The scent of blood was strongest here—coppery and sharp, barely covered by the medicinal tang of salves and herbal ointment.

And there, in the middle of it all, was Reid.

Paler than before, he'd been propped up on a pile of pillows. Bandages were wrapped tightly across his chest and neck, and his half-lidded eyes were locked on me with startling clarity.

Placing one hand in the center of his hunter-green sheet, Reid rasped, "I need to speak with Ember and Briar. Alone."

The silence that followed felt like a fuse being lit.

Ryker moved.

A snarl ripped from his throat, deep and raw. His arm jerked forward, the tendons in his neck bulging like he was seconds from lunging.

Gage grabbed him from behind, arms locked around Ryker's chest. "Don't."

Kendric stepped in front of him, palms out. "Think this through. He just wants to chat with them."

"Let go of me," Ryker snarled, his gaze locked on Reid like he could tear him in half with just a thought.

"No, I agree with *him*," Sun spat and pointed at Ryker while glaring daggers at Reid. "You've got some nerve. You're near death and in our home and bed, and you want alone time with the girl you were fated to—after claiming me? No. Not happening."

Reid's eyes hardened. "There's a reason, and you know what it is. There's a lot that needs to be—"

"No," she snapped. "Not without me."

I stepped forward, but Ryker surged again, this time hard enough that Kendric joined Gage, both of them holding Ryker back with every ounce of strength they had.

"Calm *down*." Xander exhaled, shaking his head.

"I swear to Fate, I will rip him apart," Ryker snarled. "You think I'm gonna stand here while he tries to—"

"Bro, he has a *mate*," Gage growled. "He's not going to try to make off with your girl."

"I'm not going to even fucking risk it. I'll finish him off before he gets time alone with Ember." Ryker broke free and reached the side of the bed.

"That's enough!" Cassi shouted and waved her hand. Ryker suddenly lost his balance and stumbled sideways. He managed to catch himself but barely.

Everyone froze.

She stood in the doorway, arms tense and face taut. "We all need to take a deep breath."

"A *breath*?" Sun barked a humorless laugh. "There's no calming down when your *chosen mate* nearly completed the fated ceremony with *his* fated. Or did you forget how sacred that is?"

Cassi picked at her lip. "You're all reacting to something that isn't real."

Sun blinked. "Excuse me? Have you lost your mind? I know—"

"They're not fated," Cassi interjected. "Reid and Ember were never fated mates."

The room spun.

"What the hell are you talking about?" For a moment, I might as well have been back in calculus class with how hard my brain was trying to make sense of what she'd said.

Ryker stilled.

Wrinkling her nose, Sun shook her head. "Don't lie. Reid *felt* it."

"I know." Cassi's shoulders sagged. "But only because I made it that way."

The air vanished from my lungs.

Reid looked like he'd been punched.

"I forged it," Cassi said, her voice soft. "I faked the bond."

Silence filled the room as we tried to process what we'd just heard. Even though, individually, each word made sense, the combination left me reeling.

My knees weakened, and my vision blurred. "That's not possible."

"What are you talking about?" Reid tried to sit higher,

but he grimaced and plopped back down on the pillows. "You can only influence emotions."

Briar rubbed the back of her neck, her confusion wafting through our connection and adding to my own.

"I can do the basics." Cassi pressed her lips together like she was contemplating her next words. "But all witches can. My specialty isn't common, so I limited how I explained my magic."

"*Limited?*" Sun's face flushed. "I'm going to need more than that."

Cassi lowered her hand and drew in a ragged breath.

As soon as her hand dropped, Ryker stood up straight once more. "Use your magic on one of us again and see what happens." He bared his teeth, his eyes glowing as his wolf surged forward.

"I couldn't let you attack Reid for no good reason."

"No *good* reason." Ryker snorted.

"Get to the point, Cassi." Reid lifted his chin.

Cassi's gaze swept around the room, landing on me last. "I did it to protect the Blackwoods," she said softly. "To repay them."

My breath hitched, and Briar glanced at me.

"What the hell does that mean?" Ryker's growl returned in full force.

Sun rolled her eyes and clenched her hands. "Just come out with it."

Cassi fidgeted. "The Blackwoods took me in when no one else would. When my sister tried to kill me, I had to leave home and survive on my own. I had no one I could trust or rely on. The Blackwoods gave me a home, a family, and safety. I wanted to give something back. Something that would last."

"So you *manipulated a mate bond?*" Sun's voice climbed into something shrill. "You decided to play Fate?"

"No!" Cassi's voice cracked. "I didn't do it for power or personal gain. I did it because I believed—because we *all* believed—that Reid was meant to be more than just the next alpha. That he could lead all the packs. But he needed the right kind of bond to do that, and everyone wanted Ember to take the throne, so it was win-win."

"You manipulated my sister—let her be humiliated—for a chance for him to become king?" Briar rubbed her hands together as her anger and annoyance constricted our pack link.

Cassi lifted both hands in surrender. "The bond would have given him legitimacy. He'd have had a powerful mate —someone with lineage strong enough to back him. Someone the other alphas would rally behind."

I blinked, trying to make sense of it. I'd never imagined that someone could make me feel fated-mate tendencies for someone who wasn't my fated.

Reid's expression darkened, the veins in his neck twitching. "I never asked for that. Why the hell would you put Ember and me through that?"

Cassi's shoulders curled inward, and her voice dropped so low I had to strain to hear it. "I know. You didn't. But I thought..."

"You thought *what?*" His tone wasn't a growl—but it was worse—cold and clipped. "That I'd want my entire future and mate bond built on a lie?"

Her breath caught. "I thought you'd want to help the packs since wolf shifters were being slaughtered. We needed a strong leader to keep all of us safe."

"And you thought faking my fated-mate bond was the

answer?" His voice broke into a rasp that echoed far deeper than just physical pain. "Did my father put you up to this?"

Cassi flinched like he'd slapped her.

She shook her head hard. "He didn't know about it, including what my special magic is. And when I influenced your emotions, everyone was happy, so I didn't think it would cause harm."

"Because you made sure it felt real." Sun's arms were crossed, her voice venomous.

"Wait." I rubbed my eyes. "Then why did he reject me at the cliff?"

"Something I hadn't accounted for." She picked at her nails. "As soon as Sun and Ryker showed up, there were complications. When you four met, my spell started to unravel. The magic couldn't hold. The closer each of you was to your true fated mate, the weaker the spell became, and then the forced bond began to repel Reid and Ember from each other."

"So you allowed him to humiliate her?" Ryker pointed a shaky finger at the witch. "You let her suffer. You let the entire damn pack believe she wasn't good enough. You let him tear her apart."

"I didn't mean for that to happen," Cassi said, sounding broken. "I was trying to give us all a chance to survive! I didn't know it would hurt so many people."

"Man, this is fucked up," Gage whispered not so quietly behind us.

Reid looked like Cassi had kicked him in the chest. "You think I wanted that? That I'd agree to bond myself to someone I wasn't fated to just for a chance to be king?"

"You wouldn't have," she said softly. "But that was the point. Neither you nor Ember would've accepted power for power's sake. Which meant you were the ones who should have it."

His growl vibrated through the room. "You're wrong. If you really believed in me, you would've told me the truth."

Sun paced beside the bed, shaking her head, eyes narrowed like slits. "You humiliated Ember, Reid, and me at the ceremony. And now we find out the only reason the bond existed was because some witch decided to play matchmaker with magic?"

Ryker flinched, his entire body vibrating with tension. "You didn't just screw with Reid and Ember," he ground out. "You messed with all of us. You know what that rejection did to her? What it nearly did to me, watching her fall apart from a lie?"

My throat burned. My chest ached so fiercely it felt like I was back on that cliff again, staring at the man who was supposed to be mine as he looked at me like I was nothing.

"I thought I was going insane," I whispered. "Because when you rejected me, I could feel it slipping. The bond. I thought it meant I wasn't good enough. That Fate made a mistake—or I had. And then I met Ryker and couldn't trust anything I was feeling."

Reid's expression crumpled.

Briar stepped forward, brows furrowed. "So your magic just... forges fake bonds?"

Cassi stiffened. "No."

Everyone went still again.

Ryker narrowed his eyes. "Then what else can you do? What else have you messed with?"

CHAPTER FIVE

Cassi stiffened, her throat working like she was trying to swallow her words before they ever left her lips.

I inhaled deeply, steeling myself for something else that would make us all question reality.

"Dammit, Cassi." Reid's nostrils flared. "Just tell us everything. You withholding information is only going to worsen things between us."

She flinched and closed her eyes. "I can... feel true fated-mate bonds."

"What exactly does that mean?" Gage asked, moving to the other side of Briar so that the four of us stood between the door, Reid and Sun.

"When two people who are meant for each other are in close proximity, it's like electricity under my skin. I can see it. Like golden threads stitching the air around them."

My breath caught. That sounded very similar to what I felt when Ryker and I touched.

"I knew Ember and Reid weren't truly fated." Cassi's gaze flicked toward the bed. "Not in that way. That bond didn't spark. Not until I forced it and, even then, it didn't really hum."

Reid's chest heaved, his bandages stretching with the movement. "So you knew it wasn't real."

She nodded. "I thought I could strengthen it if I moved fast enough. If I got you two to complete the mating ceremony, the mate bond would take effect once you claimed each other, and you wouldn't ever know you had a fated mate."

"So you knew," he snarled. "You *knew* it was falling apart the moment I met Sun, and you still tried to get me to complete the fake bond with Ember?"

"You believed you could beat Fate to the finish line?" Sun asked and shivered.

Glancing at the wooden floor, Cassi's face scrunched. "I just wanted to give back to the Blackwood—"

"*No*," Reid interjected, his chest heaving and his face straining from what had to be pain. "Even though I would be proud to lead the wolf shifters, I would never *ever* be willing to give up Sun for that. Having her by my side is the most important thing to me."

"But if you didn't know she existed, and you completed the bond with Ember, you would never have known, and you'd feel differently." Cassi clasped her hands together. "You'd have a woman you loved and the throne."

Ryker snarled, taking my hand and edging in front of me. "Unbelievable."

"No, what's unbelievable," I snapped, my voice trembling with fury, "is that you let me stand on that cliff to be rejected in front of *everyone* there. You even knew what was going on, and you still tried to push it!"

"I didn't want it to end like that—"

"Bullshit," Ryker growled, stepping toward her. "You

didn't care how it ended as long as it served your plan. You used Ember and didn't even try to intervene and make things right, despite knowing what was going on."

Reid slammed his palm against the bed and winced. The white cloth on his neck became stained pink and then a deep crimson, proving this conversation was taking too much out of him. "You humiliated her. You humiliated all of us."

Sun's eyes burned as she stood and came to my other side. For once, her hatred wasn't directed at me. She pointed at Cassi and said, "You knew I was his fated mate and that we'd finally met, and you *still* messed with our bond?"

Cassi flinched like Sun's words were claws raking across her skin. "I didn't mean for any of it to happen this way."

"But it *did* happen this way." Ryker's voice was low, vibrating through my core. "You played Fate with all our lives and caused problems that should never have been there in the first place."

"I was trying to help—"

"You were trying to control us," Sun cut in, her voice like steel. "You wanted a perfect story. A leader. A queen. You decided who should be with whom and to hell with the consequences."

Behind me, Briar's breathing picked up, her body humming with restrained emotion.

"You didn't just lie. You changed the course of our lives." Gage smacked his lips like he tasted something bad. "Ember's. Reid's. Ryker's. Sun's. And everyone who counts on them."

My breath caught. Gage was right. Maybe if the bonding ceremony hadn't happened, my pack would still be alive and wouldn't have been targeted by the vampires. And if I hadn't been influenced during those few weeks between the slaughter of the royals and Ryker's packs, maybe I would've met Ryker earlier, before he'd had that spell cast on himself.

"I thought things would fall into place...." Cassi's shoulders sagged.

"They fell into place all right." Xander snorted without any humor.

Kendric muttered, "What the hell is wrong with people?"

Valid question.

In fact, it was more than valid. The question snapped whatever reticence I'd had. "*It fell apart.* You may believe you understand the impact, but you didn't experience or even see the repercussions on my side. You'll never know what it felt like or truly understand what I experienced watching the man I thought was my mate look at me like I was *nothing* and tell *everyone* something was wrong with me."

Ryker's body shook with rage. Any second, he might unleash his wolf.

Grimacing, Reid placed a hand on his wound. "You were right about one thing, Cassi. I *never* would've wanted a forced bond with someone. Period. Even if the option would've placed me on a throne."

Sun ran back to his side and tried to get him to lie back down, but he refused.

"A throne I didn't want, on top of that," I said, my voice caught between a growl and a human tone. My wolf inched forward, just as angry as me, hating this witch for all the damage she'd caused. Especially me holding back from Ryker, believing it wasn't possible that the connection we had could truly mean what it did.

"This is why I asked you to come here, Ember." Reid's face paled even more, but his eyes glistened. "I'm sorry for how I treated you that night. I couldn't explain it then, but the connection with you... it started to feel *wrong*. Like my instincts were trying to break free, and every time I tried to push past it, my wolf became more agitated. I wanted to go after you to explain, but chaos erupted. I never meant to make you feel shame or anger or to embarrass you."

A lump formed in my throat, and my eyes burned with tears. All this time, I'd condemned him and his pack when they were just as much victims as I was. "It clearly wasn't your fault. I'm sorry that I blamed you." I turned to face Cassi again.

She frowned. "None of this would've been a problem if both of your fated mates hadn't shown up at the ceremony."

My stomach twisted, nausea crawling up my throat. "You mean... if Fate hadn't gotten in the way."

"You were racing Fate," Reid muttered, voice filled with contempt. "You actually believed you could outpace her?"

"I just wanted..." Cassi whispered.

"Don't you fucking say you wanted to give back to the Blackwoods again." A muscle in Ryker's back twitched. "If you say that again, I won't hold myself back."

I had to agree with him there. She'd done so much damage. My wolf was trying to take control, but my newer, warm magic pulsed once more, holding her back. "You made me doubt myself. My instincts. My heart."

"And me," Reid added bitterly. "You made me doubt everything I felt for Sun. Like maybe I was betraying some higher plan by choosing her over Ember."

Cassi folded in on herself, shrinking under the weight of every word. "I know."

The silence that followed was deafening.

Even though I wanted to dwell and release more anger, we couldn't keep circling the same pain. Not with the dead still unburied and the vampires hiding in the shadows.

I sucked in a shaky breath. "Why were you in our territory that night, Reid?" My voice cut through the quiet, rough and raw.

Reid blinked like I'd yanked him back to the present. "I was coming to apologize."

My chest hollowed, and Ryker took my hand once again. As soon as his skin touched mine, some of the anger eased.

"After the way everything happened, I couldn't explain anything to you that night," he continued, his words slower now, like his injury was catching up to him again. "My parents were horrified by what I'd done, and I couldn't ignore the pull of Sun. I felt guilty about all of it."

"Because of that *bitch*," Sun bared her teeth and glared at Cassi.

"Dad—" Reid's voice faltered. His chest shook with a sob he had to be holding in. "We were coming to talk with you and your father. It was late, but we agreed the longer we waited, the worse the situation would be. When we crossed the edge of our property near yours, we caught a scent—faint but definitely wolf shifter. Not ours or yours. Dad and I called for more of our pack because something didn't sit right with me, and that's when we heard the howl."

My spine stiffened. I didn't need to hear anything else. My throat tightened, and my breathing turned ragged.

"That's enough." Ryker pulled me to his side and placed an arm around my waist. "She doesn't need to relive it."

"Yes." I lifted my chin, knowing we had to have this discussion. We needed to know everything we could. "I do."

I bit my lip. Briar's emotions intensified, adding to my own, breaking through and reminding me that I was being selfish. I'd been so focused on my own trauma that I hadn't been paying attention to her well-being. What a shitty sister and alpha I was turning out to be. "If Briar is okay with it." This conversation would be just as hard on her.

"I'll be okay." Briar moved to my side, taking my other hand. "Please continue."

My chest squeezed more, but this time from comfort. I had the two people I loved most holding my hands and standing at my side.

Reid's fingers curled over the sheets. "Like I said, we heard a howl. Long, agonized, and laced with warning. It was meant to alert anyone within range that something was wrong."

Inhaling sharply, Briar squeezed my hand harder as her pain merged with mine.

"We raced toward the sound and onto your pack lands."

My mouth parted, but no sound came out. I hadn't expected this. Everything I'd thought I understood unraveled, making me question all of it. "But I saw you lunge at Rosa."

"Ember, we didn't attack your pack." Reid's jaw clenched, guilt flashing behind his darkening eyes. "We couldn't see the attackers—it was wild and scary. The only way we could help was to wait for someone to be attacked and try to defend the area where it seemed the attacker would have to be."

I wanted to fall apart and curl up on the ground, but I couldn't do that. Not now.

"Like we had to do when we were shooting guns during the last attack." Kendric pursed his lips.

"Exactly." Sweat beaded on Reid's forehead. "That was the problem. The vampires were only targeting your pack. I didn't realize why until tonight. I rejected you, claimed something was wrong with you, and our pack scent was all over the place where the Sinclairs all lay slaughtered. They *wanted* people to think we were responsible. But we only engaged when we had no other option."

Just like that, everything made sense.

I thought back to every snap of teeth, every scream, every body that hit the ground. My grief had warped my vision. My rage had turned Reid into the villain like the vampires wanted.

But he'd been trying to help.

"I saw you two run toward the river," Reid said, voice hoarse. "I tried to get to you. But it was like... they were using us against each other."

Sun placed a gentle hand on his arm. Her jaw was tight. "I think enough has been said tonight. We can meet again in the morning after Reid gets more rest. He needs to heal. His wound is already oozing again."

"Here." Cassi moved past Ryker when Sun lifted her hand.

"Do *not* come any closer." Sun scowled. "You've done enough."

Cassi flinched and stopped.

I couldn't blame Sun. I wasn't thrilled to be near Cassi either. Not after what she'd tried to pull.

"I'm sorry—" Cassi started.

"Cassi, go," Reid said groggily. "You said you wanted to help, then go spell the perimeter. If the vampires try to come back, I want to know the moment they get within fifty yards of anyone."

She hung her head. "Okay. I'll go reinforce the wards now." She turned and slipped out the door without another word, her shoulders hunched like she might fold into herself entirely.

The moment she was gone, the air seemed to lift just a little. Still heavy but breathable again.

Sun looked at me, her expression unreadable but no longer hostile. "I'm not trying to be rude, but he needs rest. I've asked Jerry to meet you outside and take you to a house where you can stay. It's just a couple of doors down from us."

"Of course. Thank you for that." I forced a smile, but I knew it didn't reach my eyes. This whole night had been a disaster.

"Come on." Ryker's voice was soft but firm as he tugged me toward the door.

We filed out quietly, the others falling in behind us. No one spoke as we walked down the hallway again, past the navy blankets and blood-soaked air.

Outside, the night hit me like a wave, along with the stronger stench of blood.

Cold. Heavy. Death.

A Blackwood shifter, who had to be Jerry, was waiting by the stairs. He gave us a single nod before leading us to a two-story house in the middle of the neighborhood. No one spoke. No words were needed. Not on a night like this.

We reached the white house with a porch light on and a woodsy scent that hinted of cedar and pine. "There are three bedrooms and a couple couches."

Gage patted Jerry's arm. "Thanks, man."

The six of us climbed the wooden steps to the front

porch and went inside. The front room was empty but clean, with two mismatched couches and a chair.

Another door opened into a hallway with multiple bedrooms.

"It's been a while since we've been in a place that feels like a home." Xander sauntered over to the mustard-yellow couch, flopping onto it.

"True, but don't get too comfortable," Kendric added.

"Well, I will tonight," Gage slumped onto the burnt-orange couch like he might fall asleep right there.

Ryker's hand tightened around mine again.

"We're taking the master." His voice left no room for debate as he led me in the direction where the large bedroom had been in Reid's house.

Are you okay? I linked with Briar, knowing Ryker probably had a lot of stuff he wanted to talk through about what we'd just discovered.

Yeah, I'm going to take a shower and go to bed. I'll stay in the other room down the hall.

Ryker and I entered the primary bedroom, and the door clicked shut. He didn't hesitate to lock it.

His chest rose and fell like he'd been holding his breath for hours.

He turned toward me, his eyes dark with anger, then released my hand and took a step back.

My heart dropped. I didn't know what I'd expected to happen once we were alone, but it definitely wasn't *this.* "What's wrong?"

He tilted his head back and grimaced. "Oh, don't worry. I'm going to tell you. In fact, I have a *lot* to say."

CHAPTER SIX

Ryker's chest heaved as he stalked across the room, running both hands through his brown hair like he couldn't stand being in his own skin. The air felt thick—charged—and not in the way it usually did when we were alone.

This was different.

Harsher.

Colder.

Like a wall had been constructed between us.

I swallowed hard. "If you're angry with me, I get it. I'm disgusted with myself for falling for all that so hard."

He froze mid-step and slowly turned to face me, jaw locked tight. "You think I'm angry at *you*?"

I hugged my arms across my chest. "You've barely looked at me since we left Reid's. You let go of my hand the second the door shut. You're breathing like you're going to explode. So yeah... I think you might be regretting all of this, and I'm sorry. That's all I can say."

His eyes widened, then narrowed as disbelief crashed over his face. "Regretting *you*?"

I stared at the floor, not wanting to see his shock wear off and true disgust slide into place. I wasn't strong enough to handle it, not with my entire world being ripped apart and making me question everything I'd ever known.

He moved so fast I didn't even register it until his hands cupped my face, his thumbs brushing my cheeks. The gold blazed in his eyes as they burned into mine. "Ember. I'm furious. But not at you."

My breath hitched as so many emotions poured into me. "You should be. I was weak and let myself get manipulated by magic. I doubted you."

He shook his head. "Lil rebel, I've been under a spell for almost two months now. I know exactly what that does and how it twists you up and makes you question your own instincts. I'm mad because you were forced into this night-mare, and you had to walk through hell thinking your heart betrayed you. That *I* would betray you too."

My knees went weak.

"Your feelings were manipulated," he growled, voice raw. "You should've been able to trust them without second-guessing every emotion. But she stole that from you."

I tried to blink away the tears that blurred my vision, but one slipped free.

He caught it with his thumb, his touch sparking some-thing primal in me.

But he wasn't done. "And then she let you stand there—on that damn cliff—humiliated, broken. Alone."

I grabbed the hem of his shirt, fisting it in my hands. "I wasn't alone. Not really. You were always there, Ryker. Even when I didn't know what we were. You kept showing up."

His hands slid down to my waist, gripping tight like he was afraid I'd disappear. "Because I felt it," he rasped.

"Even when it didn't make sense. I felt you in my bones. I've tried so hard to protect you despite you running straight into danger, but I couldn't protect you from that." His voice cracked on the last word.

I leaned into him. "Well, now we know what happened, and what's brewing between us makes sense," I whispered.

That must have released something in him because his mouth crashed down on mine, not gentle or soft but desperate. Consuming.

I didn't hesitate, and our tongues collided. I clawed at his back, dragging him closer. The kiss deepened, full of everything we hadn't said, everything we'd feared.

When he pulled back, he searched my face. "I'm so damn tired of fighting this. I want this. I want *you*. But I need to be sure it's what you want too, and I know I promised you time."

"I don't need more time." My voice came out stronger than I expected, surprising even me. "I've wasted enough time doubting and trying to ignore what I already knew in my soul."

I stepped closer to him, pressing my palm against his chest where his heart thundered beneath my touch.

"Ryker." His name felt sacred on my lips. "I'm done waiting."

His eyes darkened, the gold flecks swirling and expanding until they nearly consumed the brown.

A growl rumbled deep in his chest, vibrating against my palm. "Are you sure?"

The question hung between us, heavy with meaning.

"More sure than I've ever been," I whispered, the words barely audible yet somehow filling the entire room. "It's always been you."

My wolf surged forward with such force I nearly staggered. She'd been waiting for this moment—recognition, completion, bonding with our fated mate.

Ryker's pupils dilated, and his nostrils flared as he caught the change in my scent. His hands tightened on my waist, fingers digging into my skin as if anchoring himself.

Our lips collided, and this time, it felt different... maybe because we knew there would be no stopping what we'd started.

My hand fisted his shirt, but he pulled back slightly. He rasped, "We've both been injured. We should take a shower to get the grime off us."

I pouted as he released me and headed to the door. My wolf whimpered. When I'd told Ryker I was certain I hadn't expected him to leave my side until we'd completed our bond.

He jiggled the door handle, making sure the lock held, and turned back to me. A crooked smirk on his face and his forehead lifted, causing the scar through his left eyebrow to become even more pronounced.

The one imperfection made him look deadly, dangerous, and delicious.

He came straight to me and hoisted me against him, and I wrapped my legs and arms around him willingly. His mouth covered mine once again, and we headed toward the bathroom.

Time seemed to stop as our mouths danced together and electricity jolted through my body. Need knotting in my core, making me wish he was already sunk deep inside me.

In the bathroom, he turned on the lights and set me on my feet. The bathroom's stark white tiles gleamed under flickering fluorescent lights.

He pulled away from me again and turned on the

shower, and I leaned against the beige granite countertop and groaned, not wanting him to leave my side. With the water warming, he came back to me and skimmed his fingers along my sides until he gripped the hem of my shirt. He slowly lifted it over my head and then carefully removed my clothes, piece by piece, until I stood bare before him. The vulnerability should have terrified me, but in his eyes, I saw nothing but reverence.

"You're beautiful," he whispered, his fingers tracing the outline of a bruise on my ribs. His touch was featherlight, contrasting with the dangerous power I knew those hands possessed. The same hands that had torn through our enemies now trembled slightly as they mapped the landscape of my body.

Steam billowed around us, fogging the mirror and creating a dreamlike haze. I reached for him, tugging at his shirt and lifting it upward with eager hands.

Inch by inch, his tanned skin was revealed. For the first time, I truly got to take in his hard frame and notice every place scarred from countless battles. I couldn't help but stare at the magnificent expanse of his chest. My every cell seemed to spark to life, and I wanted to freeze this moment.

I traced a particularly jagged mark on one side of his ribs. The very scar that was the result of him jumping in front of my sister to protect her for me.

Heart clenching hard, I wanted to scream. I should've known after he'd nearly died for me that there was no reason to hold back from him any longer. I had been so foolish and misled, and I planned on making that up to him every day for the rest of my life.

"See something you like?" he teased.

"I guess it's all right," I whispered, trailing my fingers down the ridges of his abdomen.

"Just all right?" he murmured and kissed me before I could answer.

I traced the curves of his hard abs and lower, his muscles tensing as I slid my fingers into the waistband of his sweatpants.

Ryker's breathing quickened as I lowered it over his taut ass.

When his pants hit the floor, I pulled away from the kiss, wanting to see him completely bare. As I took in the handsome man before me, I grew dizzy.

He was more perfect than fresh brownies. And when my attention focused on his arousal, my wolf howled in approval.

I couldn't help but stare, heat flooding my cheeks even as my core tightened with want.

He stepped forward, closing the distance between us, and I traced every ridge and plane of muscle until my fingers wrapped around his dick.

Ryker hissed as his mouth found mine again, and he moaned, "You're going to be the death of me."

My thumb circled over his tip, and he bucked into my hand. Steam swirled around us, the shower almost forgotten as my fingers explored his length, learning what made his breath catch and his muscles tense.

"Shower," he managed to growl between kisses, his self-control slipping. "Before the hot water runs out. I want to take care of you, please."

With reluctance, I released him, and he guided me backward into the shower until the warm water cascaded over us both. His hair darkened under the spray, and water droplets clung to his eyelashes as he watched me with an intensity that made my knees weak.

"Turn around and step back," he commanded with a

voice full of desire.

I obeyed, feeling his solid presence behind me. His hands slid up my sides, leaving trails of fire in their wake.

The shampoo bottle clicked open, and I heard the soft sound of the liquid being squeezed into his palm. His fingers tangled in my hair, massaging my scalp with firm, circular motions that sent tingles down my spine.

"Close your eyes," he whispered, his breath hot against my ear.

They closed of their own accord, and I surrendered to his touch. He shielded my face with one hand while the other guided the suds away. There was something achingly intimate about it.

"You have no idea how long I've wanted to do this." His lips brushed my ear as he reached for the conditioner. His fingers worked through my hair, massaging my scalp until I couldn't help the soft moan that escaped me.

I leaned back against him, feeling his hardness press against my lower back. Fire flamed through my body.

He took his time rinsing the conditioner from my hair. When he finished, his hands slid down to my shoulders and began to knead the tension from muscles I hadn't realized were so tight.

His hands slid around my waist...and turned me to face him.

Steam swirled around us as he reached for the bodywash, squeezing a generous amount onto a soft washcloth. The clean vanilla scent filled my nose as he began to wash me, starting with my shoulders and working his way down. The rough texture of the cloth contrasted with the occasional brush of his fingers against my skin, each touch igniting sparks that traveled straight to my core.

He moved me forward, and the washcloth glided over

my shoulder blades and down my spine, lingering at the small of my back before continuing lower. His free hand followed in its wake, tracing patterns on my clean skin that made me shiver despite the warm water.

When he finished, he dropped the cloth and replaced it with his lips on my neck, causing me to gasp. His mouth was hot against my wet skin, his teeth grazing my pulse point before soothing the spot with his tongue. I pressed my neck to his teeth, desperate for him to claim me.

"Not yet," he breathed as his hands slid around to cup my breasts. "I've dreamed about this," he murmured against my skin, his thumbs brushing over my nipples until they hardened beneath his touch. "About you. About us."

I let out a shaky breath. "Me too."

His hands wandered lower, tracing the curve of my waist. One of his hands splayed across my stomach, holding me against him while the other dipped between my thighs. When his fingers found my center, my body shuddered, already slick and ready for him.

"So wet for me," he rumbled.

I reached back, threading my fingers through his wet hair as his touch became more deliberate. One finger circled my entrance before sliding inside, making my knees buckle. His other arm tightened around me, supporting my weight as a second finger joined the first, stretching me in the most delicious way.

Desire increased, demanding more than just his fingers. "I need you," I whimpered, my head falling back against his shoulder as his thumb found my spot and circled with just enough pressure to make stars dance behind my eyelids.

His teeth grazed my earlobe before sucking it. "You'll have me. All of me. But first..."

His fingers curled inside me, finding that spot that made

my entire body tremble. The dual sensation of his fingers thrusting while his thumb worked had me climbing toward release faster than I'd thought possible.

"Ryker, I'm—" My words dissolved into a moan as he increased his pace.

"Let go for me. You're safe with me." He turned me around and lowered his mouth to my breast and said, "I want to feel you come apart in my hands." Then he sucked on my nipple, pushing me over the edge.

My back arched as pleasure crashed through me in waves. His name tore from my throat as my entire body shook with the force of my release. He held me tight against him and began kissing my shoulder as I shuddered through the aftershocks.

"Beautiful," he murmured, slowly withdrawing his fingers as I came down from my high. "So fucking beautiful."

Legs unsteady, I pressed my forehead to his chest. The water cascaded over us both, washing away the evidence of my pleasure. When I'd caught my breath, I looked up at him, taking in the hunger in his eyes. The tension in his jaw as he held himself back.

"Your turn," I whispered, reaching for the soap.

He raised an eyebrow, that dangerous smile lifting one corner of his mouth as I swirled the soap between my palms until they were covered in lather.

I placed my hands on his chest and took my time tracing his muscles. My soapy hands glided over his broad shoulders, down his powerful arms, feeling the strength beneath my fingertips. His eyes never left mine, darkening as my touch became less about cleaning and more about exploring.

"You're enjoying this." His voice strained as my hands worked lower, tracing the defined lines of his abs.

"Immensely." His muscles tensed as my fingers dipped just below his navel.

My hands slid lower and wrapped around his dick again. His sharp intake of breath sent a thrill through me, a surge of power at knowing I could affect him this way. I stroked him slowly, taking in his changing expression.

I tightened my grip slightly and quickened my pace. His breath came in shorter bursts, and the water poured over us, smoothing my movements as I worked him.

His response was a strangled sound, somewhere between a groan and my name. Emboldened, I experimented with pressure and pace, cataloging every twitch, every hitch in his breath.

"Fuck, Ember," he managed, his voice rougher than I'd ever heard it. One of his hands braced against the shower wall while the other tangled in my wet hair.

I marveled at the contrast between us—his large frame towering over me, muscles coiled tight with restraint, while I explored him with deliberate movements. Steam wrapped around us like a cocoon, creating our own private world where nothing existed beyond this moment, this connection.

His hips rocked against my hand. I could feel him growing even harder. The way his jaw clenched and the tendons in his neck stood out in stark relief told me how close he was getting to the edge.

"You feel incredible," I whispered, mesmerized by his reaction to my touch. "I could do this all day." My free hand traced patterns on his chest, and I raked my teeth against his neck.

His body tightened and he jerked away, causing me to damn near stumble.

Had I done something wrong?

My heart felt like it was breaking in two, the agony on par with losing my pack. A sob built in my chest, and his eyes widened.

"Babe, what's wrong?" he asked and cupped my face.

"If you need more time, I get it." I tried to swallow my sob and hold back the tears. He'd given me additional space when I'd needed it. Doing the same for him was only fair.

"More time?" His brows furrowed as the water ran over his body. "That's not it at all. I just didn't want to finish like this."

"Like what?" He'd pleasured me, and I wanted to return the favor.

His hands dropped to my waist, and he stepped forward until my back was pressed against the cool tile wall. The contrast between the cold surface at my back and his burning hot body against my front sent shivers racing along my spine.

"I want to be inside you the first time I come for you," he growled. "I've waited too long for this—for you—to rush it."

The raw hunger in his gaze made my heart slam against my ribs and my body nearly combusted. Water continued to cascade over us, steam filling the small space until it felt like we were suspended in some dreamlike realm where only we existed.

His mouth found mine again and demanded even more this time. Desperation built to a throbbing ache. One of his hands tangled in my wet hair while the other slid down my back, cupping my ass and lifting me effortlessly. I wrapped my legs around his waist, my core pressing against his hardness.

"Ryker," I whispered against his lips.

He pressed his forehead to mine, his glowing golden eyes locked with mine as he positioned himself against my entrance. He rasped, "Tell me you want this. Tell me you want me."

"I want you. Only you. No one has ever made me feel like this." The words tumbled from my mouth.

"I've never wanted anyone but you," he confessed and entered me slowly, inch by agonizing inch. The stretch and fullness made me gasp, my fingers digging into his shoulders. When he was fully seated inside me, he stilled.

Somehow even more desire blasted through me, and I tried to buck against him, but he held firm.

"You feel like home," he murmured.

I couldn't speak, could only feel. The electricity jolted between us, intensifying to a level I'd never experienced before.

He began to move with agonizing slowness, drawing almost completely out before sinking back in. Each thrust was measured, deliberate, as if he wanted to memorize every sensation between us. I clung to him, my body trembling with need, but he maintained that torturous pace, making the build slow and intense.

I wasn't sure my body could handle much more.

"Ryker, please." My voice broke.

"No." His lips brushed against my ear. "I've waited too long for this. I'm not rushing anything."

He rolled his hips, sending sparks shooting through my every nerve ending. The water continued to rain down on us, droplets catching on his eyelashes and trailing down the sharp planes of his face. I watched, mesmerized, as a bead of water slid from his collarbone down to where our bodies were joined.

His free hand cupped my breast, thumb circling my nipple while his mouth moved to my neck. I gasped as his teeth raked against my beating pulse, the sharp points of his canines extending just enough to remind me of what was to come. Beneath my skin, my wolf stirred, eager and wanting.

"Dammit, Ryker," I begged, tightening my legs around his waist.

A growl rumbled deep in his chest as he gently pinched my breast and commanded, "Look at me."

I gazed into his eyes, which had darkened to a molten amber.

"I need—" My words dissolved into a moan as he suddenly increased his pace with newfound urgency. The controlled rhythm was gone.

Tired of him being in full control, I braced my hands against his shoulders and pushed back, just enough to create a whisper of space between us. His rhythm faltered as confusion flickered across his face.

"My turn." I unwrapped my legs from his waist, separating us, and planted my feet on the floor.

Before he could protest, I spun us around and pressed

his back against the wall. His eyes widened, then darkened with renewed hunger as I took control. I lifted a leg around him, guiding him back inside me as I set my own pace—slower, deeper.

His hands found my hips, his fingers digging into my flesh, but he didn't try to quicken my movements. Instead, he watched me as he panted.

"Ember," he breathed my name, causing my wolf to break free.

I rolled my hips and quickened my movements, pulling him in deeper as I arched my back. Our bodies slid against each other, and something primal took over.

No more waiting. I couldn't take it.

I grabbed his hair and pulled his head toward my neck.

"Bite me." If he didn't do it this second, I wasn't sure I could take much more. "I'm ready to complete the bond if you are."

His teeth scraped against my skin again, the pressure increasing as our movements became frantic.

"Are you sure?" he asked against my flesh. Even as he asked, his teeth sank in a little deeper.

The sting added to my pleasure, and my head spun.

"Yes," I gasped, my body trembling on the edge of release. "Make me yours."

His teeth sank into my flesh, breaking the skin. The initial sharp pain transformed into something else entirely—a flood of warmth that surged through my whole body. My chest cracked open like a dam breaking, and Ryker's emotions crashed into me—his desire, his possessiveness, his relief, and his love. The intensity of feeling both his pleasure and mine simultaneously sent me spiraling.

"I love you," I whimpered as waves of ecstasy tore through me, more powerful than anything I'd ever experienced. My body convulsed around him, my vision blurring at the edges.

My wolf took control, not satisfied yet. I buried my face against his neck and sank my teeth into his wet skin, tasting copper as the bond completed. His blood filled my mouth as my orgasm continued to pulse through me, each wave stronger than the last.

Ryker's grip tightened painfully on my hips as his body went rigid. A guttural roar tore from him and reverberated through the shower as he shuddered against me. His release surged through him in powerful waves that intensified my own. Our bodies remained locked together as we rode the aftershocks together.

With our bond formed, I could feel warm spots that had to be Xander, Gage, and Kendric. No! My stomach knotted; I did not want to be the alpha of the merged pack. Some instinct inside me pushed the bonds away, not accepting them, as my eyes rolled back and euphoria flowed through my body.

I collapsed against Ryker's chest, both of us sliding down to sit on the shower floor. The tile was cold against my legs, but I barely noticed. Our chests heaved, and our hearts raced at the same frantic pace.

Mine, he linked, resting his head against my shoulder. His arms wrapped around me, holding me so tightly I could barely breathe. Hearing his words in my head meant so damn much to me.

Yours, I agreed, my fingers tracing the fresh mark I'd left on his neck. *Always and forever.*

As the haze wore off, three new links warmed in my chest at an even level, indicating they were fellow pack-mates, and Briar's cooled marginally back to the fellow packmate level.

Softer. Steady. Familiar.

After so long, with almost nothing but cold after losing my entire pack apart from Briar, the sensation nearly undid me.

My eyes fluttered shut as I curled tighter against Ryker, my forehead resting against the damp skin of his chest as the water sprayed us. For the first time in what felt like forever, I didn't feel hollow.

Ryker was our alpha. That truth settled inside me like a balm, like something my soul had always known but hadn't let itself believe until now.

I hadn't wanted to lead. All I'd ever intended to be was a beta or an alpha's mate.

I just wanted this.

Him.

The sudden shift of the water temperature jolted me, pulling me from the daze. Cold droplets replaced steam, and my breath caught.

Ryker grunted and adjusted himself beneath me. "Water's cold."

"Mmm." I didn't want to move, but the chill started to bite.

With a sigh, he eased us upright. Muscles trembled as the final shivers of magic and release worked themselves out. He brushed his lips over my temple before reaching for the knob and twisting the water off.

We stepped from the shower, the air hitting like a cold blanket. Goose bumps covered my body, and I shivered.

Ryker grabbed a towel from the hook and wrapped it around me before taking another for himself. I leaned into the gesture and the solid weight of him beside me.

Conflicting emotions surged through me. I'd never been

so content or happy, but my parents weren't here to cele-brate Ryker's and my union.

Ryker stilled. *What's wrong?* He lowered his hands, the brown returning to his irises. *Do you regret—*

No. I cut him off and tried like hell to hold back a sob. *I... I just wish my parents were alive to celebrate our bond.*

His expression softened, and he dropped the towel and pulled me flush against him. He wrapped his arms around me and placed his chin on my shoulder.

I know. He kissed the mark he'd made that claimed me as his. *I want mine here too. They would've loved you.*

His pain mixed with mine, and once again, the sensation of drowning hung over me.

We stood there, water dripping from our bodies and puddling at our feet, but I didn't care. His touch was enough to keep me together when the pain threatened to splinter us apart.

"I can't bring them back to us," he vowed. "But I *will* get justice for them. Every vampire who laid a hand on our packs will pay for what they did. I swear it, Ember. I won't stop until they bleed and I've taken their lives with my own hands."

Tears finally fell, hot against my chilled skin. His words released the grief I'd been suppressing for too long. Some-how, this time, it didn't feel like it would kill me.

"No, *we'll* make them pay." I didn't want to be left out. They'd tried to kill my entire pack, and only Briar and I had gotten away. "For every name, every howl cut short, for every mother, father, pup—"

He placed his hands on my cheeks. "We'll do it *together*. Like we will from here on out. Side by side."

Promise, I linked, afraid of how the word would sound if I spoke it out loud.

Lil rebel, your wants and needs are the most important thing to me, above everything and everyone else. I don't give a damn if that's wrong for an alpha because you are now my entire world. I revolve around you, and if you need a hand killing those who did you wrong, then I'll be there with a smile.

A few weeks ago, that would've scared me, but not anymore. I finally understood Ryker. He'd gotten the spell cast on him to avenge his family and pack. Everything he'd done had been to ensure he didn't hurt those who didn't deserve it.

A shiver racked my body, and he stepped back, leaving me even colder.

"Let's see if we can find clean clothes instead of putting the dirty ones back on." He motioned toward the bedroom.

I wanted to pout, but we'd had a long day and night and needed rest. There was no telling what would happen tonight or tomorrow.

We padded back into the bedroom, and Ryker went to the dresser on our left and opened the top drawer. Folded inside were several pairs of dark sweatpants and a few worn shirts, clearly left behind by a pack member.

He grabbed a sweatshirt and a pair of black shorts that he tossed at me, then he grabbed sweatpants and a shirt.

We slipped on the clothes and climbed into the bed, sinking into sheets that held a trace of cedar and smoke. He pulled me against his chest, and I breathed in his intoxicating scent as well.

My eyes fluttered shut, exhaustion beginning to take hold.

Congrats, Briar linked gently into my mind, *about time. I hope I waited long enough and am not interrupting anything.*

A small laugh escaped, and Ryker lifted his head to look at me. He arched a brow.

Thanks. And your timing was perfect, I replied while smiling.

"I'm not complaining, but what's this all about?" Ryker tilted his head.

"Just Briar congratulating us." I snuggled deeper against him and let the warmth of his body and the bond we'd sealed wash away the last traces of cold I'd been carrying.

He kissed the top of my head. "Well, I'm not upset about that."

In his embrace, I finally felt like I'd found another home, and for the first time since I'd watched my world burn, I didn't feel like I was drowning.

Something tried to tug me awake, but Ryker's body pressed against mine, and the comforting thrum of our connection lulled me back under.

But then something hit me.

A scent.

Floral... but not common. I breathed deeper, my eyes still shut. The scent was beautiful, like roses steeped in magic and lilacs blooming in the middle of a lightning storm.

My heart leapt into my throat, and a shiver coursed down my spine.

That scent—I'd smelled it twice before.

I forced my eyes open.

The room was dim, bathed in the faint blue-gray light of dawn creeping through the window blinds.

And *he* leaned over me.

A scream lodged in my throat as a warm palm clamped over my mouth.

Golden skin shimmered faintly in the low light. Dark-auburn hair framed sharp cheekbones and ears that narrowed to elegant points. His glowing, otherworldly eyes bored into mine.

Unblinking.

Unmoving.

I wasn't even sure if he was breathing.

My body went rigid, instincts screaming, bond flaring with panic.

Ryker—

But he didn't stir. He remained completely still beside me, his breathing deep and even—asleep.

Like he couldn't hear me or sense the danger.

The strange man's hand remained soft over my mouth as he stared at me like he was silently willing me not to panic, and the strange, warm magic inside me responded, surging forward, appeasing me.

Then, softly, he pressed a finger to his own lips. A silent command.

Don't scream.

My pulse thundered. Magic crackled at the edge of my awareness, my skin buzzing where his body hovered too close.

He was real.

And I had no idea how he'd gotten inside.

Or what he wanted.

CHAPTER EIGHT

The man didn't move; he merely stared like he could see everything inside me.

Warmth exploded through me. It wasn't anything like the sensation I felt with Ryker. This wasn't a tug and attraction but more like familiarity that shouldn't be possible. A whisper threaded through my veins, the intensity stronger than anything I'd ever felt before.

My new magic stirred like it recognized him and wanted to go to him.

His hand fell away from my mouth—slow, deliberate.

I needed to scream, but I wasn't able. The noise just wouldn't come. I was locked there, staring into his glowing eyes while something unseen passed between us. My magic seemed to pool into him as he returned the favor.

For a heartbeat, we just *existed* in this strange moment of knowing and not knowing. My skin prickled. I was both petrified and freed, as if a part of me that had been hidden was finally being seen.

Somehow, I realized he wasn't here to hurt me.

Just as quickly as the warmth bloomed, Ryker stirred beside me, and it disappeared. The stranger's eyes flashed—liquid gold catching the light—and then he was gone. Vanished into thin air with no trace of a shadow to denote his presence. No sound of movement, nothing but a faint swirl of floral scent and the lingering imprint of his presence ebbing from within me.

My lungs finally worked on their own as Ryker's concern slammed into me.

He bolted upright, searching the room for danger. *Is someone in here?*

Of course, he'd suspect it to be a shadow. Heart pounding like a drumline against my ribs, I scanned the room, searching for some hint of *him*. He couldn't really just vanish, but shouldn't I be able to see him if he was cloaked?

Still, there was nothing.

The room was empty.

"No, no one is in here right now." I let out a breath, and my hands shook. "At least, I don't think so."

"Ember?" Ryker's voice grew sharper now. His hand gripped my arm, turning me toward him as he rasped, "What the hell just happened?"

I couldn't answer. I shook my head, my pulse screaming, then opened my mouth to respond, but nothing came out. I wasn't sure how to describe what had just passed between me and the stranger, but he'd done something to me. The warm presence I'd come to recognize inside me had calmed, but it was stronger than it had been before his arrival.

Baby, you're scaring me.

I blinked, trying to force words to form. "I..." My throat closed again, the words sticking to the back of my tongue like ash.

His thumbs brushed my cheeks. "I don't feel pain, but are you hurt?" Cold tendrils of fear flowed into me from him.

I had to get my head on straight. Worrying him like this wasn't right, especially with everything going on right now. *The strange man. He was here. I tried to wake you, but you didn't stir.*

Ryker's body snapped taut like a wire about to break. "What? What do you mean? Was it a dream?" He scanned the room again like he expected to find the man hiding in a corner.

It wasn't a dream. If my warm, strange magic wasn't still sparking within, I might have believed it was. *I woke up, and he was leaning over me. He clamped a hand over my mouth so I wouldn't scream.*

His nostrils flared. "He *touched* you? I'm going to *kill* him."

The thought of the man being harmed caused my heart to drop. "*No.* You can't." I grabbed his wrists, forcing him to look at me. "He didn't do anything but... watch me. And then he touched me. But it wasn't threatening. It was like... my magic knew him. Then he vanished into thin air without even a shadow defining him."

Something unreadable passed into me from Ryker. My blood turned cold as the sheen appeared over his eyes.

"You think he wasn't a threat?" His voice dropped low, more dangerous than I'd ever heard. That's when I realized what he was feeling—fear and bloodlust. He wanted to kill the man for putting me in danger.

He wasn't, I linked, but the second the words left, I knew I'd made things worse.

Ryker reared back slightly, shaking his head, disbelief—and something deeper—burning through our bond.

"That's what has you shaken like this?" he ground out. "Because someone broke into this house while we were sleeping, and *your magic liked it?* Why the fuck would your wolf like it, Ember? You completed the bond with me. That shouldn't be possible."

My mouth opened. Closed. I didn't know how to defend what I'd *felt,* but I understood why he was feeling that way. A strange man had appeared in front of me while I slept in bed with my mate, and I'd shared my magic with him with Ryker by my side. "It wasn't my wolf magic." I winced, realizing I hadn't actually told him about the warm, strange magic within me.

Betrayal shot through our new bond. "What do you mean it *wasn't your wolf magic?*"

I reached for him again, needing to touch him, to anchor us both. When I touched his hand, he moved a little like he was going to pull away, but then he didn't. The buzz between us sprang to life.

"I don't know. There's... something else inside me. Something that woke up after you pulled me from the river that day. It's warm. Not wolf. Not witch. Different. I didn't say anything because I didn't know what it meant. And I thought—" My voice caught. "I thought maybe it was just my mind playing tricks on me because of my grief."

"When did you figure out it wasn't?" His expression strained as his eyes examined me, looking for any sort of reaction.

"Tonight." The ache in my chest threatened to fracture me. "Just now. The part that I thought resembled the way how we carry our pack inks flared within me like I recognized him."

Ryker's lips parted, but nothing came out. Our bond

throbbed, channeling pain, betrayal, fear. All tangled into a knot so tight it nearly strangled us both.

"I need to keep you safe." His voice was hoarse. "A witch must have put a spell on you or something. You're not thinking clearly."

"But I am." I clasped one of his hands in mine and continued. *I don't know how to explain it, but I could sense his intention, and it wasn't to cause harm.*

His mouth tightened. "From here on out, I need you to promise to tell me if anything strange happens again, even if it's internal. I need to know we're a team. That's what I signed up for, and I won't allow another man to come in and ruin it."

"I promise." I looked him in the eye, needing him to know that I meant it. "And I swear, I have *no* romantic feelings for this man at all. No one could *ever* take your place."

Some of the tension left his shoulders. "I swear, if he tries anything with you in any sort of way, I'll take pleasure in killing him slowly."

I wanted to argue with him, but that would make him more steadfast in that decision. The best thing I could do was downplay my connection with the strange man. I couldn't fault Ryker because if I were in his shoes, I'd be acting the same way. However, something inside me *recognized* that man.

He threw the covers off and kicked his feet over the edge of the bed just as his voice popped into my head, along with the other four pack links. *Everyone, get up. We have a threat to chase down.*

I tilted my head and spoke out loud so the other four couldn't hear me. "What are you doing? Everyone needs rest, and we haven't been alerted that there's a breach."

"But there has been a breach." He lifted his chin.

What's going on? Briar replied, and I heard her door open down the hall. *Are we being attacked again?*

I bit the inside of my cheek, but I suspected I knew where this was going. I didn't like it one bit, but I had to stop pressing, or he'd be more determined.

Yes, but your sister doesn't agree. Ryker crossed his arms, daring me to say something.

If Ember doesn't think it's a big deal, then I agree with her, Gage added, still not wanting to listen to Ryker.

"Ryker, please." I jumped out of bed with my hands up. "Don't do this."

"I have to protect you." He walked over and kissed my cheek. "I know you don't agree, but I can't just sit back and then have something happen to you, especially when he got away without a trace."

The comment hit me in the chest because he was right. If even I couldn't see the man, he could attack, and we'd never see it coming. But I *knew* he wouldn't.

Someone just came into our bedroom and vanished. Not even Ember could see him once he disappeared, and he didn't set off the perimeter alarm. Ryker took my hand and gently squeezed. "I don't mean to upset you. I love you more than life itself, but I can't risk something happening to you. What if he turned on me or Briar?"

The walls seemed to close in on me. I hadn't considered that, and I couldn't argue. *Let's go.* Still, I knew it would be futile.

Some of the tension melted from his face when he realized I wasn't arguing. He took my hand, leading me out to the hallway. The wood creaked beneath our steps, and soon, we entered the living room where the other four waited.

Gage sat up on the couch, his hand wrapped around the grip of his gun. "What's wrong?"

Jaw tight, Xander stood. "Are we under attack?"

Emerging from the hallway with his shirt half on, Kendric flexed muscles that strained against the fabric.

Briar stood near the archway, her braid a mess, but her eyes alert and already scanning for a threat.

"No one's attacking yet." Ryker stepped closer to me and continued, "But someone got inside this house while we slept."

"How the *fuck* did that happen?" Xander nabbed his gun from the couch.

I interjected, filling them in on the events from earlier.

Kendric nodded. "I agree with Ryker. He had to be taunting us. I can watch over Ember while we're running around so you can stay focused, Ryker." He stepped close to my other side.

"No." Ryker snapped his head toward him. "She's coming with me. There's no way in hell I'm separating from her now. Briar can go with you."

"What?" I blinked. "I thought you wanted me to stay here."

"I want you to be safe," he said, teeth clenched. "And you're safest with me."

The others stilled, but no one dared to argue.

"But Briar—" The thought of something happening to her made me nearly lose my mind.

"Will be fine since the man is fixated on you." Ryker's wolf surged forward as if he might use alpha will.

He linked, *You think I'm going to leave you behind after that thing got that close?* Frustration and anger constricted my chest from his emotions. *I didn't even feel him, Ember. He slipped past me. That's not happening again.*

Gage exchanged a glance with Xander, who gave a tight nod.

"We move quietly," Ryker continued. "Briar, Kendric—flank us. Eyes sharp. Nothing gets near Ember unless it wants to die."

Kendric nodded once, already pulling his knife from his belt and tucking it into his boot.

"Let me grab my boots. I thought we might be shifting." Briar darted back down the hallway toward her room.

Ryker turned to me, his jaw still tight. "Get your shoes. I'm not letting you out of my sight."

I didn't argue. Not because I was afraid but because, deep down, I knew he was right. Whatever that man was, he'd seen something in me. Reached something I didn't understand.

And I wasn't ready to face that alone.

Gage bent down and produced three more guns. He handed one to Ryker and another to me. The cold metal bit into my hand, feeling foreign despite my history with it.

Briar came down the hall, boots laced, a knife strapped to her thigh. Her expression was grim, and the sharp lines on her face confirmed she felt similarly to me.

"Here, take this," Gage said, handing her a gun.

"Let's roll." Xander headed to the door and opened it.

The six of us went outside, and for a second, we all stared at one another.

Be safe, everyone, I linked. *Let me know the second something feels off, anything at all.*

I followed Ryker, the others falling in behind us.

The moment we stepped off the porch, the world looked different.

Twilight crept along the horizon, streaks of pink and gold trying to paint over the horror of last night. But I could've sworn the shadows still clung to the edges of the trees, and the scent of blood hadn't faded.

Bodies.

Dozens of them still lined the clearing across the neighborhood—some wrapped in sheets, others barely covered. The wolves hadn't had a chance to bury their dead. Not yet.

A low growl rumbled in Ryker's chest as we passed them, his eyes flicking to each one.

We walked in silence, the only sounds our boots crunching over gravel and the wind rustling through the trees.

When we reached the edge of the woods, Ryker stopped and raised a hand.

Stay human, he ordered. *If we encounter shadows or worse, we need to be able to shoot. Shift only if absolutely necessary.*

Everyone nodded, weapons already drawn.

My fingers twitched on my pistol, nerves dancing in my blood. The weapon didn't feel right, and I wanted to drop it. However, I had to be strong.

We stepped onto the forest path, the trees closing in around us.

The air changed.

Became colder. Heavier.

That familiar sensation hit first, like a gaze pressing into the back of my neck. The warmth I'd felt earlier stirred again, telling me someone was watching.

Him.

As I tried to locate him, I didn't see any sign or sense any evidence that he was near. But the sensation intensified. Then came the chill, a creeping, icy dread that wrapped around my spine.

My breath caught. I didn't need to see red eyes or shadows to know.

Vampires.

They were close, and they had to be hunting.

Hunting *us*.

CHAPTER NINE

Do you sense something? Ryker linked as he turned toward me. His fingers brushed mine as we moved, low and silent, through the thick oak trees.

Our connection sprang to life, and the connection in my chest shrank and coiled, affected by tension from both of us.

Yes, both the vampires and the strange man. I honestly hadn't wanted to tell him that last part, but I refused to keep things from him anymore. We were partners... one soul, completed now, and I wouldn't take our relationship for granted.

My fingers clenched tighter around the gun I held. The coldness of the metal might as well have been an icicle.

Are you fucking serious? Uncomfortable heat seeped into the already-strained bond. *The psycho who was watching you sleep and covering your mouth is around too? How do you know?*

That answer wasn't going to go over well, but what could I do? *That strange magic feels a tug toward him.*

A snarl ripped from Ryker's chest despite us needing to

be quiet. Granted, if we smelled them, they'd probably already caught our scent or would soon.

I'm going to kill the motherfucker. Ryker's back muscles quivered in front of me as he continued, *You're mine. No one will ever take you from me.*

I wanted to reassure him it wasn't anything like that, but I already had, and clearly, it hadn't helped. Even though I wished he would listen to and believe me, a part of me—my wolf—was thrilled with his possessiveness. Fated mates were meant to make you feel special and worthy.

Every step we took made the hair on my arms rise. The familiar pulse of Ryker's presence next to me grounded me —but barely.

Something else stirred beneath my skin, and it wasn't my wolf.

Everyone, stay on high alert. Ryker slowed his pace, scanning the area even more thoroughly. *We've got both vampires and the weird man on our trail. Neither of them can be seen.*

I glanced over my shoulder and saw Kendric and Briar scanning the flanks while Xander and Gage guarded the rear, silent and sharp-eyed.

But I couldn't stop my head from turning toward the trees, toward the feeling that we were being followed.

Unlike last time, the cold, disturbing magic wasn't advancing on us. It was more like they were watching us. As if they were trying to get answers themselves.

The warm pulse of the strange man's magic brushed mine again—soft and too pointed to be anything but deliberate.

Ryker stopped short and extended an arm to block my path, and I almost slammed into him.

My shoulder bumped into his, but I planted my feet into the mulch to prevent myself from moving farther.

The coldness increased, as did the warmth. As if they were coming from the same direction.

Strange.

Were the man and the vampires working together? Maybe Ryker had been correct that the strange man was using something to influence my mind.

What's wrong? Kendric inched forward so he could see both Ryker and me.

I don't want to get too far from the neighborhood in case we need backup. Ryker's eyes glowed as his wolf surged forward.

His frustration built, bubbling over.

He was trying to hide that he was upset, but why? *Do you see something?*

You're joking, right? He looked at me, his face lined with what had to be concern. *You're the only one who can see them... unless your morning visitor somehow took the vision from you.*

Before I could stop myself, I flinched. I hadn't expected him to take out his frustration on me. It was unacceptable, but we would address that later. We didn't need to lose focus on the actual threat. *You feel frustrated.*

He exhaled. *This whole bond thing is going to take some getting used to. I can feel your emotions too, and I let you down.*

What do you mean? Out of every response possible, I hadn't expected that one.

Because I was so desperate to find this man you keep talking about that I rushed out here without thinking to alert the Blackwood pack.

We're close to them, and if we don't leave the perimeter,

we should be fine. I tilted my head in the direction of the houses, where I could hear a couple sets of paw prints running not too far away from us. *If we scream, they'll know.*

I don't understand why the perimeter wasn't broken. Briar's voice interjected into our private conversation, pulling us back with the others. *If Ember can feel them, shouldn't they be right here?*

That was when it hit me. They weren't sure how I knew either, beyond seeing the vampires in cloaked form. This had to be the vampires trying to figure out both my abilities as well as the barrier that sometimes came to our aid.

No, I can feel them a ways off, but I think that's what they're testing as well. If that was the actual case, I couldn't react until they revealed themselves. *They're somewhere near the perimeter to the left of us, but they haven't crossed it yet. That's why Cassi and the Blackwoods haven't been alerted.*

Ryker swallowed. *I bet you're right. Is your sense of the strange man coming from the same direction?*

Irritation flashed through me, but I yanked it back to indifference. Ryker already wanted to kill the man, but I believed he was an ally, even though I was beginning to see Ryker's point. *Yes, he is.* I wanted to say more. If he was on our side, he could be watching them for us, but Ryker might see it another way. In the end, we didn't know anything about the man, so it was best to not rush to any sort of decision—including killing.

I blanked my expression and kept surveying everything, trying to glance in their direction the same length of time as all others.

We continued to move. About twenty yards from the

perimeter's end, the cold pressed on me like a wave slamming into me and trying to drag me under.

Ryker stumbled, clearly feeling the same sensations. The mate bond was even more connected and intense than the pack members' bond, which took me by surprise.

Keep moving. They've got to be close to the perimeter. It feels as if I've been hit by a tsunami. My lungs screamed as if tons of pressure had settled over me, but the warmth that had to be coming from the strange man pulsed into me and warded off some of the discomfort.

No, we're just gonna stop— Ryker started, but I noticed the wisps of shadows edging from spots behind the perimeter tree line.

They're here, I linked with everyone, *but don't react. Not yet.*

Dark, smoky outlines crawled behind the perimeter like ink bleeding through air. The shadows danced just far enough away to not set off the alarm.

I clenched my jaw, every instinct screaming to raise my weapon. *Everyone, keep watching. They aren't coming over yet to attack.* I didn't need to react. Not yet. Not until I *had* to.

What if they have weapons this time since we know who they are? Gage asked, and I could hear his steps becoming a little less steady behind us.

With the rising sun and the lightening sky, the darkness of the shadows thickened as more vampires arrived. None of them came any closer, but the magic pressed harder on me as more and more came.

A shimmer caught my eye, going back and then propelling forward like someone flicked their wrist.

My heart seized.

Knife, I linked as it soared toward me. I dove sideways as the blade ripped through the air, and it whistled past the place my throat had just been and embedded in the trunk behind me with a sickening *thunk.*

I hit the ground hard, shoulder skidding through mulch and wet leaves. Pain flared, but adrenaline kept it distant as I rolled to my feet, gun already raised.

I aimed and pulled the trigger, knowing that I wouldn't be able to make out which one had tried to kill me. I merely had to make a stand.

A dark blob dropped while the rest of the shadows floated backward.

I hated that they now knew I could see them.

Ryker squatted at my side, his snarl slicing through the trees as he and the others fired in the same direction. Gunfire cracked through the woods like thunder—sharp, raw, relentless.

Xander and Gage kept firing toward the retreating shadows while Briar dropped to my other side, scanning me for injuries.

Calm down, I linked, needing them to stop. The Black-woods had to be panicking at hearing all the commotion out here, and we had no way of contacting them to let them know they weren't at risk. *They've retreated. All you're doing is wasting ammo at this point.* Ammo we probably didn't have a ton of, as wolf shifters, in general, preferred fighting in wolf form over using weapons. This was an exception because we couldn't see them.

Smoke curled from the ends of gun barrels, scenting the air with metal and gunpowder even as my pack stopped shooting.

The warmth I'd felt from the strange man vanished with the vampires like it'd never been there at all.

Ryker grabbed my arm, spinning me toward him. *Are you hit? Did they injure you?*

No, I dodged it. I shivered, trying not to focus on what could've happened if I'd missed seeing the glint of the blade. *I'm fine.*

He cupped my jaw with one hand, gaze darting across my face like he didn't believe me.

We need to get the fuck out of here. Xander kept his gun aimed as if he expected them to come back at any second. *We're low on ammo now.*

A warning howl pierced the air, and paws pounded on the ground toward us, not bothering to be quiet.

We need to meet up with them, I linked. The sooner we headed them off, the better. I could only imagine the panic that had to be pounding through all the survivors right now, wanting to protect their home and their dead while losing no others.

Ryker helped me up and placed a hand around my waist as if I couldn't handle my weight on my own. Even though I was fine, the whole situation had terrified me, and his embrace was like a safe haven.

As we went to meet the Blackwood pack, I looked over my shoulder, ensuring the vampires weren't sneaking up on us. The cold magic they emanated wasn't strangling me, but I didn't want to be careless in case something changed.

Knowing we needed to hurry, I did the one thing I didn't want to do. I pulled away from Ryker and linked, *We need to move faster to meet up with them.*

I don't give a damn if they're pissed, lil rebel. His gaze settled on me. *You were just attacked, so if you need a minute to collect yourself or be rattled, that's what we're fucking going to do. The Blackwoods may be our allies, but you trump them in every way.*

In less than a few hours, he'd made this declaration twice. The cold man I'd first met had completely vanished... at least, for me, and I liked that he wasn't like this with everyone else.

Still... the idea of leaving families to panic didn't sit well with me. *I know, but I know how I'd feel if I thought the vampires were coming and I needed to protect my family. I promise I'm fine. I dodged it, remember?*

The fact that they aimed for you is bad enough. He growled faintly, taking my hand, and we all picked up our pace.

A hundred yards away, the Blackwood wolves burst through the trees, snarling and sniffing the air. Dozens of them in wolf form circled out wide, noses in the air, hackles raised. They looked at me and stalked toward us, eyes wild and teeth bared. They were ready to fight.

"It's okay! They're gone." I lifted both hands, but it probably wasn't as comforting as I wanted it to be with a gun in one hand.

The wolves slowed, their eyes locked on Ryker and me. I hated that we couldn't communicate both ways, but we no longer had a royal pack to intercede, so two-way communication was impossible when one pack was entirely in wolf form.

Two larger wolves who had to be some of Reid's top in command circled us in tight formation, eyes glowing and breath heaving from the run. Their teeth weren't bared, but their stance screamed accusation.

Ryker inched closer beside me, and I could feel the tension coiled through him like a live wire. We had to be careful how we handled this. We'd gone on a search for a potential threat without alerting them. Granted, I hadn't considered it because I didn't believe the strange man was a threat, but I should've considered that the vampires would be searching for answers.

"We need to go back to the neighborhood," I said quietly, lowering the gun. "We need to talk to Reid and Sun about what happened."

The largest dark-blond wolf shook his head in what seemed to be frustration but then nodded, indicating we should walk ahead.

Ryker exhaled, shoulders tight. "Let's go then."

The other wolves broke formation, two of them darting ahead to signal the pack, the rest falling in behind us like a silent escort.

We walked in tense silence, the forest thinning as the Blackwood neighborhood came into view.

What remained of the previous night's horror was everywhere—makeshift bandages, fresh graves, the scent of blood and grief still thick in the air. Shifters stood on porches, some in human form, others not. All watching as we approached.

Their eyes narrowed. Not just at us.

At *me*.

A dozen conversations cut off the second our boots hit the main path. Faces turned. Chests rose with tight, shallow breaths. They didn't speak either. The silence was worse than a snarl.

And then he appeared.

Reid stepped out of his house at the end of the row, a cane tucked under one arm, shoulders hunched but steady. The flannel hanging off his frame couldn't hide the bruises or the pain etched into his every step, but his eyes burned with something stronger than hurt.

Sun stood beside him with one hand clenched in a fist at her side.

Ryker's grip on my hand didn't tighten. It didn't have to. His pulse through the bond was steady. Fierce. Unapologetic.

But Reid's gaze locked on mine, and the storm that gathered there promised that we had to answer. "What the hell happened, Ember? And why weren't we informed that a threat was nearby before you ran straight into danger, risking us all?"

CHAPTER TEN

My heart skipped a beat. How much more damage had we caused between our packs? Relations were already teetering on the edge due to the manufactured fated-mate bond.

The shifters who stood outside their homes stared our way.

Sun stood beside Reid, jaw ticcing and eyes cutting straight through me.

I stopped. We needed to give them space right now. They were upset, and the worst thing we could do was come up on them like we were trying to dominate the conversation.

"We didn't mean to put anyone at risk." I kept my voice measured, but the words landed with less impact than I had hoped. "Vampires were scouting the area and stumbled upon us. They didn't cross the perimeter, and we couldn't alert you since we didn't have a phone." I didn't mention that we'd been looking for a possible threat in the first place.

"Why were you near the perimeter?" Sun lifted a brow. "We informed you we would be handling security."

I opened my mouth to answer, trying to figure out how to respond without telling them someone had come into our room undetected. It would only cause more problems among us.

Ryker stepped forward with an unreadable expression. "It was my decision."

Sun's head tilted back. "So you all decided to scout the area. Why?"

"It wasn't a full hunt." Ryker's jaw flexed. "It was a check-in. Quiet recon. I felt that something was off. We kept close and didn't cross the perimeter."

Reid's cane struck the porch with a dull thud. "You didn't think to tell me? To tell any of us? If something felt *off*, we deserved to know."

Ryker's arm brushed mine. "I did what I had to do. Ember was in danger. Something had breached the house— something we couldn't identify. I wasn't about to wait around and risk it happening again."

"Something *breached the house*?" Reid's gaze cut through him. "And you didn't care that my entire pack—or what's left of it—was in danger too? You just left without consulting or informing us?"

Ryker took a step forward. "It wasn't after your pack. It was after Ember."

A growl rumbled low in Reid's throat. "And how the hell do you know that?"

"I just do," Ryker snapped. "He watched her sleep and didn't make a sound. Didn't stir anyone else. If he'd wanted blood, he would've taken it then. He was there for her. No one else."

Are you going to do anything, Briar asked, moving to my side. She glanced back and forth between the two alphas.

"And you're just...trusting your gut?" Reid shot back.

"That's the kind of reckless logic that gets people killed. You don't *know* his intent."

Gage muttered under his breath. "Of course he's causing problems. The spell must still be working."

"I know enough," Ryker growled, eyes glowing now, his wolf skimming just beneath the surface. And he linked, *Shut the fuck up, Gage,* before speaking out loud. "He didn't lay a finger on anyone else. He had the chance and didn't take it."

Tension coiled like a whip, a mere breath away from snapping, and it came from within our own pack as well as the Blackwoods'. All this conflict was tearing us apart from both sides.

As if this wasn't bad enough, a tingle slid down my spine like a warm breath. The exact warmth that only the strange man caused.

I turned my head, eyes sweeping the trees at the edge of the clearing, and came up with *nothing*.

Not a glint of light. Not a flicker of movement.

Still, I *felt* him. The urge to seek him out rose, but I couldn't do that.

Not here.

Not now.

If I admitted I felt him, both packs would take their frustration out on him.

I took a breath and stepped between the two males, lifting both hands. Reid was still several feet away, but I placed one hand on Ryker's muscled chest, hoping my touch would ease some of his anger.

"That's enough." My voice rang clear but sounded tighter than I'd intended. I didn't need Ryker to sense my distress right now because there would be no reasoning with him.

I exhaled, focusing on Reid and Sun. "We should've told you," I continued. "You're right. If there was a threat—any threat—you and your pack had every right to know. What we did... it wasn't just reckless. It was disrespectful, and I'm sorry."

Ryker stiffened but didn't interrupt.

We were on the same side. We had to get over the animosity manufactured by the vampires in order to get through this.

We, the Blackwoods, and the Shae pack had all lost too much. None of us should be left in the dark any longer.

Reid stared at me. His jaw worked like he wanted to keep pushing, but my words—my tone—had landed.

Finally, he gave a tight nod. "We'll talk inside," he said flatly. "All of us."

"Are you serious?" Sun's mouth dropped. "They—"

He cut his eyes to her, and she stopped talking. He frowned, clearly not liking being questioned in front of his pack.

I understood his situation. He'd become an alpha because of his father's death, and he was injured with a huge threat looming at his property line. He couldn't seem weak, not in the slightest.

Sun cleared her throat. "Of course, let's talk."

Reid limped toward the house with Sun shadowing him. She glanced back at me with a look just as guarded as his.

We followed in tense silence and filed into their home one by one. The scents of blood and herbs still clung to the air, thick and acrid. A reminder of the night they'd lost so many and how injured Reid had been himself.

Ryker stayed close to me, the tension in his body making him move as if he had to force himself to go forward. I took his hand and tried to push calm toward him, hoping to take off the edge. I could feel how much he hated this—being called into another alpha's space and expected to fall in line.

Remember, this is about aligning and keeping all shifters and witches safe. Not all the witches are as bad as Cassi, and the vampires are a whole other ball game, I linked only to Ryker. *You're my alpha now, and I'm asking you to consider the needs of all. If you don't, we may not be able to achieve justice for the loved ones we lost.*

He exhaled and closed his eyes for a moment as Reid eased into a chair at the head of the room, shoulders rigid, cane resting beside him. Sun stood to his right, arms folded, her gaze cutting through every one of us like she was daring someone to step out of line.

Xander growled, clearly feeling similar to another alpha giving commands.

I didn't want to overstep, but the bridge between Ryker and the other three men of our pack needed to be repaired. *You may want to caution them to be rational.* I didn't want to be the one to inform them of what was needed.

Reid straightened his spine, trying to look strong despite his injuries. "If you aren't going to respect our pack, especially since we extended a home to you for safety, then you'll have to leave. I've lost too much to gamble what little we have left."

Clenching his hands, Gage bared his teeth, and Briar grabbed his forearm like she was preparing to hold him back.

Hand tightening, Ryker linked with all of us, *Calm down. I don't like it either, but we're not going to be able to take out the vampires by ourselves. We need allies, and the Blackwoods have extended their home to us.*

Satisfied that he'd taken the lead with our pack, I interjected, knowing that saying the words out loud would be harder. "You're right, and we understand."

Sun's and Reid's heads jerked back as if they hadn't expected that.

Ryker tilted his head and inhaled deeply. "To be honest, my pack isn't used to having to coordinate with other packs. We give orders, and others obey."

Fair. I hadn't thought of it that way. His pack had been the protectors of the royals and had obeyed the king and no one else. They didn't have to work with other packs; they'd ensured the others stayed in line.

"Well, that's not the case anymore, and we need a royal fast—before our power begins draining." Reid sighed. "But we need to address one problem at a time. From now on, I want full cooperation and transparency. If anyone in your group senses a threat—whether it's a vampire, shadow, or your weird magical stalker—you come to me."

Gage, Xander, and Kendric huffed a little, but Briar held her breath like she hoped Ryker would agree.

I did too, but I couldn't push him. He was the alpha. I'd given up that right by rejecting the bonds when they'd tried to come to me.

Ryker's mouth twitched, but he gave a stiff nod. "Fine."

His displeasure twisted between us as he swallowed hard.

Silence stretched a beat too long before the front door creaked open again.

Every head turned.

A sharp, citrusy scent rolled in first—bitter orange and dried herbs—followed by the thud of heavy boots. Bruce, the Shea pack's alpha, entered the house, his broad shoulders filling the doorframe. His normally groomed hair was a mess, and the dark-black circles under his eyes were even more pronounced. His usually sharp green eyes were dulled. "Sorry it took so long to get here." He ran a hand through his salt-and-pepper hair. "Another pack member died."

My heart cracked further. Another life lost, and for what? I wasn't even sure what Queen Ambrosia's end goal was.

"I'm so sick of this. What the hell does she even want?" Xander snapped, dragging a hand through his hair. "Is this just about slaughter? Or is she after something bigger?"

Silence followed. The kind that made us feel like the air had thickened.

"Fuck if I know." Gage ran a hand over his face. "Every time we saw her, she seemed so considerate and friendly."

"There's no telling how long she's harbored this hatred." There had to be *something* we were missing, but I didn't know what.

"She's going after the strongest packs," Ryker murmured.

"Maybe anyone she views as a threat?" Briar asked, glancing between Reid and Ryker. "It started with the royals and the protector pack, right?"

"Every attack has been deliberate," I mused. There had to be something we weren't seeing. Something that would make it all make sense. "None of this has been random."

Ryker pursed his lips. "She's hunting something—or someone."

Bruce walked into the room and leaned against the wall. "You're not wrong, but why kill the vampire nest? Those were her own people."

My heart stalled, and a sour taste filled my mouth. Flashing back to the nest killing had my stomach churning. It had been so bloody and devastating. "It did kind of solidify in my mind that the attackers were a shifter group, especially with the strange scent."

"Wait." Briar lifted a hand. "How do they smell like shifters? Is that witch magic?"

Bruce crossed his arms. "Yeah, and it was like we couldn't make out individual scents."

"Like it was blended." I remembered that it had been faint, but I'd assumed that was because of the cloaking spell.

Sun placed a hand on Reid's shoulder and muttered, "It couldn't be part of the masking charm, right?"

Shoulders sagging slightly, Reid shook his head. "There's only one way to get that answer."

The room went quiet, and I had no doubt we all knew what that meant.

Getting Cassi involved.

Ryker snarled, sharp and low. "You've got to be kidding me. Did we not just learn that witches can't be trusted?"

"The best way to get answers is to talk to one of them," Reid snapped, eyes locked on Ryker. "Because none of us knows, and she's been with my pack for years and never messed up before."

"That was a *huge* fucking mess up," Gage interjected.

"I agree." Ryker held an arm out. "She manipulated fated-mate bonds. The most important connection."

"She might also be the only one who can tell us what kind of magic can make a vampire smell like a shifter," Reid said evenly. "So, unless you want to keep playing in the dark, she's our best option."

I bit my lip and looked between them. They were both right—and I hated it.

Reid's eyes glowed, indicating he was using the pack link.

"Are you sure?" Sun wrinkled her nose.

"I am." Reid's irises returned to their normal blue. "Cassi should be here within minutes. A pack member is fetching her."

This isn't a good idea, Kendric linked.

At least that's something we can agree on right now, Ryker replied.

Xander added, *Then why the fuck are we waiting here for her to arrive?*

Because we can't do this alone, I replied, realizing how quickly my words had changed in such a short time. I'd been ready to take Briar and run, but now I understood what Briar believed. If we ran, there would be fewer people to fight for what was right. *And Reid's right. What other option do we have? We'll smell it if she lies, and I can see the shadows when witch magic is activated.*

So there's not much chance she can fool us if we ask the right questions, Briar added, coming to my side.

Good point, Xander replied, rocking back on his heels. *What could really go wrong?*

For the love of Fate, please don't challenge her. Gage blew out his cheeks, reminding me of a puffer fish.

I smiled a little, but I understood the sentiment. I firmly believed that Fate hated me—we didn't need to tempt her further.

"All I want are some fucking answers because I'm tired of losing pack members." Bruce scratched the scruff on his chin. "I don't care how we get them."

Ryker scoffed. *I understand that all too well.*

He had to be talking about his own soul-cloaking spell.

We lapsed into heavy silence for several minutes until the front door creaked open.

Cassi stepped in slowly, her expression unreadable. Her eyes flicked to me first, then Ryker, and finally to Reid. She folded in on herself, not looking like the strong, confident witch I'd seen before.

Reid stood and winced. "We need to know how the vampires are masking their scent to smell like shifters. Is there a spell that can counter the one they're under?"

Cassi blinked. "Witches can't cast a spell to make someone smell like a different species. It's about the balance of power. We can't manipulate what the goddess inhibits."

My stomach dropped, and the walls seemed to close in on me.

Reid frowned. "So you're saying it's not possible?"

Wringing her hands, she nodded. "Unfortunately, no."

"So we're back to nothing," Gage muttered.

Cassi's gaze shifted to me. "Not exactly."

I narrowed my eyes. "What do you mean?"

Her face lit up a little. "I stayed up all last night, and I came up with a plan."

CHAPTER ELEVEN

I waited with bated breath but tried to keep my head on straight. She'd already manipulated us once; who was to say she wouldn't do it again? We had to play it cautiously and check for hints of lying or manipulation.

Ryker didn't say a word, but a flare of annoyance burst through our bond like lightning licking across my skin. Sharp. Hot. Dangerous.

"Care to elaborate?" Reid arched a brow.

Is he being serious right now? Xander's surprise could be felt in his words.

Yeah, Gage chimed in. *We can't trust the witch bitch.*

The corners of Cassi's lips tipped upward. "Since Ryker has that spell on him, I can use it to locate the witch who cast it. We might get some answers from her, even if she's not with the vampire queen. And if she is, then we'll know where they're hiding and restrategize."

Hope bloomed in my chest...which had to be dangerous. Every time I thought we had a way to get answers, it never seemed to pan out.

The fact that no sulfur had permeated the air made it even more challenging to squash that sensation.

"What do you mean exactly?" Bruce pushed off the wall and stood upright. "No wordsmithing or tricks."

She nodded. "I can do that." She lifted both hands in surrender. "When a witch casts a spell, they use a piece of their magic. When the spell is used, it leaves a faint essence of the witch who cast it, but you can't locate them with it because it's not tied to them any longer."

All nine of us studied her intently, searching for any sign of a lie—avoiding eye contact, touching her mouth or throat, or scents that shouldn't be there.

"However, the spell she cast on Ryker uses a strong magic that only a handful of witches have. Limited powerful ones who are one of a pair of twins," she continued. "When twin girls are born, one of them will be gifted with a super rare and strong power, one of which is cloaking. When a permanent spell is placed on an individual, a thread of power constantly links them to the witch, unlike when a temporary one is placed. As soon as the spell is used, the connection vanishes."

I tilted my head, trying to understand, but it sounded similar to what the last witch we'd talked to had explained. "Someone else already told us that, since the spell on Ryker is still in place, it means the witch who cast it is alive."

"Well, yes, but there's more to it than that." Cassi closed her eyes for a moment, like she was steeling herself.

Briar leaned forward. "What is it?"

"It's something that we aren't supposed to share with outsiders, but these are extenuating circumstances now that everything is coming out." She wrapped her arms around her waist.

Reid stood, his face twisting. "If you aren't going to be helpful, then you need to—"

"No, I'm going to tell you." She dropped her hands. "Your pack took me in and sheltered me when my coven abandoned me. That means something to me, but the witch practices have been so ingrained."

My heart ached for her. She was warring with two parts of herself—the beliefs she was raised with and the family she'd chosen outside of blood. I was curious why she'd needed to be taken in.

"Any day now," Ryker snarled as his annoyance strengthened even more.

"I can track her using the thread that connects her magic to Ryker." She wrung her hands together. "It's just a pulse, but if I use a location spell and focus on the magical essence, we'll know where she is."

My blood turned cold, and a lump lodged in my throat.

"Wait." Sun's hand trembled. "If you can track her, can she track Ryker?"

That was the exact same question I had.

"Yes." Cassi rubbed a hand down her charcoal shirt. "But there's nothing I can do to prevent that. She'd have to remove the spell."

The silence that followed was deafening. Time halted as understanding finally broke through the shock.

"You mean to tell us we've been walking around with a fucking beacon on our backs?" Gage's voice boomed.

Xander snarled. "You've *got* to be kidding me. You should've started with that."

Kendric stepped toward Ryker and narrowed his eyes as he gritted out, "I hope you're satisfied with the fucking decision you made behind our backs."

Ryker didn't flinch. Didn't move. But the energy pulsing

from him was lethal. "If she's had access to me this whole time—"

"She knows where you are at all times," Reid bit out. "That would've been nice to know before you came here."

Anger swirled from Ryker and toward me through our bond, and he dropped my hand. "Are you fucking kidding me?" His words were such a low growl that they were almost inaudible.

Guilt crashed over him, surging through me as well, and I wasn't sure what to do.

He glanced at me, his expression twisting. "Is she messing with us? Is she hiding the scent of lies with magic?" I could hear the desperate hope that clung to his words.

My eyes focused back on Cassi, confirming what I already knew. "She's not."

The mix of emotions that slammed into me weakened my knees. There was so much there, anger... disdain... embarrassment... and shame. He stood there, rigid, his jaw clenched so tightly I half expected his teeth to crack.

I glanced at Xander, Kendric, and Gage, who showed varying expressions of anger, each with deep lines in their foreheads and flared nostrils.

If you'd talked to us— Gage started.

Stop. I wouldn't stand here and allow them to rip Ryker apart. *This is not the time or place. Focus on what we can do now instead of on the past, where we can't change a damn thing.*

"They won't expect us to use it against them." Cassi cleared her throat. "So that should give us an advantage."

Reid nodded once, curt and clipped. "What do you need?"

Cassi met his gaze. "A sample of Ryker's blood. A

binding stone. Sage—fresh from the garden. And a map or something to ground the magic."

"That's it?" Sun pursed her lips.

Cassi nodded. "It's a simple setup. I'll do the gathering myself so no one else is put at risk. I know where to find everything I need."

Reid studied her. "How long will it take?"

"If I leave now and nothing gets in the way, I can be back in a few hours." Her voice stayed even, but I could hear an edge of anxiety buried beneath it.

"We'll do the spell tonight then," Reid said, nodding once. "That gives us time to coordinate and make a plan for the morning."

Xander shifted his weight, glancing between me and Ryker. "And what exactly is that plan?"

"We use the location to track her down," Sun answered before Reid could. "We don't act until we've scouted out the situation properly. Hopefully, she won't be with a ton of vampires, but if she is, at least they shouldn't be cloaked."

"Will you have enough of us ready for scouting in the morning?" Briar bit her lip. "So many are injured."

"We have enough strength," Reid finally said, breaking the silence. "Bruce, do you have any people you can call here?"

"Not a ton, but I can try to get a few more. Though probably not by tomorrow." Bruce shook his head. "Whoever I ask to join is pretty much signing their own death warrant. We have to stop all these deaths."

His words were the equivalent to a kick in the gut. I hated that so many lives had already been taken. "Well, the vampires are still reeling from what happened last night and trying to figure out how the barrier works. That should keep at least some of them occupied."

"What if the witch tracks Ryker while we're on the way to her?" Kendric scratched at his beard.

"We'll contend with that if it happens." Even though I wasn't one for elaborate strategies, I did know that every plan had flaws. Right now, we just needed an advantage.

Reid let out a long breath, rubbing his temple like the tension was starting to weigh more than his own weight on the cane he was leaning on. "Then we reconvene after the burials. Let the dead rest before we plan to risk more lives."

No one argued.

The heaviness in the room didn't lift, but it settled into mutual understanding.

"I'll get the supplies," Cassi said, voice low. "I know what I need and where to find it. I'll be ready to perform the spell at sundown."

"Go," Reid muttered. "And be careful."

She nodded and slipped out the door without another word.

The moment the door closed, tension cracked through the room like a whip.

"Rest while you can," Reid said, his tone final. "We all need to be in the best shape we can be for our next move."

He was right. A lot of us were still injured, and sleep would be the best way to rejuvenate us.

Xander and Kendric fell in behind Ryker and me as we followed Briar and Gage toward the house. The weight of what we'd learned, what was coming, pressed against our backs.

When we stepped out into the fresh air, Ryker's hand found mine again, but it wasn't the comforting gesture it usually was. Despite the fated-mate connection buzzing between us, his grip wasn't strong, and the sludgy feeling of guilt weighed on our bond.

Briar's eyes flicked toward the path to the house, where so many people stood over the dead, crying.

Tears stung my eyes. I wished we'd had the same opportunity to mourn our own pack.

The second we crossed the threshold of our house, the door shut with a snap.

A beat past tense, stretched thin.

Gage marched into the living room and stood between the two couches. Accusation flared into his eyes. "You put all of us at risk without informing us of what you'd done."

"No wonder they always found us," Xander said and grimaced.

Ryker dropped my hand and moved behind the couch closest to the door. His face flushed, and his hot anger rolled through me.

I had to step in before he said something he'd regret.

But Briar rushed past me and stepped between them, placing a hand on Ryker's and Xander's chests. "Enough," she said, her tone sharp. "We can argue later. Right now, we need to remember who the real enemy is. Ryker made a call. It was the wrong one, yeah, but he's not the only one in this room who's made a mistake. He lost his entire pack. Became alpha in the middle of chaos. And he's been carrying the weight of keeping the rest of us alive. Maybe try giving him a damn second to breathe and realize people do stupid things when they're grieving."

"*You* haven't." Kendric slumped against the hallway wall. "And Ember hasn't either. So I'm not sure you're making your point."

I laughed over both statements and in surprise that Briar had spoken up. I'd expected her to take more time to warm up.

"What's so funny?" Gage leaned on one leg.

"A few days ago, I just wanted to take Briar and leave." It felt like it'd been forever. "That was my plan, and it was stupid. If not for Briar, I'd have made a mistake I couldn't come back from. But my mistake was one of cowardice. Ryker's wasn't. He was trying to gain an advantage to avenge your pack. In my eyes, my decision was far worse than him not knowing more about how the spell would work."

Ryker exhaled, rubbing the heel of a hand down his face. Tension bled out of him, slowly, like a dam leaking under pressure. *You don't have to set yourself up to look worse just to save me.*

I'm not. Ryker, I don't agree with what you did, but I understand your motivation. It didn't hit me until I said it that I actually did understand. Sometimes, you felt like there was only one solution, and you didn't give a damn about the consequences. *You did it out of love and to honor your dead.*

Gage looked away, and Xander pressed his lips together. Kendric eventually sat on the couch, resting his elbows on his knees.

"You're right." Kendric rolled his head. "Raven didn't even die, and I feel like she did. I'd do anything to get revenge... even use a spell."

"I guess," Gage muttered, sliding one shoe along the wooden floor.

"For what it's worth...." Ryker grimaced. "I'm sorry. You're right. I should've spoken to you and included all three of you in the decision. I was just so angry. My focus was on taking down the assholes who killed our pack and our royals. It was all I could think about, so I made a dumb decision that actually helped the people I wanted to hunt keep attacking us."

Xander's eyes widened, and then he grinned and cupped his ear. "What did you say again?"

"Nope." Ryker crossed his arms. "I'm not saying it again. If you didn't hear it, that's your loss."

"Dammit." Gage frowned. "That might be the only time we ever hear him say that. We should've gotten a recording."

I smiled, not even trying to hold it back. This felt right... like we had a pack and a family again.

Ryker's mood lightened, and he watched me for a second.

"We should rest." I hated to ruin the moment, but we didn't have time to relax. Another battle was brewing. "We need to prepare."

The teasing stopped, and each of them nodded.

I took Ryker's hand and led him toward the room in the back, brushing my shoulder against his.

You okay? I linked as we shut the door.

The second it clicked closed, he pulled me into his arms.

No. But you're keeping me sane right now.

I leaned into him, letting the warmth of his body melt away some of the cold that had sunk deep into my bones. He lifted me and carried me to the bed, and I rested my head on his chest. His heartbeat pounded steadily beneath my cheek.

"We'll fix it," I whispered.

"We have to," he murmured, brushing his lips against my forehead.

Oh, and congratulations on the bond. Please make sure your sleep doesn't keep the rest of us up, Gage suddenly linked.

I rolled my eyes, but the happiness came back. Even in

all the chaos, some joy had found me. *Thanks, and no promises.*

"Really now?" Ryker lifted his head.

I placed my palm on his forehead and pushed his head back down. "Nope. Just giving him a hard time. We need sleep."

His chest shook, and he wrapped his arms tighter around me.

And sleep took me under.

We woke to dusk spilling through the blinds. Pale-orange light streaked the floorboards, and for a moment, everything seemed still.

A knock echoed through the house.

The two of us groaned, not wanting to get out of each other's arms, but Kendric linked, *It's time. Cassi is back and ready to perform the spell.*

Ryker tossed off the covers, and we jumped to our feet and headed down the hall. This was the first time that we might actually come out ahead, if only slightly.

When we reached the living room, Gage stood near the window. Kendric and Xander sat on their designated couches with strained expressions.

Briar stood at the circular wooden dining table with Cassi, who placed a leather pack on the surface. "I got everything."

Reid, Sun, and Bruce entered the house and moved to the other side of the table.

"So we're ready?" Even more of Reid's color had returned.

Cassi nodded and laid out the supplies: the stone, fresh

sage bundled tight with twine, and a cloth map that spanned the surrounding region. She then lit the herbs. Smoke curled into the air, earthy and grounding.

She removed a small silver dagger from her satchel and held out her free hand. "All I need is Ryker's blood. Ryker, please come here."

Dread replaced my contentment, and I kissed his cheek. I linked, *This is our best chance.*

The last time a witch did something to me, I gave her a way to find me at any time. He rolled his eyes, his frustration with himself returning. Then he swallowed and stepped forward, putting his hand in Cassi's.

My wolf surged forward, snarling, not liking another woman touching my man. *Whoa, calm down there,* I chastised her. I had to remind her this was a spell to help protect us and all the other shifters.

We all circled close, the room thick with the scents of sage and old paper.

"Everyone be quiet," Cassi said softly.

She whispered under her breath, words I couldn't make sense of, and held the tip of the dagger to Ryker's palm. Tendrils of shadows danced around her, indicating that her witch magic had been activated.

She then pressed the blade into his flesh as her attention moved to the map. Guiding Ryker's hand over the center, she turned his palm face down. Blood dripped onto the map, shimmering like it wasn't liquid at all but alive.

Then, slowly, it rolled.

It pulsed once—then slid across the surface and just...stopped.

I blinked. Holy shit. This has to be a joke.

CHAPTER TWELVE

My heart seemed to stop as awareness prickled through me.

All eyes locked on the dark red drop of blood, now perfectly still—sitting on the map over one place that my pack all knew too damn well.

The vampire queen's mansion near town.

The very one we'd walked through, slept in and strategized in with Raven and the queen.

Kendric swore under his breath. "You've got to be kidding me."

"Are you saying they kidnapped the witch moments before Ember, Ryker, and Raven arrived at her cottage and brought her to the mansion while we were *there*?" Briar's voice cracked.

Reid leaned closer, his face paling. "She was right fucking there. And we didn't know."

A cold shudder crawled down my spine.

The magnitude of the vampires' betrayal still hadn't hit completely because this crushing new sensation all over my body made me want to drop to my knees. The mixture of both Ryker's and my emotions was overwhelming.

The vampire queen had completely fooled us. Even my wolf had paced inside her walls and hadn't sensed a thing. Queen Ambrosia had managed to pull the wool over our eyes perfectly. But some things still didn't make sense.

When we'd left the second witch's house after discovering that this witch had vanished, Raven had been attacked with us. She'd even been injured... But then a knot formed in my stomach. Maybe they'd hurt her so we wouldn't be any wiser. What else were they capable of?

"They've been ten steps ahead of us this entire time." Gage clenched his hands. "And we just walked in and made ourselves comfortable."

"And now we know why the attacks were so precise." Xander shook his head. "We actually told them exactly what we were going to do."

My chest tightened. "We didn't just miss the signs with Raven. We trusted her. We gave her everything she needed to plan the vampires' next move."

Ryker's fists trembled at his sides. His rage coursed through me, icy and volcanic all at once. He stepped closer to the map and stared at the blood. "This time, they won't see us coming." His voice was low and lethal.

"They staged the attack on the royals and your pack and drew you away so it would appear as if you were guilty." Reid wrinkled his nose, and the lines in his face deepened. "None of us trusted you anymore, and they leveraged it to get you to go to them."

"They played us all," Bruce growled. "Every single one of us. I even believed Raven for a minute."

"At least..." Briar hesitated, her gaze flicking to me, then to Ryker. "They don't know how the barrier works."

I laughed, the sound raw and hollow. "*We* don't even know how the barrier works, but some of the guards are preoccupied, attempting to figure it out." I glanced out the window. The sun had set, and it was now that shadowy time between night and day. Twilight seemed to blanket us, and for some reason, it made me feel more unsteady. "But we do know it's the only reason we're still standing."

Reid ran a hand down his face. "That's a problem. We can't rely on it. None of it comes from us."

The warm magic in my blood increased in temperature, similar to how it reacted when the strange man was near.

What are you thinking about? Ryker linked. *Your emotions just changed, and I can't tell what or why.*

Of course he'd notice. I now sensed every small change within him, and our fated-mate bond was way more intense than my alpha bond with Briar had been when I'd had it. If I hadn't experienced being an alpha for a short time and gotten used to sensing heightened emotions, I would've been more disturbed. *I believe that the strange man is creating the barrier. Every time the barrier happens, it's like a part of me responds to him.*

Cold tendrils of fear shrank the bond while the greasy feel of jealousy caked over it. Ryker replied, *I'm going to kill this guy.*

It's not like that, Ryker. I'm not attracted to the man whatsoever. His presence just feels familiar, and for some reason, he's protecting us.

"I'm just glad whatever happened is keeping some of the guards distracted," Bruce muttered. "They're scrambling to figure it out too."

I didn't have time to reassure Ryker. He could feel how much I loved him and should feel my dedication. I shouldn't have to explain that my feelings toward the stranger weren't even close to romantic.

"And we suspect they're trying to determine why Ember can see them," Ryker added, focusing back on the conversation. He took a step away from me as hurt blossomed through our bond.

Bruce focused on the map. "Then we don't give them time to figure it out. We move fast before they realize what we're planning."

"Agreed," Reid said, leaning against Sun. "With the number of lives they took and the change in alphas, they won't expect us to strike this quickly, especially since I was so severely injured."

Ryker nodded. "We can't take everyone. A smaller group has a better chance of leaving here undetected."

"Do you have any idea where on the property she is?" Reid asked. "You're the only ones who've been inside the vampire mansion for any substantial length of time."

"I do." The corner of Kendric's eyes tightened. "I know exactly where they would keep her. It's a prison on the same property, about a half mile from the main house. It's in the western quadrant, below ground, cut into the rock."

"Is that where they took Felix?" I remembered the night when I'd been attacked by a former human Queen Ambrosia's son had turned into a vampire. She'd punished her son in front of everyone on a live stream for committing the heinous crime.

Lifting a brow, Bruce inhaled deeply. "You think they'd keep a witch in the same cell block as a rogue vampire?"

Kendric nodded. "That prison was built to contain supernatural threats, not just vampires. If she's dangerous, that's where she'd be. No windows. No light. Reinforced walls. Raven said the witches protected it from the inside out with wards."

"Damn witches," Gage spat. "The goddess just needs to kick—"

"Witch here." Cassi spun around and glared, turning her back to the map. "I just helped you locate a witch and now will help you with some of the wards, so a little bit of respect would be nice."

"You have a spell to get through wards?" Sun tilted her head back.

"Most of the time, when wards are done by witches against their will, they have a workaround for others of our kind. It recognizes our witch magic and will let us in without alerting anyone. That doesn't mean that we'll get around any security inside, but at least they won't be alerted immediately. If I go with you, I can cast my magic out to cover you as we enter and as long as the witch who spelled it is loyal to us, we won't be at risk immediately."

"Wait." Briar lifted a hand. "I thought you said that you can impact fated-mate bonds."

"Yes, but part of that is spreading my magic out." Cassi placed a hand on her heart. "I will *not* mess with any bonds; I'll merely extend my magic like I might do during any sort of normal spell, like encouraging rain for the plants and such."

Reid studied her, and unease lined his face. "And you're confident you won't trip anything and that you won't mess with our fated-mate connections?"

Cassi straightened. "As confident as I can be without seeing the wards firsthand, but that's what all witches are taught to do under duress. And I *swear* not to mess with any bonds of any sort."

"Then we should go before sunrise to help avoid detection." Ryker rubbed the cut on his palm. "I say the group here goes, and if Reid isn't well enough, then he can have one of his pack members replace him."

Reid straightened. "I'm going. I'm not sitting this one out. Not when my pack has suffered losses and needs time to heal. I'm the alpha, and the responsibility falls on my shoulders. I need to see this through."

"Reid—" Sun started, but he raised a hand.

"My pack will survive a few hours without me. What everyone here needs more than anything is closure—and this witch might have the answers to stop this from ever happening again. If I'm not willing to go, then I have no business asking one of my pack members to take my place."

"Fine. But Reid, it won't do us any good if you wind up being a liability," Ryker said and moved to stand beside me.

"Then that means we need to put more ointment on you, eat a huge meal, and get some sleep," Sun said with a scowl and tugged Reid toward the door. "Because if you can't walk normally in the morning, you're not going anywhere. I don't give a damn if you're my alpha or not. I refuse to let you head into danger like that."

Gage snorted. "I can see how Cassi might have thought Ember would pass as his mate. That's something she'd say."

Deep, threatening growls came from both Ryker and Sun just as Xander smacked him upside his head.

"You fucking dumbass." Xander's voice was strained, and I wasn't sure if it was from anger, surprise, or trying not to laugh.

Ryker's eyes glowed and landed on Gage as I stepped between them to redirect the conversation.

"We don't have time to waste energy now." I lifted my chin, allowing my wolf to surge forward so they could feel my power. Even if I wasn't the official alpha of our pack, I had a strong wolf, and they'd know it. "We need to conserve ourselves and rest. All of us are tired, stressed, and still in mourning for all the people we've lost." I then linked to Gage, *I know you were teasing, but no more of that. Not right now.*

Fine. He sighed. *But I still think it was funny.*

Not helping. I pressed my lips into a firm line so there was no mistake that I didn't find it humorous.

"She's right, but I swear to Fate that if you make a joke like that again, I will kill you with my bare hands." Ryker bared his teeth, letting every ounce of his anger show. "Let's meet outside Reid's house an hour before sunrise."

"I'll have a few more pack members run the perimeter tonight so we have a clear idea of where the vampires are by searching for faint wolf-shifter scents by the time we leave." Reid went to the door, moving slowly with his cane.

"I'm going to head back to the house with the others," Bruce said and followed the Blackwoods. "I'll try to bring one additional person with me in the morning, but I can't risk more than that right now."

"Understood." Ryker sighed. "We've all been pushed to the limits."

As the others filed out under the night sky, our pack was left alone.

For a moment, we all stood there in silence, finally able to breathe, processing everything that we'd learned and decided.

Xander moved first, crossing to the fridge like a man on a mission. "I'm starving. Let's see if there's anything edible in this damn place."

He pulled it open and whistled low. "Well, look at that. We've got a stack of raw steaks. Someone must've thought about us eating."

Gage peered over his shoulder. "Hell yes. Let's throw them on the grill just long enough to warm the edges. I'm starving."

"Rare and bloody," Kendric added, stretching with a groan. "Only way it should be."

"I'll get the fire going." Xander opened a few of the old wooden cabinet doors, found the plates, and took one. He filled it up with the raw meat and went out the front door, opening it with his elbow.

The rest of the guys headed outside, the screen door creaking and snapping behind them as they stepped into the fading twilight.

Ryker stayed by my side, his eyes locked on the door.

Go with them, I linked, kissing his cheek. I enjoyed the rough prickles of his scruff against my lips. *You need some time alone with them to reconnect after that misunderstanding.*

He sighed and rolled his eyes. *That's your nice way of saying mistake, isn't it?*

I smirked. *However you want to take it. But go, I need some time with my sister.*

Fine, but only because I won't be gone long and we'll have the night to cuddle.

He kissed my lips and then headed out the door as I headed to the small pantry in the corner of the kitchen. The room was bare, but I hoped to find the ingredients to bake something sweet. I missed working in the local bakery. I needed to do something normal, completely separate from blood and war.

My fingers landed on a dusty box of chocolate cake mix, half a bag of flour, and a few other basics.

Briar came to my side, her eyes catching the box in my hand. "Really? Cupcakes?"

"It's the only remotely comforting thing I've seen in this whole house." I gave her a tired smile. "Want to help?"

She began searching the cabinets until she found a mixing bowl, mixer, and measuring cups. "Let's bake."

We moved around the kitchen, falling into an easy rhythm like we used to at home. Briar cracked the eggs while I melted the butter, and for a little while, things felt almost normal.

"Feels weird," she murmured, stirring the batter. "Being here. Laughing a little. Knowing we're going back into hell in a few hours."

"I know." I leaned against the counter beside her. "But I think that's the point. We hold on to whatever bits of peace we can... even if they're small and soft and covered in chocolate."

She smiled. "I'm glad I'm here with you. No matter what happens next."

I reached over and squeezed her hand. "Me too."

The scent of sizzling meat drifted in from outside, mixing with the warm chocolate filling the kitchen. The guys' laughter—deep and raw—floated through the open window. It was the sound of worn-down protectors trying to remember who they were before all of this.

When the cupcakes were done and the meat had been pulled off the grill, we sat together around the scratched dining table. Plates were loaded, and laughter mixed with low conversation. No one talked about battle. Or loss. Or betrayal.

We were just a pack, enjoying a meal and feeling like things could be normal again... at least for a little while.

Later, when the dishes were stacked and the house had gone still, Ryker pulled me into his arms and led me back to our room.

He didn't speak as we climbed into bed, didn't loosen his hold as I curled against him.

"I won't let anything happen to you," he whispered into my hair. "Not again. Not ever."

There was no stench of a lie because he meant it. But even I knew that it was a foolish promise to make. The one thing I'd learned was that there were no guarantees of tomorrow. A hard lesson I'd had to accept ever since I'd lost my childhood pack.

Still, with Ryker's arms wrapped tight around me and his heartbeat steady against my cheek, I let the weight of the day fall away. Sleep came quickly, but even in dreams, I sensed him protecting me like a life vest in a sinking boat.

Hands shook my shoulders gently, and I opened my eyes to find Ryker standing over me. His face was grim and set in determination. "It's almost an hour before dawn; we need to get moving."

I rolled out of bed carefully, letting out a ragged breath. "Let's get this over with."

We went into the living room and found the others waiting. As soon as they saw us, we all headed out the door, not needing to make a sound.

At the alpha house, Reid was leaning on the porch rail with no cane. Bruce flanked his right, arms crossed and face carved from stone, while Sun's gaze kept darting around from the other side of her mate.

When we reached the bottom of his steps, Reid whispered, "The scouts say the vampires are on the eastern side of the property. If we move fast and cut around the western edge through the tree line, we'll avoid their line of sight."

"What about getting to the mansion?" Kendric asked. "We don't have a vehicle. Vampires will notice if we take one."

I grimaced. He was right.

The vampires might catch us if we didn't take a vehicle, but the noise of one would alert them too. We'd been so focused on the mansion that we hadn't considered a way out of Reid's territory.

If there was something we could—

My stomach dropped. There was one answer. An answer that lodged in my throat, making it difficult to voice.

CHAPTER THIRTEEN

I swallowed hard, bile burning the back of my throat. The last thing I wanted to do was suggest this, but the situation was bigger than the impact it would have on Briar and me.

"If they're west, that means the area toward the Sinclair pack territory should be clear." I swallowed hard, but I had to get the rest out before I changed my mind. "We can use vehicles from there. There's a back way out of the territory, so we won't even have to drive down the main road."

Everyone turned to look at me, and Ryker's concern spiked.

"No." Ryker shook his head, already feeling how the thought alone had impacted me. "We can find another way."

Reid bit his lip like he was weighing what to say, and Bruce wrung his hands.

Sun bowed her head slightly, her focus remaining on me with something like respect gleaming in her eyes for the first time. "That's our best bet, so if Ember is willing, then we should take her up on the solution and move fast before the vampires change course."

I linked with Briar, *If you aren't up for it, you can hang back. There's no weakness in that.*

No, I agree with you. It's not something I want to do, but we need to find the vampire queen before she harms any others and get justice for our packs.

"That's too much to ask of her and Briar." Ryker shook his head as he took my hand and tried to move in front of me. "We can run in wolf form." His determination flowed through our bond.

This wasn't something he would budge on, so I needed him to know that we'd be okay.

I turned and locked eyes with him. His golden flecks almost looked like real gold with the intensity of his concern.

I smiled sadly, placing my hand on his chest. "It's all right. I need to do this. Not just for the group but for me as well. Going back..." I paused and grimaced. "It's going to hurt. But avoiding it won't bring them back, and it won't stop the queen. This is how I prove I'm not broken, and it'll help us get to the witch faster. We can use things from my home pack to make them pay."

His jaw clenched, the muscles twitching. But he didn't speak.

I cupped his face and linked, *You risked your soul with a spell to find justice for your pack. Let me do something for mine as well.*

The bond between us pulsed—hot, thick with emotion. The others remained silent, no doubt knowing that the two of us were communicating via our connection.

If you so much as waver, you tell me. His brows furrowed, and he grabbed my wrists, holding them gently but with enough pressure to make sure I heard every word. *You tell me, and we alter plans.*

I nodded once, my heart growing twice its normal size because he was listening to me. *Deal.*

Ryker sighed. "Ember is convinced that it's the best way, so who am I to argue against that?"

"I think it's the best strategy too," Briar added, taking the spot on my left side so we presented a united front.

"Then I won't argue." Bruce karate-chopped the air. "I agree. It's our best bet. Running in wolf form would take us too long and exhaust us physically."

Footsteps broke the silence as Cassi rounded the corner and hurried toward us with her satchel. "Sorry I'm a little late. I thought I detected something on the way here, and I was trying to investigate."

"What was it?" Reid walked down the steps.

I couldn't help but notice he still strode slowly compared to normal, but at least he was moving sufficiently without a cane.

"Nothing." She shrugged. "I had to be hearing things. I didn't feel any witch magic, just a hint of rose and lilac."

My stomach dropped... It had to be the strange man. Why did he keep appearing?

Ryker's head snapped in my direction. *What's wrong? Do you know that scent?*

My instinct was to play with words so I could navigate the truth, but I refused to allow myself to do that. I wouldn't want Ryker to do that to me, and he deserved the same respect in return. *The strange man—he smells of that mixture and wet earth, but I don't sense him right now.*

Of course he does. Ryker scowled.

Everything inside me screamed not to, but I informed the rest of the group about the man. If we were going into a fight, they needed to know there could be a lurker somehow magically appearing and watching us.

"Great." Gage shook his hands with a sarcastic, happy face. "Another enemy we can't really see and who can appear at random. It's not like we don't have enough stacked against us."

"Either way, it doesn't change our plan." Reid crossed his arms. "We still have too much to risk by remaining idle."

Making her way to the grass, Cassi pulled out a map and laid it on the ground. "Can I get two people to hold this?"

Xander and Kendric each took a side, anchoring the map so the breeze wouldn't take it away.

Not needing to ask, the rest of us gathered around, Ryker taking the spot next to Cassi with his hand held out.

I scanned the area, searching the darkness for any signs of shadows or the strange man. I didn't feel the warmth or the cold pressure that would signify either of the threats were around. Even though I didn't think the strange man posed harm to us, I couldn't deny that his actions did, in fact, seem threatening.

Cassi lit the sage, a burst of orange and red against the dark of the sky, and then blew out the flame and laid it on the damp grass. She then removed the silver dagger and took Ryker's hand. As soon as her hand touched his, a sensation of discomfort and dread pulsed through our connection, though his physical demeanor didn't change.

She whispered the incantation under her breath, her words blurring as if we weren't supposed to hear them. Shadows curled out from her body, and she pierced the edge of the dagger into his palm once again. The blood shimmered and rolled across the surface of the map... and stopped in the exact same place.

"She's still there," Cassi breathed.

I let out a breath that I hadn't even realized I'd been holding. With our luck, they would've moved her to a different location we knew nothing about. We were already heading in with limited knowledge.

"Then we move now," Reid said. "Every minute she stays in their custody puts us at risk since she can track Ryker."

A jolt of pain shot through our bond, followed by embarrassment and regret.

"We need to head to the middle of our neighborhood." My mind raced as I thought through the best strategy. "If they do come by the neighborhood to do recon, they'll likely focus on the perimeter, so taking a car from somewhere in the middle shouldn't be noticeable."

Briar nodded. "And we'll take that back-road exit. It was barely used, and they may not even know about it."

My chest squeezed. Our pack had made sure to stay out of politics, but Dad had feared something might happen someday and had prepared an escape route. He'd never anticipated what the vampires had managed though.

"You all had an alternative exit?" Reid's brows rose. "You guys never told us that!"

"It wasn't anyone's but our pack's business." I crossed my arms. "Are you trying to tell me that you shared everything about your pack with us?"

Silence fell, and then he nodded.

"Light will be here fast." Bruce gestured in the direction of the Sinclair pack land. "If we want to blend in with the darkness, we need to go."

"Are we waiting for anyone else?" Xander asked.

"No. No one was well enough to come with us." Bruce's

face seemed to become paler each day, signifying that he wasn't doing well with the stress either.

We could all relate. I was so damn tired of being hurt, running, and hiding.

"Then let's go," Ryker rasped, taking my hand and leading me toward the woods. His concern heightened even more.

No one disagreed, and the entire group moved in silence. We set out through the trees as the darkness settled over us. In the next thirty minutes, the sun would rise and cast a few minutes of twilight over us all until it rose higher.

Every snap of a twig and rustle of brush made my heart jolt. I kept my senses trained outward, scanning for movement and shadows. The cold, pressing feeling of the vampires. And that strange ripple of energy that always preceded the stranger's presence.

Nothing came.

The woods were quiet. Almost too quiet. There were no scurrying mice or other animals trying to settle in before the day, nor even a gentle breeze to drift across our skin.

We moved as fast as we could in human form, with not even Reid slowing us down, mainly because Cassi traveled with us. Witches couldn't move as quickly as wolves in general. Still, my muscles seemed to weigh me down more with every step closer to the ruins of my home.

When we breached the invisible territory line into the outer fringe of my pack's territory, my breath caught in my chest.

The land looked exactly the same—unchanged, untouched, too quiet. I expected to hear the padding paws of the wolves on guard duty rushing toward us.

They never came.

Briar moved to my other side and took my hand as we

walked the familiar track to our childhood home. Memories coursed through my mind. Briar and me, running along with friends in animal form. Dad taking me out to learn how to track. I could hear my mom's voice in my head, telling me to head in for breakfast.

I would never walk through that door and see them again. Never sit with my family around the table and hear my mom's laugh echoing through the kitchen. But I could make sure the monsters who tore that life away from us paid for every scream and every drop of blood.

We broke the final line of oak trees. My parents' house came into view, and my chest tightened. The firepit outside hadn't been touched since the night I'd burned my mating dress after Reid rejected me.

Everything seemed untouched as the sky around us lightened with the first hint of sun.

Briar squeezed my hand tightly as we trekked past the only home we'd ever known and walked deeper into the neighborhood.

Houses stood like ghosts. Hollow. Still.

Ryker had started caring for the dead, and Reid had told me they'd finished the burials. I knew that. But still... It felt like, any second, my dad would walk around the corner, or my mom would leave Tricia's house down the street and head back home.

No one came.

Briar made a strangled sound, gripping my hand even more tightly, her knuckles white. Every step pressed memories into me. Laughter. Warm meals. A life that was safe and full—until it wasn't. My wolf paced inside, anxious and uncomfortable.

I didn't realize I'd stopped moving until Ryker touched

my back. He linked, *I'm here for you, lil rebel. Whatever you need.*

And those words were enough to help me keep moving forward. *I love you so damn much.*

Ryker stepped closer. I could feel his tension, the ache to take this pain away from me, but he couldn't. Instead, he stood beside me and let me look.

Gage moved to the left, Kendric to the right, while Xavier stayed behind with Cassi, Sun, Reid, and Bruce.

"Kevin's two vehicles should work," Briar whispered and dropped my hand.

Good idea, I linked back. He'd always left the keys in his cars, saying that if someone was dumb enough to try to steal one, they didn't deserve to live. He'd been one of Dad's best friends, and we'd spent a lot of time in his house while growing up.

We followed Briar down a narrow path behind a row of houses. Gravel crunched beneath our boots, louder than anything had a right to be.

I scanned the area once again, searching for any signs of a threat. So far, this had been easy, which never happened for us. Maybe Fate was going to let us have a win.

Kevin's house came into view, and Briar jogged over to it. The black Honda Accord and dark blue Mazda SUV were parked in front of the house as usual.

"What's the plan?" Reid's voice was barely above a whisper.

"Briar and I need to drive the cars." No one else would know the dips and turns of the dirt track. Hell, I wasn't sure I would remember them because it'd been over a year since I'd driven the path. "We'll split into two groups. I want Cassi with me to make sure she doesn't try to use any magic."

"I want to be with Reid," Cassi insisted.

Ryker rolled his eyes. "Fine, Reid and Sun can come with us too. Everyone else rides with Briar."

No one argued as the sky lightened further and we hurried into the vehicles. Ryker climbed into the front passenger seat of the Mazda beside me while Cassi, Sun, and Reid took the back.

Next, we needed to try to leave before anyone heard us.

You ready? I linked to Briar.

Now, she replied.

Our engines rumbled softly to life, and Briar pulled out of her spot first. I may have scouted the lands and handled more pack business than she had, but Briar thrived on learning all the secret facts about our pack. She found things like the backup exit fascinating, along with how our pack theology resonated differently than most packs.

I pulled in behind her, and we eased down the familiar track. Briar cut into the grass, increasing her speed to drive around the trees and swerve around potholes.

The cold pressure suddenly pressed against my body and lungs.

"Ember?" Ryker turned toward me, his eyes wide. "What's wrong?"

The sensation increased.

Four shadows stepped onto the track in front of Briar, and then I noticed something a slightly lighter shade of gray than the dark shadows. Something that resembled a hand grenade.

Briar, stop. My heart tried to lurch from my chest. *We need to turn around.*

But it was too late. The vampire launched the grenade, and it barreled straight for the Accord.

CHAPTER FOURTEEN

Hysteria took over my mind as I linked to our entire pack, *Grenade! Stop!* Cold tendrils of fear choked me as I watched my sister barrel toward her death.

My wolf howled in my head, and the warm magic within me started churning.

The red brake lights flashed, but it was too little, too late. The grenade was right on it.

I screamed, "No!" hoping like hell to somehow stop it.

The grenade hit the car with a sound that resembled metal skidding across stone... and ricocheted back toward the vampires.

The grenade spun, flipping over itself once... twice... and then exploded.

"What the hell?" Ryker gasped, twisting in his seat just as a deafening *boom* shook the earth.

Fire erupted several feet in front of the cloaked vampires, spraying flames toward their shadows in a blast of blinding light. Mulch and dirt sprayed upward in a violent cloud as shrapnel exploded, embedding into the trunks of trees, slicing off branches that crashed to the ground, and stripping bark.

The vampires screamed—high and sharp—but the noise cut off fast as smoke rolled through the woods.

"What was *that*?" Cassi gasped, peering between the front seats.

"A grenade hit the other car and somehow blasted back toward the vampires." The words felt like sandpaper against my throat. I linked with everyone again, *Are you guys okay?*

Yes, Briar replied, but that was all I got.

"They're fine." Ryker reached over and rubbed the tops of my hands. "I can feel them. They're just in shock."

I tore my gaze from the Accord and looked at my hands, noticing how tight I was holding the steering wheel. Despite their death grip, my hands were shaking, and that's when what had just happened truly hit me. I had nearly lost my sister and three of my packmates.

That was fucking badass, Gage interjected.

"How was that even possible?" Sun asked, her breathing ragged.

"All I can come up with is the strange man," Reid growled. "He's still watching Ember."

"He protected our people again," I added, wanting to believe this stranger had good intentions.

Still, his help could vanish at any time. We couldn't depend on it, especially when everything else around us broke so easily.

"Not trying to be inconsiderate—because I know we almost lost half our group—but we need to move," Reid said urgently. "That blast will bring more of them, and I suspect they'll alert the vampires at the mansion."

He was right. We took a moment to collect ourselves; dealing with the emotions would have to come later.

Ryker's frustration flared, causing more anxiety to race through me as he linked, *We gotta go. The surprise could be ruined, so we need to get there and get this done quickly.*

Briar's Accord shot forward, the tires ripping into the soft earth as she veered around a burning tree limb. I floored Kevin's old Mazda, which jostled over roots and narrow trails like it remembered the path as well as I did.

"They'll be coming faster now." Ryker scanned the woods despite his inability to see the shadows. "We need to ensure they're not chasing us before we hit the road." His frustration continued to grow.

My heart slammed against my ribs as I tore through the woods behind Briar. The backup exit sat hidden behind a collapsed barn on the outer edge of the Sinclair land with no signs and no markers. Just a narrow path between two trees that led to a forgotten gravel service road.

What's wrong? I asked. I couldn't figure out what was bothering him so much.

Reid had to tell us to drive. Ryker's disgust seeped through the bond. *I'm the alpha protector. That should've been my call.*

I'd always thought Ryker was hard on himself, but feeling his emotions made me realize it was worse than I'd ever imagined. *You almost lost four of your pack members.* He wasn't going to lose any of his. *That's completely different.*

That's why I had the fucking spell placed on me. He fisted one hand in his lap. *But I couldn't even get it to pull up when I tried just now.*

My gut clenched hard, but I couldn't take my eyes off the trail to glare at him. Instead, I pushed toward him all my hurt and disgust. *Even after everything, you're trying to use the magic? She said it would change you.*

All of a sudden, Briar jerked to the right and linked, *Fallen tree!*

The Accord skidded around it, revealing a huge-ass oak tree lying in front of us. Luckily, we were at the end where the roots stuck out, so I yanked a hard right like Briar to get around.

Our car tipped and rolled up on the passenger-side wheels as the driver's side tires hit the tips of the roots, causing a few to break off and fly. One hit the windshield and cracked it as we cleared the tree by inches.

The Mazda slammed back onto the dirt path with a sickening thud, and Reid groaned painfully from the back seat.

"Is everyone okay?" I rasped, focused on watching for other surprises that might appear out of thin air.

"We're fine, seeing as we're all still alive." Sun sighed.

I didn't need to look in the rearview mirror to know that her words were sincere.

"For the love of the goddess, please tell me we're almost out of this path from hell?" Cassi's voice was tight and timid.

Before I could answer, Briar pulled out onto the gravel road just about ten yards ahead.

"We're here." I sagged slightly, thankful that we were on an actual road. I'd known the secret path would be challenging, but I hadn't expected a grenade.

Our tires spat gravel as we raced toward the end of Sinclair territory.

Ryker's emotions were still on edge, but a little bit of peace seemed to envelop us.

Babe, having emotions isn't a bad thing. Now that I didn't have to focus on the road so intentionally, I could pick up our previous conversation. The sun was rising, blanketing the sky in pinks, purples, and oranges. *Sometimes, emotions help us focus on what really matters. Cutting them off can have you making a decision that you will regret for the rest of your life.*

Being a leader means making hard calls, lil rebel, he replied, placing a hand on my thigh. *You know that. It's easier to not let emotions confuse things.*

Like when you wanted to leave me for dead after pulling me from the river? I arched a brow.

Intense agony shot through our bond, and guilt returned. He inhaled sharply. *Point made,* he replied.

Briar cut left onto the main road that led past town and toward the vampire mansion. I followed, tires spitting dust and tiny rocks, creating a cloud behind us.

For a second, everything went still. All we could hear was everyone's breathing, heartbeats, and the rumble of the engine.

The oak trees thinned as the terrain changed, the shadows growing smaller as the sun continued to rise.

If the drive is any indication of what's to come, I want everyone to know that I'm not above shrieking before being blasted to pieces. Gage popped into our heads.

Man, not funny, Xander shot back. *Don't go freaking out before we even get there. We need to keep our heads on straight.*

I understood that Gage joked as a coping mechanism, but right now, I didn't think any of us were in the mood.

Too soon, Ryker replied. *Not all of us deal with stress the same way as you.*

All I care about is getting that spell off Ryker, Kendric added. *I don't want them to be able to track us. I hate that we've informed them of everything to this point as is.*

I didn't need the alpha link to know Raven's betrayal

was making Kendric extra bitter. In fairness, we'd all been sucked in by her act, especially after that night when we'd retrieved Briar and Ryker had nearly died in the back seat of a car. She'd had all these words of wisdom about love and what was important, like she'd wanted to guide me to do what was best for me. When all she'd really wanted was to get me to trust her. *We need to focus on the goal and not let our mistakes get in our way. Take our actions one at a time.*

I agree. Ryker smiled tightly as we passed by the small downtown of Shadow Brook.

A few lights were on. A lot of people were getting ready to start the day.

A lump formed in my throat. We were nearing the mansion, and we wouldn't have the dark to cover us. Getting out had taken longer than expected.

Everyone, gather your thoughts and get ready for what lies ahead, Ryker commanded.

I couldn't help but notice that Briar remained silent, so I linked to just her. *Is everything okay?*

No, not really. But I'll be fine, I promise. I'm coming to grips with the fact that there are going to be more chances of death as we continue this fight. The explosion brought the risks to the forefront of my mind.

If only I could reassure her and vow that it would never happen, but I couldn't. We were at war, and death would be the cost. We could beg Fate to not take any more lives, but even I understood that would be foolish.

Freedom came with a cost. History has proven that time and time again.

The town disappeared in the rearview mirror, and tension began building in my body once again. We'd be in vampire territory soon.

"Can you utilize your magic so Ember isn't the only one who can see the shadows?" Reid asked Cassi.

"That's not possible. I'm not even able to see them. I can just sense their magic."

"Cassi's magic use needs to be limited until there's no other option." Ryker looked over his shoulder. "The vampires have guards in place to detect magic. I know it works because they detected the cloaking spell over me."

"Wait." I just realized a huge issue with our plan. "Cassi mentioned that other witches may have a safeguard in place to allow access for other witches, but as soon as she uses her magic, they'll know we're on the premises." The fact that I hadn't considered that until now made me want to scream.

"Then we'll need to move quickly." Sun fidgeted in her seat. "Because our plan stays the same. We've got to get that witch to remove the spell from Ryker."

Kendric, tell Briar where to park and enter to get us to the prison fastest, Ryker linked. *We need to move in and out quickly because they probably know we're coming, and they'll sense Cassi's magic.*

Got it, he replied.

Soon, the familiar woods that marked the queen's territory appeared. My stomach roiled. This was going to be messy. I could only hope that our small group could get in and out without detection.

We drove past the road we'd normally take to the mansion and headed toward the other end of the land.

My heartbeat quickened. This would probably turn out abysmally.

Soon, Briar pulled onto a grassy shoulder and parked. I followed suit, pulling up behind her.

We all climbed from the cars, and I glanced upward to see the fading signs of sunrise. Morning had started pushing through, and the air felt wrong—thick and sharp—like it knew what was coming.

Ryker caught up to the rest of our pack and Bruce.

Bruce shook his head. "I should've brought some men after all. The vampires have to know we're coming."

"Yes, but they don't know we were able to locate the witch." Ryker rubbed his hands together. "So they'll be expecting us to attack the mansion."

A little bit of tension was released from my body. He was right. They wouldn't expect us to go for the prison.

Reid leaned against the Mazda. "How far away are we from the entrance?"

"It's about two miles in the woods from here." Kendric crossed his arms. "So, about a mile from the mansion. There were no guards around, at least that I could see. It was hidden."

I linked with Ryker, *Even though Reid is holding up well, I don't think he should come. He's still injured, and if we're traveling four miles total, he'll slow us down.* I turned to look at Sun, Cassi, and Reid, and I could see Sun's strained expression as she studied Reid.

She had to be worried about the same thing as I was.

You're right. Ryker pivoted and tilted his chin up, ready to play alpha.

Yeah, that wouldn't go over well, so I spoke before Ryker could. "Reid, I know this is important to you, but with all the pack-link connections and everything, it would be best if you and Briar stayed here for when we return. We're going to need the cars ready to take off and not try to be fumbling with everything then."

Ember, no, Briar linked. *I want to be beside you.*

Selfishly, this plan helped ease some of my worries. *Reid is sweaty and pale. He's not going to make it, and you know the area and its hiding spots better than most. We're one of the packs that know the surrounding areas well. It makes sense for you to stay with him.*

"What? No—" Reid started.

But Sun jumped in. "I agree with Ember." Her eyes glowed, and I had no doubt she was speaking to him.

After a moment, he frowned and exhaled. "Fine, I can do that, but I need Bruce and Ryker to swear they'll take care of Sun."

Both alphas agreed, and Ryker pushed his pride toward me.

He knew what I'd done.

"Then let's move. Time is running short." Bruce pointed to the lightening sky.

"Gage, Xander, and Kendric, I need you three to shift. Leave your guns on the car so the rest of us can double up." Ryker rocked on his heels. "Ember, Sun, and Bruce can have two guns each."

Everyone nodded.

Kendric removed his holster and placed it on the trunk then jogged to the tree line. Xander and Gage followed suit, and the three of them yanked their shirts over their heads as they disappeared behind three large trees. Within seconds, bones began to snap.

While we waited, Reid and Sun hugged, and I could see the lines of worry already deepening on his forehead. He didn't want his mate to go, but at the same time, he knew he couldn't stop her.

Taking my hand, Ryker turned me toward him. He kissed my lips and linked, *Please, don't do anything reckless. I can't handle losing you.*

I won't do anything I consider reckless. I returned his affection, but I couldn't agree to his terms. There were things I'd done in the past that he'd thought risky, and I hadn't agreed with him.

He huffed. *I guess I'm going to have to accept that.*

The guys emerged in wolf form and waited for us.

Kendric's massive black wolf shook his head, his hackles already raised. Xander's wolf—a dark brown—flanked him, and Gage's blond coat bristled.

Do you want us to scout ahead? Xander asked, pawing at the ground.

No, but we do need your enhanced hearing in animal form. Ryker stepped back. *If they're cloaked, only Ember can see them, and I don't want to put you at unnecessary risk.*

Maybe Cassi should ride on one of their backs? I bit my lip. Since Cassi was a witch, she couldn't move as quickly as we could. We needed to be as fast as possible. And silent.

She can ride me, Xander trotted over.

Ride you, aye? Gage laughed, sounding more like choking.

Rolling her eyes, Briar hung her head. *So not funny right now.*

Xander stopped in front of Cassi and hunkered to the ground. Cassi tilted her head back.

"He wants you to climb on his back so we can move quicker," Ryker explained.

Placing her satchel around her body, she obliged, and Xander stood with no problem despite the additional weight.

"Let's go." Bruce walked to Gage and Kendric.

Briar threw her arms around me, and I heard similar movements from Reid and Sun.

You better come back, Ember. Briar tightened her grip even more.

I returned the squeeze and pulled back so we were eye

to eye. *I will do everything possible.* Knowing that if I didn't leave now, it'd be harder, I spun on my heels and went toward the woods. Ryker appeared at my side, taking my hand as Sun flanked my other side.

We ran.

No one spoke, and no one stumbled. Our feet fell in perfect rhythm on the mossy earth, muffled by the thick undergrowth and damp morning dew.

The sun filtered weakly through the trees in ribbons of gold and pink, casting long shadows between the trunks. However, none of the shadows were the threatening kind.

But the woods themselves were silent—too silent.

No birds. No insects. Not even wind.

The kind of quiet that warned of blood ahead.

Still, we pressed forward.

Kendric led us with long, purposeful strides, his black wolf weaving expertly between the trees. Gage and Bruce flanked him while Ryker, Sun, and I trailed close behind. Xander padded just ahead with Cassi, who gripped his thick fur tightly, scanning the woods.

The closer we got to our destination, the colder the air grew.

The trees thinned as we neared the rise where Kendric had said we'd find the prison entrance. A boulder the size of a small car was supposed to mark the trailhead, though it was concealed in vines and half-covered in moss.

But when we reached the top of the incline, we all stopped short.

Cold pressure slammed into me just as Kendric linked, *The rock is gone.*

CHAPTER FIFTEEN

The cold pressure pulsed against my skin—sharp, familiar, and wrong. My breath hitched as I staggered forward a step, trying to fill my lungs once more.

Ryker placed his arm around my waist, anchoring me to him. *What's wrong?*

"Why have we stopped?" Bruce frowned. "We don't have time for lollygagging."

If only that were the problem

"The rock is supposed to be here." Ryker gestured with his free hand to the area. "But something is wrong with Ember."

I inhaled, though it didn't feel as if I should be able to with the pressure mounting over me. *It's a cloaking spell.* There was no doubt in my mind. We were in the right space; they had just taken extra precautions.

"Maybe he's confused." Sun pursed her lips and closed her eyes in defeat. "We came all this way for *nothing.*"

"No." Cassi lifted a hand. "There's something here."

"Ember says she can feel cloaking magic." Ryker's arm tightened.

I slowly scanned the area, searching for something to stick out. I squinted at a patch of moss-covered earth with divots that looked as if something were lying on it. The others probably couldn't see it, but a large, iridescent shadow sat right on top of it.

"It's there," I said, pointing at the spot. "I can see the shadow that hides it."

Cassi slid off Kendric's back and brushed some twigs from her body, though a few were still stuck in her hair. She walked in the direction of my gesture, and her eyes widened. "Yes, I feel it getting stronger." She kept moving even when she was right on it.

"Stop." I jerked forward, trying to reach her, but it was too late.

Her shin hit the invisible rock, and she tripped over it and twisted her ankle. Her body hit the ground, and she whimpered before she could stop the noise.

Lovely. Gage appeared at my other side and panted. *We already have enough stacked against us, so why not let our witch get injured?*

I hurried toward her, and Bruce and Sun did the same. The problem was that they were heading straight to the rock as well.

"Stop," I whispered sternly. "You need to head to the left to go around it. Follow my lead." The last thing we needed was Sun and Bruce injured too. There was no telling what we were getting ourselves into, but I knew, without a doubt, that all the shifters needed to be ready and well to shift at a moment's notice.

I dropped next to Cassi and touched her ankle.

She groaned and winced. "I think I sprained it."

That's a problem, Xander linked. *Most of the time, sprains are worse than an actual break.*

My heart thundered, and I could sense Ryker's frustration, fear, and determination funneling through our bond, adding to mine.

Bruce knelt beside me as Sun walked around Cassi to her other side.

"I know you're in pain and it hurts." Her ankle was already swelling, and I hated what I was about to ask of her. "But you're at the rock. Are you up for getting this over with before we get caught?"

She nodded and slowly moved her legs behind her so she could kneel. "I can. Just know if the witch cloaking the vampires and now this rock is truly on the vampire queen's side, then..."

"They'll know we're here as soon as your magic connects," I finished for her. I wanted to scream and throw a tantrum because, no matter what we tried to do to save innocent lives, we kept getting served cruel circumstances.

"Immediately," she confirmed. Her eyes locked with mine.

"We've come too far to turn around now." Ryker rubbed his eyes as his rage boiled into me. "We can't just leave without trying. The grenade gave away that we'd left, so this may be the only chance we have to gain an advantage because I suspect they'll soon double their guards."

"Agreed," Bruce said as he reached between Cassi and me. When his hand hit the shadow, he quit moving forward, and his mouth gaped while he shook his head. "That's fucking disturbing. It's like I'm not touching anything, and yet I can't move anymore."

Cassi braced her palms on her thighs, trembling slightly as the weight of our decision pressed in. "Once I get us in, the witch performing the cloaking spell will feel my energy.

If she's loyal to the vampire queen, she'll alert them immediately."

Silence descended once again, and even the wind seemed to hold its breath.

"So what you're saying is," Bruce said grimly, "there's no way we aren't going to have a shit ton of bloodsuckers upon us very soon."

Cassi flinched. "Most likely."

My stomach sank hard. I wasn't up for another battle with vampires, but clearly, Fate didn't give a damn. It was going to happen, even if I asked her nicely not to plague us.

"If we all stay together, that will help, but we may emerge only to face a bunch of vampires ready to attack." Cassi touched her ankle and jerked her hand away as her face twisted in agony. "Either way, this isn't going to be easy."

Fuck. I placed a hand over my heart. No matter what happened, we always seemed to wind up in worse situations than we expected.

"Can you spell the perimeter to at least give us a heads-up?" Ryker nodded to the others. "So we aren't walking in completely blind."

"I... I can't." She pointed at her satchel, her ankle, and the rock they couldn't see. "I don't have enough supplies or energy. If I spell the area, I might not have enough to get the witch out. Our magic is fluid and connected with earth. It drains quickly and has to replenish to ensure we don't cause unjust harm. Either way, all it would confirm is what area is being breached. It won't give us an idea of numbers."

"Then how is the witch cloaking everything?" Sun spread out her arms to her side. "She shouldn't be able to continuously do any of this then. Shouldn't she run out of power?"

"She has to be running thin. All of her energy is funneling into the cloaking. However, she's cloaking the vampires only when needed, so that does help." Cassi tried to stand but fell back on her ass with a *thud*. Her eyes glistened, but she stayed focused, though her voice trembled. "She can't be doing any spells other than those, given how often she's using her magic now."

That had to count for something, but I wasn't sure what. Acid churned in my stomach.

There were no good choices here, but an even more disturbing thought came to me. "And who's to say the witch tracking Ryker isn't somehow tracking others?"

"You're right." Bruce rubbed a hand down his face. "She could be able to track multiple people."

"Which is even more reason not to abandon this plan." The skin around Ryker's eyes was taut. "Besides, Cassi can't even walk now on her own."

I stepped closer to Ryker, my fingers brushing his. The bond between us surged, fierce and steady.

Bruce exhaled slowly. "You're right. When we go down there, everyone needs to keep their eyes sharp. Cloaked bastards won't make a sound, but they'll still disturb the area if we look hard enough. Cassi and Ember can't scan everywhere for us."

"Kendric, carry Cassi again. You'll be in front with Gage right beside you." Ryker then pointed at Xander. "Guard our backs. You and Gage can engage in battle the fastest since you're in animal form and not carrying anyone."

They moved silently, with no questions or protests. This was war. There wasn't room for second-guessing.

"Cassi and Ember should be in front at first so they both can scan the surroundings. Once we know more about the situation inside, one of them can fall back and help Gage watch the back." Ryker's jaw was tense, and his worry crashed into me like a tsunami. "I'll stay behind them with Sun and Bruce between Gage and me."

Everyone nodded but didn't say a thing. We could pivot once we got inside and saw what we were up against.

Cassi took a shaky breath. "I'll push my magic around all of us, but just know, if they have guards inside, they'll know we're here."

Thank Fate, Briar wasn't with us. I would never admit it to anyone, but right now, I was scared shitless.

"No hesitation. We get in, get the witch, and get the hell out." Ryker removed his gun from its holster. He linked to me, *I won't let anything happen to you,* and pushed his determination toward me.

Even when he was worried, he still took the time to comfort me. *I love you.*

I love you, and I will protect you until my last breath.

My heart felt so full from his love; I touched his arm, needing to feel him. The jolt shot between us as Cassi climbed on Xander's back. As soon as she was settled, she leaned over Kendric, her hand hovering just above the shadow.

"Are you all ready?" Cassi asked, glancing over her shoulder at us.

No one responded because anything we said besides no would be a lie.

"Let's go." I nodded.

Wisps of shadows unfurled from Cassi's body. She turned her head and focused. "When I touch it, we'll fall through to the prison. The rock was meant to be a magical barrier and then it was cloaked. We'll wind up inside."

The dark tendrils of magic now circled our group, and

cold pressure brushed against my arms, but nothing like the spell that cloaked the vampires.

And then Cassi touched the rock, and the sunny outside suddenly changed to pitch dark.

A suffocating stench hit us like a wall the moment we landed, heavy with rot and iron, piss and decay. I gagged, covering my nose with my elbow, but it did nothing. The air clung to my skin—humid and thick.

Ryker grabbed my hand again, grounding me as always, but even that didn't take away the intense discomfort.

A low groan echoed from somewhere ahead, and then a whimper followed not too far away.

Slowly, my wolf surged forward and helped my eyes adjust. And what I saw was worse than any horror movie.

Cages.

Dozens of them, stacked on both sides of a narrow dirt corridor, each one no larger than a dog kennel. Every cage appeared to be occupied.

Some witches slumped in back corners while others stared blankly ahead with vacant expressions.

One of the witches moaned when Cassi stepped forward, the faint sound snapping me back into motion.

"They're afraid," she said softly. "There's no telling what's been done to them."

Ryker's gun clicked softly as he lifted it, eyes scanning the far end. "No visible guards. Yet."

Right. I needed to search for shadows. I examined the area, which forced me to study each witch. Some were young, some were old, but the one in the back right corner broke my heart even more—a child.

"No shadows as of now," I muttered low, not wanting to frighten these witches more.

"I'll look for the witch who spelled me," Ryker rasped, moving to the first cage, examining the older woman.

My heart stopped. We were going to be in here longer than we should be.

Xander paced slowly behind us, and Kendric adjusted his gait as Cassi buried her head in his neck, no doubt trying to block the awful smell.

I took another step, scanning the darkness... and then I saw it.

A thread—faint and nearly invisible—linked Ryker's chest to a corner of the room. It was stretched thin like a spider's strand of silk soaked in shadows. A magical tether.

My blood turned to ice.

"I found her," I whispered and took off walking.

Ryker's pulse spiked as the bond between us sparked like a live wire. He rushed to my side as I passed Cassi and Kendric, needing to face the witch responsible for half of our problem.

We moved together, crossing the line of cages to the other end of the cells, and stopped at the one across from the young girl.

The woman appeared to be close to my age. She was chained to the wall. Her black, oily hair clung to her face, her skin pale, nearly blue. The thin, barely visible magical link came from inside her chest, where her witch magic must be stored, connecting the two of them.

She lifted her head, eyes dull and sunken—until they landed on Ryker. Then she flinched.

That isn't her. Ryker shook his head. *She was an old woman.*

"I'm sor-ry..." Her voice cracked, so soft it was almost a ghost. "I didn't have a choice."

I see the thread. I blinked, trying to make sense of it. But we didn't have time to hang out and talk about it.

Then we'll figure it out later. "We're getting you out of here," Ryker growled. "Then we'll get around to the spell you placed on me."

Cold pressure built inside me. Faint but undeniable.

Cloaked vampires. They had to be coming. "We need to *move*. I sense something," I rasped.

Ryker aimed his gun at the lock and fired. *Bang!* The shot echoed through the cavernous corridor like a thunder-clap, and the cage door sprang open.

My ears rang. All around us, the other witches groaned, some flinching, some sobbing.

"Shit," Ryker muttered, rushing to the witch's side. He took the handle of his gun and hit the base of the chain that held her to the wall. Bruce rushed past me and started doing the same thing on the other side, though he and Ryker were pressed together in the small area. The witch's arms released, and she collapsed against them, her frail body trembling.

Gage, come here, Ryker commanded. *We need to put her on your back,*

Without a moment's hesitation, Gage backed into the small cage, half his body sticking out into the hallway. Bruce and Ryker lifted the witch and placed her on his back.

"Hold on the best you can," Ryker whispered.

The witch whispered something, but even with wolf hearing, I couldn't make out the words. Her arms moved around Gage's chest like she was trying to hang on.

Gage ran down the hall to the exit with Sun, Cassie, Kendric, and Xander right behind them.

My gaze landed on the little girl. Her brown hair was matted, and her haunting, clear blue eyes locked on me. She couldn't be older than ten. Why the hell did they have her locked in here?

I swallowed as Bruce ran past me.

Ryker took my hand, tugging me to go with him, but I couldn't.

My legs wouldn't move. My body froze in refusal.

CHAPTER SIXTEEN

"Please help us," the young girl asked clearly, despite her trembling lips.

I stared at her—at the girl too small to fight back, too young to understand why her world had become a cage.

I couldn't leave her.

I *wouldn't.*

A hand took mine, and when the buzz shot between us, I had no doubt who it was. Ryker linked, *We've got to go. You said you're feeling the vampires.*

I shook my head slowly while my heart hammered. "We can't leave them. Any of them." Something inside me screamed for justice for all these women.

He blinked. "We got her. She was the one—"

"No," I snapped, louder than I meant to. My voice echoed. "What does it say about us if we only save the ones who are useful? If we pick and choose who gets freedom like the vampires do?" My throat closed. "Then we're no better than them."

Ryker froze. A beat passed. "We don't have time."

"She's right." Sun's determined voice cut through the thick, rancid air.

Of everyone who might back me, I hadn't expected it to be her.

Sun stood near the cage of an older woman who had her fingers curled around the bars. Sun turned in my direction and nodded. "We don't leave them. Not if we can help it."

"Fuck," Bruce muttered. "They're right. Let's do this fast."

Ryker met my gaze, frustration warring with urgency in his eyes.

I hated that he didn't understand my need, but it wasn't right for us to leave all these women to be mistreated like this. *We may never get another chance to help them, and they can be used against us.* The last part was true, but that wasn't the real reason I wanted to save them. *Besides, isn't the enemy of our enemy a good friend to us?*

He softened and pushed love toward me. *We do it your way, lil rebel, but we do it fast.*

Ryker, Bruce, and Sun started shooting open the locks, moving down the hall in a coordinated rhythm. I followed them, yanking open each door the moment the chain fell, helping each stunned witch out and ushering her toward the exit.

Some collapsed. Some crawled. Some sobbed with disbelief.

The cold pressure was not upon us yet, but I had no doubt the vampires would be waiting outside the magical entrance. It would've been that way even if we hadn't taken a few minutes to free these ladies. I couldn't swear that each would make it out alive, but at least now they had a chance.

Ryker shot the girl's cage last, and she didn't flinch when I opened it—just blinked up at me with hollow eyes.

"Can you walk?" I asked gently.

She nodded slowly. I helped her out, my hand firm on her elbow, and we shuffled back into the corridor.

The entire group now waited by the exit, with Cassi and Xander up front. Cassi held the handle of a door I hadn't noticed when we'd arrived. It must be the real entrance, unaffected by the outer spell. She nodded once Ryker, the girl, and I reached everyone else.

"Is everyone ready?" she asked.

I removed one gun from my hip and held the young girl close to my side. I wasn't sure what the hell we were walking into, but we had tried our best.

Ryker placed a hand on my shoulder and squeezed. "Once we leave, all witches should disburse and get away from here as best you can. The rest of us will fight off the vampires as we all escape."

Several witches nodded, the stench of all of them huddled together somehow worse than when they'd been in cages.

"Everyone else, get your guns ready. We need to move fast and hard," Ryker continued, commanding us all.

Sun and Bruce readied their weapons as requested, and we glanced at one another. We were ready to fight like hell.

"Let's move," Bruce added from the end.

Cassi opened the door, and when the sunlight burst through, I couldn't see.

My eyes burned, stung, and watered as the sunlight hit. After the darkness of the prison, it was like someone had stabbed glass into my pupils.

I squinted hard, shielding the girl's face with my arm as she clung to my side. Ryker moved in front of us, blocking us from whatever threat might be ahead.

Shapes blurred into focus. At least fifteen vampires

stood in front of us, uncloaked. They had guns at their sides and wore black vampire guard uniforms. One picked up a mic and said, "They've let all the witches out."

Our group launched into action without hesitating. Sun and Bruce began firing as Xander leapt at the closest guard to us.

We managed to kill five vampires in the first minute because the vampires hadn't been prepared, not knowing exactly when we'd emerge.

Several vampires returned fire, but some of the witches charged right at them.

I glanced in the direction of the vampire mansion and saw dozens more barreling toward us, cloaked in shadows, like a wave of ink smearing across the tree line.

"More are coming," I rasped. "And they're cloaked."

Get Cassi and the witch who spelled me to the vehicle now, Ryker linked to Xander, Gage, Kendric, and me. *Take Ember with you so she can watch for shadows.*

My blood heated. *I'm not leaving you alone to die when a horde of shadows is heading this way.* A shadow separated from the woods, and I fired and saw it fall to the ground. *The shadows are here, and I'm the only one who can see them.*

Another shadow tore from the tree line. I fired again.

It crumpled mid-step. Ryker exhaled, his displeasure and fear swirling into me, but he didn't argue. He knew it was pointless—my ass would remain here.

Sun unloaded several shots into the chest of a guard trying to drag a fleeing witch back.

Just stay close to me, please, Ryker linked, firing at another guard. The witches created more chaos, adding an advantage to our side. All fifteen vampires died, and Bruce yelled, "Let's move. Follow the two wolves carrying the injured."

Our group moved, and I saw that one of the witches who'd been crawling away lay dead.

Tears burned my eyes, knowing that I was partly responsible for that loss of life. However, letting them stay caged like animals didn't seem any better.

I glanced behind us. The cloaked vampires were getting close. I wanted to scream in frustration.

"What's wrong?" the little girl asked, tugging on my hand. "You seem extra upset."

I bent and picked her up, knowing we needed to move as quickly as possible. She wrapped her arms around my neck, and her gaze never left my face.

She expected an answer. Our group moved, but we were a lot slower with the newly freed witches. They stumbled along with us as best they could, but the cloaked vampires would be on us in seconds, and I didn't want the little girl to be afraid.

Ryker stayed at my side. We started in the middle of the group, but each time I glanced back to gauge the distance between us and the cloaked vampires, I moved closer to the back.

Xander was protecting the rear and would be one of the first they targeted, and I couldn't lose another person.

"Fire," the girl whispered. "You're Fire. Are you scared?"

"Some vampires will be here soon to attack us, and you might not be able to see them." She seemed odd. I didn't want to scare her further, but I couldn't shield her from what was happening.

"Oh." The little girl pouted. "And you don't like that?"

"It's hard to fight an enemy you can't see." I tried to

keep my voice steady, but they were now upon us. I linked, *They're here. Xander, get out of the way.*

Before he could respond, a cloaked vampire darted forward and had its claws in a witch's back, lifting her from the ground like she weighed nothing.

I aimed and fired, but I was too late.

She slumped in its grip, lifeless.

My stomach twisted, bile rising as rage roared through me. I tried to fire again, but I was out of ammo. I needed to reload, but I couldn't with the girl in my arms.

"Here, I can help," the little girl said and lifted her hands. White tendrils exploded from her body and soared toward the vampires.

"What are you—" I started, but my words died as the white tendrils hit the guards. All of a sudden, the vampires came into view.

A collective gasp broke out from the witches behind us as the shadows peeled away like smoke from fire. Vampires staggered, no doubt unsure what was going on.

Then everything exploded into chaos.

Gunfire. Screaming. Growls.

Vampires lunged, claws slashing, fangs bared. Ryker shot one point-blank in the face, and its head snapped back with a violent *crack* before it collapsed.

Sun fired from behind a tree, killing one vampire as another barreled toward her behind her back. Bruce grabbed Sun's attacker and slammed him into the ground hard enough to leave a crater.

Three witches joined hands near the edge of the woods and began muttering under their breath. Wind swirled, ripping through the clearing with a roar.

A vampire launched toward them then froze in midair,

suspended by a shimmering wall of magic before bursting into flames.

The others hesitated.

The vampires hadn't expected this. They'd thought we were weak. That these women were broken.

They were wrong.

I ducked behind a boulder with the girl still in my arms, shielding her as I reloaded my gun. "You okay?"

She nodded quickly, eyes wide, the glow in her fingertips still sparking.

Ember, what the hell is going on? Briar linked. *Are you okay?*

Another witch screamed.

Ember, watch out! Ryker linked with fear surging to me.

I looked up in time to see a vampire blur toward us. His eyes homed in on me, making his intent clear. I raised the now-loaded gun, still not liking how the metal felt in my hand, and fired at him.

The vampires are on us, but we're fighting. I didn't have time for a conversation with Briar now.

Two more vampires approached from opposite sides. I shot one, and Ryker took down the other.

Dammit, I'm out. He grabbed the nearest vampire by the throat, drove him to the ground, and twisted until bone snapped. Blood sprayed, soaking his shirt.

A familiar male scream pierced through the noise.

Bruce was down on one knee, blood pouring from a gash in his thigh, a vampire dragging claws across his side. Sun shot it, but not before it ripped into Bruce again.

She dodged a vampire leaping toward her.

I spun and fired at the next one closing in.

Two more witches went down, their magic spent, their bodies too weak to remain upright.

But the rest—those still standing—channeled everything they had toward the vampires. Fire flared from trembling palms. Earth cracked beneath vampire feet. One witch conjured ice sharp as daggers and sent it flying.

It was working.

The tide was shifting.

The vampires—what was left of them—staggered. Some hissed and turned toward the trees.

They were retreating.

The girl in my arms whispered, "They're scared."

"Damn right they are," I said, standing taller as Ryker ran to my side, blood dripping from his jaw.

"We may not have the advantage for long," he said, breathless. "We need to hurry."

I nodded, holding the girl tighter, tension still buzzing like electricity in the air.

Xander trotted up beside us, his wolf form splattered with blood. Bruce was slumped across his back, unconscious, blood soaking through his shirt.

Shit.

I swear if you don't make it back to me, Briar linked, *I will kill Ryker myself.*

"Let's go!" Ryker barked. "Move out now!"

The witches didn't need more prompting. They lurched in the direction we were leading them, helping one another, limping, dragging along those too weak to stand. Gage stayed near Cassi and the witch who'd spelled Ryker, his coat matted, his posture protective.

I ran beside Ryker, the girl's arms looped tightly around my neck. Her cheek pressed against mine as I clutched her with one arm and kept the gun raised with the other.

The tree line broke.

The road came into view. And with it—Reid.

He limped forward from where the cars were parked, Briar right on his heels, her face pale and panicked.

"What the hell happened?" Briar's voice was hoarse.

"We were ambushed," Ryker growled. "There were more witches locked inside than we expected, and we didn't want to leave any behind."

"Damn." Reid looked past us as the witches poured from the woods. "How many?"

"Like, forty of them," I answered.

Briar's gaze landed on me and the girl in my arms, and her forehead lined with worry. She linked, *You brought a child?*

She was in one of the cages. I just couldn't... My heart sank, and tears blurred my eyes.

She hugged me on my free side. *You did the right thing. I'm so proud of you. And now we have so many more people to help us take down the vampire queen. That's amazing.*

Reid hobbled forward and opened the back of the first car. "We need to move. We can't carry all of you back, so if you go across the street and head to the playground area of the park, which should have people around by now, we can pick you up—"

"No," one of the witches said, stepping up beside me. She looked to be in her mid-thirties, her jaw bruised, one of her eyes swollen shut. "We're not going with you."

"What?" I blinked. "You all need rest and care."

"We want to form a coven together and stay off the radar." Her voice didn't shake. "We don't want to be a part of this at all anymore."

Another witch stepped beside her. Then another.

"We know the land around here. We've been held in it long enough. And we have magic."

"You don't have enough strength—" Reid tried.

"We have enough hate," the woman cut in. "And that'll do for now."

Cassi slid off Gage's back. "She's right. Their power's returning faster than I expected. It's like the land's feeding them again."

Ryker stared at the group then turned to me. His eyes weren't angry now—just... understanding.

"They just want to live in peace," he murmured.

I nodded slowly. I couldn't judge them. I wanted the same.

Sun exhaled hard. "We could really use your help."

Another witch stepped forward. "We'll head east into Hollow Pines. There's an old warded ruin there—we can hide and rebuild."

Another witch, younger than the others with burn scars down one arm, looked up from where she'd been helping one of the older women to her feet. "We were taken because we trusted too easily. Look where it got us."

Her words weren't bitter—they were bone-deep tired. The kind of exhaustion that didn't fade with sleep.

"We fought once," she added. "We lost everything."

"But you didn't lose your lives," I said quietly, glancing between them. "You could've died down there."

The witch with the swollen eye stepped closer, her gaze locked on mine. "That would've been mercy. What they did to us... what we saw..." She shook her head. "We're not warriors anymore. We're survivors. That's all we want to be."

Silence fell.

Ryker's hand brushed mine again, grounding me.

Cassi looked like she wanted to argue but didn't. Her mouth opened. Closed. Then she just nodded and folded her arms across her chest like she was holding herself together.

Reid paced a few steps. "So that's it? You'll just hide while the rest of us fight to keep the world from burning?"

"We're not the ones who lit the fire," another witch said from the back. "We're tired of getting scorched."

It wasn't said cruelly. Just the truth.

"Then at least let us help you get settled," I offered. "Supplies. Medical aid. A way to contact us."

"No contact," the lead witch said. "Please."

"But—"

"No contact," she repeated, softer this time. "We've seen what happens when witches get involved in pack wars. Vampire courts. Shadow politics. We're done for now. We need time to heal."

My throat tightened.

"We need to go." Briar gestured to the cars. "The vampires could come back any second."

She was right. Xander and Gage placed their passengers on the ground. Bruce stirred, and his eyes opened. Sun helped the witch stand and join the others, while Briar helped Bruce get to the car.

The witches began to talk together, and I hugged the little girl tight in my arms. At least I had her.

But then she suddenly moved and whispered, "Fire, I —" Her voice was full of apprehension. "I have to go with them," she whispered. "They're my coven now."

CHAPTER SEVENTEEN

M y breath caught, and my heart squeezed uncomfortably. I wanted to tell this girl that she'd be safer with me, but that wasn't true. She'd be more at risk.

She pulled away from me, and I let her drop to the ground. Her head came to just above my waist, and once again, the fierce urge to protect her came over me.

Her focus was on the other witches. Several had started walking down the road, but others stood steady and looked toward the girl, their chins raised despite the signs of their captivity—matted hair, dirty skin, and the stench of what they'd had to live in.

"I hope you understand," she added, softer now, and looked back at me.

I crouched lower, heart pounding so loud it drowned out the rustle of branches and the shuffle of feet. "You don't have to go." I placed a hand on her shoulder. "You can come with us. I'll do everything I can to protect you."

She smiled faintly, the kind of smile that cut deep. "You already did."

Something inside me cracked wide open. She reminded

me of innocence and hope. Everything I used to be until the vampires changed me.

The witch with the swollen eye stepped forward, extending a hand to the young girl. Her expression was tired but fierce. "I'll protect her. No matter what. I swear on the goddess."

The girl didn't hesitate and took the woman's hand.

"Thank you for not leaving me there," she whispered. "Thank you for seeing me. It'll never be forgotten, and one day, I'll return the debt owed."

My eyes burned as unshed tears filled them. "You owe me nothing." I hated the idea that if someone helped another, there was this burden placed on the one receiving the help. Our pack never expected anything in return for our help, and it saddened me that most supernaturals felt a sense of obligation.

The little girl blew me a kiss as she joined the other witches. My knees threatened to give out, watching her walk away. I wasn't sure how I'd connected with her so quickly and completely.

Ryker wrapped an arm around my waist, and I leaned into him. I could hear the shuffles of the others putting the witch, Bruce, and Cassi in the vehicles.

Ryker didn't say anything. He didn't need to. He just held me as I tried to keep from breaking.

Leaves crunched in the direction of the prison.

Sun stiffened. "We've got incoming."

Xander's ears perked, his nose lifting to the breeze. A low growl rumbled in his throat.

Our time was up.

"Everyone, get in the vehicles. Now," Ryker barked.

I spun around to see that Bruce had made it into the front passenger seat of the Accord, and Cassi was waiting in the back seat of the Mazda. The captured witch had been placed in the far back of the Mazda since it was a hatchback. Reid slammed the trunk shut and hurried into the car.

The final rescued witches took off at a slow gait, staying next to the road, which would have vehicles periodically driving by. The vampires couldn't attack without outing their kind.

Sun slid in the back of the Mazda with Reid, and Ryker and I hurried to the front. I slid behind the wheel as Briar opened the back seat of the Accord and Gage, Xander, and Kendric jumped in, still in wolf form.

Our engines roared to life just as a few vampires tore out of the tree line.

Tires squealed, and dirt shot up everywhere. I floored the gas pedal, but it wasn't fast enough.

A body slammed into the back of the Mazda with a force that rocked the entire car. The rearview mirror showed a blur of movement as claws scraped metal.

The vampire latched onto the trunk, claws screeching as he crawled toward the rear window.

"Hold on!" I shouted, gripping the wheel so hard my knuckles went white.

Behind us, the Accord swerved as another vampire lunged, claws raking a side mirror. Briar hit the brakes just enough to throw the woman vampire off balance, and Gage —still in wolf form—lunged out the back window just far enough to snap his jaws on the creature's arm.

The vampire shrieked and tumbled across the road.

But we weren't clear yet.

Another slammed into the driver's side of my car, his face twisted with hate and disgust. He dug his claws into the window frame and yanked hard enough that the metal crunched under the pressure and the window itself cracked and buckled.

Ryker raised his gun and fired twice, putting two holes in the window.

Blood sprayed.

The vampire crumpled to the pavement with a wet thud, but more figures barreled from the trees.

A random red car appeared around a curve in the road, heading toward us. The sedan swerved, honking loudly, and was followed by a second vehicle.

The vampires froze before retreating. They vanished into the shadows of the woods like they'd never been there at all.

Now that we were free, I twisted the wheel and turned the car around, stepped hard on the gas, and followed the two vehicles. We needed to be around humans. The vampires wouldn't risk getting more humans involved. *Follow me*, I linked to Briar.

I didn't let off the gas until we were behind the other two vehicles.

I glanced in the rearview mirror to make sure Briar was right behind us, then asked, "Is everyone okay?"

A groan came from behind Sun, who turned in the middle seat to check on the witch in the back. "Yeah, I think we're all okay, but that was close."

Reid wheezed beside her. "Next time, maybe let's *not* take the scenic route through hell."

"I'm not okay." Cassi shook her head. "All those witch-es...they had them down there in those horrible conditions."

Was anyone else injured? Ryker linked with our pack.

Bruce started bleeding more, but other than that, we're all okay, Kendric replied.

Ryker's fingers flexed over his knee while tension and concern swirled within him.

The red car we'd followed turned off the main road and headed into town, but that no longer mattered. There were no vampires behind us.

"We can't go back to the Sinclair land." Ryker leaned his head back on the headrest. "That grenade blast would have alerted the vampires to where we came from. They'll be prepared for our arrival."

"They'll be crawling over the whole damn area, including my lands," Reid muttered. "Probably already are."

Sun kept a hand touching the witch in the back to steady her. "Then where do we go? Because we can't keep running forever, and our pack needs us after all our losses."

Silence settled around us. The only sounds were the rush of wind through my destroyed window, the whir of tires on the asphalt, and the rumble of the engine.

My mouth dried. Yet another impossible decision had to be made. There were no right answers, just a bunch of risks to calculate. "What if we go straight down the main road into Reid's territory?"

Cassi snorted. "They probably wouldn't expect that, but they'll still have vampires lurking nearby just in case."

"Exactly," Ryker said, eyes narrowing. "They'll assume we'll circle back and try to sneak in like before." Some of his tension ebbed, though worry still saturated the bond.

"Not a straight shot through the main, open road." I swallowed hard.

Reid blew out a breath. "If we go that way, we're going to need cover. If they realize what we're doing, they'll attack, but we should be able to make it through the perimeter before all the other vampires can catch up."

"Your pack could be ready with weapons inside the

perimeter line to help hold the vampires off if they attack the cars." Ryker leaned toward me and continued, "They need to wait until we turn down the road so they don't alert the vampires to our plan."

"I'll tell them now," Reid confirmed.

Silence filled the car once again as Reid and Ryker linked with the packs, informing them of the plan. Everyone agreed that it was the best possible option, outside of just not returning, but we couldn't leave Reid's pack surrounded by vampires without their alpha.

Soon, we passed the turnoff for the Sinclair lands, and I noticed shadows in the corner of my eye. "We've got company," I said out loud and also linked to Briar. "Shadows are watching us and following us."

I punched the gas harder, trying to gain more distance. They'd be alerting the others to where we were heading.

Of course they are, Briar replied. *This couldn't be easy.*

The turnoff for Blackwood territory was up ahead. My heart thundered, knowing what we would eventually find.

When we reached the turnoff from the two-lane highway, the tree line exploded with visible vampires.

I slammed down on the gas pedal. "They're here!"

Gunfire erupted from the Accord behind us. Briar and Bruce both fired through the cracked-open front windows, trying to keep them back.

I weaved the Mazda around a pothole just as one vampire lunged across the hood. Ryker opened fire without waiting for a clear shot. The windshield cracked, but the vampire fell off, screeching.

"Hang on!" I shouted, just as another set of claws scraped across the roof. My ruined window left me the most vulnerable to an attack.

The pack land perimeter was maybe three hundred

yards ahead now. The final stretch, but at this rate, I wasn't sure we were going to make it.

A female vampire ran right in front of us like she expected us to stop, but I pressed harder on the gas.

The impact was sickening. A heavy, wet *thud* and a splintering *crack* that shuddered up through the steering wheel and into my arms. I felt it in my teeth. The crunch of bone against metal echoed through my open window and into the car, unreal and too loud. Like stepping on a branch magnified a hundredfold.

I gripped the wheel harder as the body slumped onto the hood, slid sideways, and then was gone—tossed aside like a rag doll by momentum we couldn't afford to lose. There was no room to stop. No shoulder to pull over to. Just a sharp drop off the edge of the road and the brutal knowledge that swerving too far would kill us too. I kept going, the entire car shaken, silent, the scent of hot metal and blood filtering into the cabin, our hearts pounding to the rhythm of what we'd just done and couldn't undo as vampires continued to attack.

Then Reid's pack came into view.

Bullets hailed from their weapons. Vampires dropped, limbs twisting, shrieks of fury and pain echoing like some kind of nightmare chorus.

But they didn't stop coming.

One leapt onto our hood, cracking the windshield even more. Another clawed at the back driver's side window, and I cringed away from the near-ruined window next to me. Cassi screamed, and I heard a gunshot right behind me.

The vampire's body hit the road, and I glanced back in time to see it crushed beneath the tires of Briar's car.

My sister rode my tail. Luckily, I'd been taking the brunt of the forward attacks, and it looked like hers had been more focused on the sides. She and Bruce continued to fire through their cracked windows, keeping most of them away.

Vampires attacked all four corners of our car, blowing the tires. I didn't stop, just kept going as the rims screeched onto the asphalt for a bumpier, skidding ride.

My heart hammered as we crossed the perimeter. A second line of bullets shredded the remaining vampires, who dared to get close to us. The vampires turned and ran off now that we were behind the protective witch magic.

I slammed on the brakes, the Mazda skidding to a stop just inside the boundary. The Accord followed seconds later, tires shrieking.

Reid's pack poured from the houses.

Two men who'd been standing at the perimeter line rushed forward, guns slung over their shoulders. One came to the Mazda, and the other split off and opened the front passenger door of the Accord to help Bruce out. The taller one, who'd come to us, opened the trunk and carefully lifted the unconscious witch into his arms.

I turned to look at him through the open hatchback. "We want the witch to stay with us at the house since she's linked with Ryker. We need her close."

The tall man hesitated, glancing at Reid.

He nodded weakly from the back seat. "Do it. We're short on people. If their pack wants to watch her, then I trust them to handle it."

The tall man didn't wait for another word. He tore down the dirt path toward the small house we'd claimed, the witch lying limp in his arms.

"I'm going too." Cassi crossed her arms like she was ready to argue. "She's a sister witch. And I want to be there for her to help her feel safe."

Briar climbed from the Accord and opened the back door for the wolves to jump out. They ran after the taller man, no doubt wanting to shift back into human form.

Ryker met Cassi's eyes and linked, *How do you feel about that? I know we don't trust her.*

I think having Cassi there to vouch for us when the witch comes to might help. I didn't want to think about all the horrible stuff that had been done to her.

"That's fine, but if you try to manipulate any bonds, you'll regret it," Ryker growled, allowing his anger to show.

"I swear to the goddess, no more manipulating bonds... *ever*." Cassi placed a hand on her heart.

That was a big promise for any witch to make. I didn't need to be around them much to know how important the goddess was to them.

Cassi followed the others down the path, limping slightly but determined.

"Do you need anything else from us?" Briar asked the group as she came and took the other spot next to me.

For the first time, I turned and looked at the cars. There were claw marks and dents everywhere, broken and cracked glass, and a chunk of hair stuck in the grill of the car I'd driven.

Vomit inched up my throat as I remembered how it had felt to run over the vampire.

"We're as good as we can get," Sun answered. She looped her arm through Reid's. "We just all need rest and answers when the witch wakes up. Will you inform us?" For some reason, Sun's focus landed on me.

"Of course." I smiled, though it was strained. Something had changed between Sun and me, though I couldn't quite put my finger on what. "And you're right. We all need to rest and eat because I suspect the vampires won't stay gone much longer."

Reid hung his head. "I agree, unfortunately."

"We need some time before we begin planning again." Ryker placed his gun back in its holster. "Maybe we meet up for dinner?"

"That sounds good to me," Reid answered and patted Ryker's shoulder.

Taking my hand, Ryker led me toward the house, Briar falling in on my other side. The small house came into view —quiet, secluded, just far enough from the main pack's chaos. It felt like the first real breath of peace we'd had all day.

Then something shifted in the air.

Warmth pulsed through my chest, a soft thrum of magic, not my own but one all too familiar.

The strange man again.

I glanced toward the trees where I sensed the magic, but as usual, no one was there. Not even a shadow, but the warmth clung to me like sunlight on skin, buzzing against my ribs like a warning—or maybe a promise. I reached out with my senses, but the presence vanished before I could pin it down.

Ryker noticed. "You okay?"

I nodded, forcing a breath. "Yeah. Just searching the area."

"For now, we should be safe, or Cassi would be running out to alert us," Briar replied, bumping her shoulder into mine.

We reached the porch and pushed open the door. The house smelled like old cedar and dust, but it was dry and safe.

The witch had been placed gently on Kendric's couch.

A blanket was draped over her, and her pale face was turned toward the window. She was very still.

Cassi settled into the chair beside her, eyes locked on the woman as if she was willing her to awaken.

"Let us know if you need anything," the tall man said as he walked out the front door, not even taking a moment to glance back.

For a moment, we all stood in silence.

"I'll get a meal started." Briar went into the kitchen.

There was no way I wasn't going to help her. That was one thing we'd always done growing up—when one of us cooked, the other came to assist.

I kissed Ryker's cheek and followed her.

Breakfast? she asked.

When would I ever say no to that? I teased as I opened the refrigerator and grabbed eggs, bacon, milk, and butter.

She pulled out two frying pans, and we began working as the men sat at the kitchen table, discussing everything that had happened earlier.

I didn't want to hear it. I needed a break.

The vampire. The impact. The sound.

That bone-splintering *crack* still echoed in my chest, in my teeth. I could still feel the way her body had slammed against the hood, still see the blur of limbs as she rolled out of view.

My stomach twisted violently.

I dropped the spoon I'd been holding and backed away from the counter. "I need some air."

Briar's eyes snapped to mine, filled with concern. But she didn't stop me.

Babe, are you okay? Ryker linked as I opened the front door.

Yeah, I just need a minute by myself, please. I didn't

want to hurt his feelings, but I didn't want anyone to see me fall apart. At least, not right now.

I let the front door swing shut behind me and walked into the woods beyond the porch.

The cool morning air wrapped around me, biting through my sweat-dampened shirt. I bent over slightly, pressing my hands to my knees, trying to breathe through the nausea churning deep in my gut.

"You shouldn't linger too long out here by yourself," a soothing voice said from behind me. The voice held an accent I'd never heard before.

I spun around, and *he* was there.

The strange man.

Golden skin caught the light like polished stone and surrounded eyes that screamed of wisdom. His hair shimmered like the first stars at dusk.

The now familiar lilac and rose mixed with damp earth scent washed over me.

And then I realized I was alone, outside, with a man who didn't seem to be from this earth. A man who'd stalked me while I slept.

I opened my mouth to scream, but no noise came out.

CHAPTER EIGHTEEN

The sound was lodged in my throat. My heart pounded against my ribs like a drummer announcing war.

His eyes softened. "If I meant you harm, Ember, you would've never made it to that prison."

My mouth snapped shut. He had to be talking about the force field that had surrounded the Accord when the vampires had thrown a grenade at it.

Ember, are you hurt? Ryker linked, and the front door opened.

No. It's the strange man—he's here talking to me.

I'm on my way, Ryker responded.

Only you right now, please. I want him to remain willing to talk, and he helped us earlier with the grenade. I pushed my worry toward him. *I need to give him a chance to explain. Please.*

My wolf was still growling low in warning, but my instincts... they didn't scream danger. "Who the hell are you?"

He smiled, but it didn't reach his eyes. "Names hold

power, and I've given enough of mine away. But you may call me what you like."

"Stalker? Creeper?" I shot back, voice sharper than I intended. My hands trembled, but I didn't lower my guard.

He tilted his head. "Fair. But I wasn't following you. I was observing. There's a difference."

"And why, exactly, were you observing me?" I needed answers before I went insane.

His gaze shifted toward the house. Ryker's frantic footsteps came toward us.

He focused on me once more, brows furrowed. "Did your father not tell you anything about me?"

I took a step back. "My *father*? You're not making any sense." What did Dad have to do with this man?

The man's expression softened, almost regretful. "You were supposed to be told when you came of age."

My pulse stumbled. "Told *what*? And what does 'come of age' even mean?" I had no clue what this strange man's definition of that would be.

"Told that your blood carries more than just wolf magic." He took a careful step closer, his voice quieter now. "That you were never just one thing."

My panic heightened, and Ryker reached me, tugging me behind him.

"What have you done to her?" he snarled.

"Nothing." The strange man shrugged and rolled his wrists. "Just informing her of her heritage."

"Bullshit." My voice cracked, and I stepped to Ryker's side for a clear view. "My father would've told me if—"

But then memories popped into my head. Different times when Dad had told me he needed to tell me something alone. Right before I was rejected and everything went to hell.

I staggered back, breath catching in my throat.

"I kept waiting for you to locate me, and when I was going to approach you for the first time, I saw you were with *them.*" The strange man wrinkled his nose. "I could not believe that you would choose to join a pack full of violence, but for some reason, your magic still called to me. But after what I saw you do today—what you've done these past weeks while also changing the violent nature of your new pack—I realized we must meet."

I don't like this, Ember. Ryker's concern and worry weighed on our bond. *I think he's messing with you.*

Though I knew he had every reason to believe that, something inside me resonated with this man. *I need to hear him out. I hope you understand.*

Ryker took my hand and moved so close to me that our arms rubbed and the fated-mate bond flared between us.

"Why do I feel a connection to you?" I was tired of the vague answers and needed the truth. "Dad did tell me he needed to speak to me, but he died before he had the chance."

The strange man's eyes glistened, making his irises look even more otherworldly. "Ah, that makes sense. You are confused and have no clue what's going on inside you."

"Ever since Dad passed, a warm sort of magic has filled me. One that isn't my wolf." I'd thought it had to do with grief, but now I was certain it was whatever linked me to this man. "None of this makes sense."

Ryker's jaw twitched.

"My dear girl, of course it doesn't." The man frowned. "When your father passed, your dormant magic activated."

The world tilted. "My what magic? And why did Dad dying turn something on inside me?"

"Many centuries ago, I fell in love with a human." The

strange man pressed his lips together and stared into the distance as if he'd gone back in time. "And then I returned to my realm without knowing she was pregnant until months later, when something yanked at me."

With a dry snort, Ryker placed an arm around my waist and drew me even closer. "Realm? What are you fucking talking about? Are the vampires using you to mess with our minds?"

"Vampires have been vile creatures for many centuries." Strange Man wrinkled his nose. "They've grown more courageous over the years."

"What?" I felt like my brain wasn't working anymore. Maybe with all the fighting and chaos, it had fallen out, and I wasn't aware. "Your words have meaning, but they aren't making sense put together."

"Of course. Let me continue my story." The man crossed his arms. "Needing to investigate what called to me from Earth, I returned and learned that I had a son. He was half wolf and half fae, and his pack name was Sinclair."

My breath punched out of me. "Are you saying you're my great-great-great-great-great-grandfather?" I had no clue how many greats to add because he'd mentioned "many" centuries.

"You're lying," Ryker barked. "Fae aren't real. They're in storybooks."

"Fae are real, but we don't visit Earth often. Though we do enjoy seeing how different you all are." The man shrugged. "But our magic works differently here, which is why only one of my descendants at a time can have their magic activated. When your father passed, Ember, you were the oldest, and thus, your magic activated within you."

I couldn't breathe. Not because I didn't believe him.

Because I *did*.

The way his magic felt familiar. The way his voice settled something buried deep in my bones.

The way my father would look at me sometimes—like he was on the edge of revealing something that never quite made it to the surface.

"I don't understand," I whispered. "Why talk to me now?"

"Because you've proven that your instincts lean toward justice, not vengeance. That matters, Ember, to fae like me because we are of the Aureline line. A very special line where we do Fate's bidding and ensure that everything is balanced between good and evil."

My brain buzzed. "What about Briar?"

"Your sister." He rubbed his hands together. "She is of the same line as you, but her fae magic won't ever activate if you have children. If you die before having children, then the magic will activate in her upon your death."

Ryker tensed. *I don't trust him.*

Before I could respond, Briar's voice came through the link. *Breakfast is done, and Cassi says the witch's pulse is steady. You guys coming in or what?*

I exhaled, heart thudding. Ryker looked to me for direction, and I hesitated only a second.

We're coming, I linked back. The last thing I wanted to do was worry her or try to explain this right now. I kept feeling like I was hitting my head against a wall, but if this man—our Many-Greats-Grandfather— came inside, he could tell her. "You should come in with us. You could speak with Briar and tell us more."

Do you really think that's a good idea? Ryker's arm tensed.

Strange Man's smile faded. "No."

"Why not?" I asked, frowning.

"There are witches inside." He gestured to the house.

Ryker stepped forward again, shielding me slightly. "How the hell do you know that?"

The man's lips twitched. "Because I watched two ladies with darkness attached to them walk inside. Their magic works similarly to ours but is of this Earth and can't be used in our realm. I can see it. Mine is stronger and I can use it here, though not for very long."

"So that's why you didn't contact me 'til now?" I asked, trying to make sense of all this.

"No. I stayed away because I needed to see if you were neutral and on the side of justice for everyone. Seeing you influence these men to change and how you released every witch proved that you're worthy of learning about your fae magic."

I bit my lip. I didn't want him to go, but at the same time, I needed a moment to catch my breath. "Will you come back?"

"I will return when the sun sets, but only if you're alone. I'm interested in discussing your role on Earth."

"Absolutely not." Ryker bared his teeth. "I have to be with her. She may want to trust you, but I don't. I won't allow anything to happen to her."

A lump formed in my throat. The last thing I wanted was for Ryker to scare him off, but I also understood how Ryker felt. If our roles were reversed, I'd be saying the same thing.

"So much anger resides in your soul." Strange Man's shoulders sagged. "I'll be glad when it's eliminated. But yes, I will tolerate you because you care for her and protect her. But no one else."

"Thank y—" I started.

"*Never* thank me." He cut me off. "I don't want my family to be in debt. I will see you soon." Then he vanished.

No pop. No shimmer.

Just... gone.

Ryker let out a growl and pulled me into his arms. "I don't trust him."

"I kind of do, which is why I want you with me when I talk to him." I rested my head on his chest. "I think I need him. I believe some of what he's saying because this magic inside me is definitely not wolf."

Ryker's chest rose against my cheek, and he murmured, "Then I'll be by your side the second he steps out of line."

We stood there for a breath longer before turning back toward the house where breakfast waited.

Are you two coming or what? Briar linked again. *If you're out there having sex with wolves constantly on patrol, you'll be giving a ton of people a show.*

Ryker snarled and yanked the front door open. *No other man will ever see Ember that way. I refuse to share, even visually.*

We stepped inside, and the warmth of the house wrapped around me. The scents of bacon and eggs wafted through the air, cozy and grounding after everything that had just happened outside.

Kendric, Gage, and Xander were already at the table, heads down, forks scraping plates. They looked up as we entered and gave us brief nods, no questions.

Briar handed me a plate and offered one to Ryker. "Eat."

He muttered thanks under his breath and took the seat beside Kendric. I sat next to him, still shaken but trying not to show it.

Briar sat across from me and studied me, her expression unreadable. "Something wrong?"

I forced a smile. "Nothing I'm ready to explain yet. Today's already been too much. I just want to sit here and eat." I reached for the spoon that was dug into the eggs and scooped some onto my plate.

She gave a curt nod. "Okay, but I want you to tell me later."

"Okay." I grabbed some bacon, using the trick of saying *okay* as a form of acknowledgment of what she wanted, not that I'd actually do it.

Cassi joined us last, moving slower than usual. Her ankle was now the size of a grapefruit, and she limped noticeably as she crossed the room and dropped into the empty chair near the couch. She didn't touch a plate; just tore at a piece of bread like she wasn't really aware of what she was doing.

I looked around the table. It was clear we were all beat up. The rescue mission had lasted almost two hours, but it felt like it'd taken an entire day.

Halfway through the meal, Kendric set down his fork and looked around. "Anyone else wonder why the vampires weren't cloaked when we came back?"

All of us glanced at one another as Gage added, "That's a damn good point. They came at us loud and proud. No hiding."

Cassi glanced up, dark circles prominent under her eyes. "The little girl. When she revealed the cloaked vampires earlier, she disrupted the spell holding the magic in place. The witch doing it... she's been draining herself nonstop. That kind of sustained cloaking over a wide area—especially with combat happening—would rip through her reserves."

"So she finally had to recharge?" Ryker leaned back in his seat.

Cassi nodded. "Exactly. She can't cloak and fight. Not like that. Especially if she's been working alone or without magical relay points."

"Which means we have a small window," Briar said. "To move, plan, and maybe strike."

I was about to agree when a sound cut through the air.

A groan.

All our heads turned toward the couch.

The witch moved slightly beneath the blanket, her head turning against the pillow. Her mouth opened, cracked lips forming words too soft to hear.

Cassi was on her feet instantly, limping toward her. "She's waking."

Ryker stood as well, heading over to monitor the exchange.

I chased after them, and everyone followed behind me.

The witch's eyes fluttered but didn't open. Her face twisted as if she were caught in a dream that hurt. "Need to break free and help."

I grew dizzy.

Leaning over, Cassi placed a hand on the woman's cheek and asked, "Help who?"

"They need help," she whispered. "Quickly. They won't last much longer."

My heart slammed into my ribs. "Who are *they*?"

The room stilled. Every breath held.

Her lips moved again, barely audible. "The royals."

A shiver ran down my spine.

"The royals?" Briar echoed, voice hushed. "What royals?"

"Captive." The woman's words were almost inaudible.

Ryker gripped the woman's shoulders and shook her a little. "Who's captive? What royals? The vampires?"

"No." The woman groaned. She muttered something else, but I had to have misunderstood. There was no way she said what I thought I heard.

I spun to Ryker and asked, "Did you hear the same thing I did?"

CHAPTER NINETEEN

Ryker's expression was unreadable. He stared at the woman like her face might rearrange itself into something that made sense.

My knees buckled. This had to be a sick joke, but there was no smell of a lie.

"What did she say?" Cassi's head lifted and she stared at us. "I couldn't make it out."

"Royal wolf," Ryker rasped, and then he grimaced.

The words settled into the air like a death sentence, and no one spoke a word.

Kendric's face paled. "She has to be delirious. That can't be right."

"She's out of it." Xander crossed his arms around his stomach. "Rambling nonsense. There are no more wolf-shifter royals."

"Either that, or she's making a fucking sick joke." Gage cracked his knuckles. "Throwing our failure in our face when she's on the brink of death. The vampires wiped them out, and we were called away to look like the guilty culprits."

"And then we felt our pack links vanish and came rushing back to find the dead bodies." Ryker grimaced. "So many of our people and the royals shredded to death, to the point they were unrecognizable."

My stomach dropped. "Did you have a final tally of the dead?" They hadn't mentioned the physical state of their pack before.

All four men flinched.

"We weren't in the mindset to count, and with how shredded some bodies were, it was hard to tell what belonged where." The iridescent sheen faintly came back to Ryker's eyes.

Our bond muted ever so slightly, like something had blanketed the connection. The hot spot in my chest muted to almost the same level as the other pack members in our pack. *Are you really trying to use her magic?*

The unconscious witch whimpered in pain like someone was torturing her.

Ryker's attention flashed to the witch, and he closed his eyes and shook his head. Immediately, his irises turned to normal. And our bond returned to its usual temperature, which somehow heated up my blood even more and not in a sexual tension kind of way.

He'd tried to cloak his soul again after *everything*. And here I'd thought he wanted to fight for all of us and not cut himself off from being an alpha who wasn't in tune with his pack members' needs.

"Something's wrong." Cassi dropped to her knees and leaned over the older witch. "The vampires may have a way to drain more of her power."

I glared at Ryker. It wasn't the vampires who were causing that problem.

The witch's breathing returned to a steady rhythm, and Cassi relaxed marginally.

"At least they've stopped for now." Cassi tugged at the ends of her hair. "Why are the vampires doing any of this?"

That was the huge question. I was dying to know the answer. Power was the primary motivation, but the way they were slaughtering shifters seemed personal.

"Think about it though." Briar twirled her pointer finger. "Our packs haven't lost any magic... we haven't weakened a bit, and everyone has been freaking out, expecting to feel the impact immediately. If the royals are alive—"

"No," Ryker shouted. "We need to stop having this conversation. They're dead. Pretending like they might not be won't change anything." His shame and pain slammed into me, showing me just how broken he really was.

The pain combined with my own and had me bending over from the sudden intensity. Ryker always seemed so confident and put together, and I'd felt his heartbreak, but nothing had prepared me for the raw feeling that exploded from him.

No wonder he'd wanted his soul cloaked. The guilt was heavier than anyone could carry.

He cleared his throat and reeled some of the emotion back in. "Besides, what would be the point of keeping them alive?"

Something screamed at me, making me think even more that this was personal to the vampire queen. But why?

I took in Xander's, Kendric's, and Gage's expressions, twisted into regret and pain. They had to be feeling similarly to Ryker. They all believed they'd failed the royals and their pack.

"We need rest." I straightened. Trying to figure something out when we were all tired, sad, and braindead wasn't going to do any good. "We're all full, and the witch is unconscious again. Let's get some sleep and figure out the next step when our brains aren't fried."

No one argued.

Instead, Kendric grabbed one of the throw pillows off the loveseat and sank down to the floor, exhaling like he'd been holding his breath for hours. Gage handed him a blanket without a word.

Briar walked toward her room without hesitation. She paused in the doorway and looked back at me. "Wake me if something changes."

"I will," I promised.

Cassi hadn't moved from the chair by the witch. She looked too hollow, too quiet.

"Cassi, if you're tired—" I started.

But she shook her head. "I'm fine. I want to keep watch. If she wakes, I want her to know a fellow sister is here."

Ryker tentatively reached for my hand, almost like he was unsure if I'd take it. My fingers laced through his as I led him toward our room. But even as the door shut behind us and the soft light filtered in from the window, his emotions didn't settle. If anything, they twisted tighter. Coiled like a wire wound too far.

I didn't say anything, thinking he needed a minute. He needed to process his feelings instead of keeping them locked away. Ignoring emotions just made them intensify until they burst out, and I suspected Ryker might have hit that point.

I stepped into the bathroom and turned on the shower. The water thundered to life, and steam quickly filled the room. I stripped down and stepped beneath the stream, letting the water wash away the day. But I could still feel him on the other side of the door.

Tense.

Pacing.

I dried my hair and then wrapped the towel around me. When I stepped back into the bedroom, I found my mate sitting on the edge of the bed with his hands clenched on his knees. The moment his eyes lifted to meet mine, he linked, *How mad are you at me?*

I paused mid-step and clutched the towel a little tighter.

You think I'm mad? I replayed everything I'd done, trying to see what made him think I was angry. Maybe that was why he hadn't joined me in the shower.

The disappointment running through you is like a fucking freight train.

Needing him to not only feel my emotions but to hear my tone, I switched to speaking out loud. "I'm not mad. I'm... worried."

He flinched like that word hit harder than anger. "Because I tried to cloak myself again?"

"That, and because you keep carrying all of this alone." I walked over to him and continued, "You're trying to protect us by cutting yourself off. That doesn't make you stronger, Ryker. It just makes you more likely to break. And I hate that you felt like you had to try to cloak your soul again instead of relying on me to help you."

He looked down, jaw flexing. "You shouldn't have to carry that burden."

"You don't think that I get it?" I patted my chest. "You lost people. I lost people. You blame yourself. I do too, because I ran while my pack got slaughtered. But we're here together, and I want to help you handle your pain. You don't have to hide it from me. I want us to be together in everything."

The silence stretched between us. Then he leaned forward and gripped the edge of the towel at my hip, just enough to anchor himself.

"You felt it, didn't you? When I slipped." He hung his head.

"Yeah." I dropped to my knees in front of him. "Our bond was affected."

He rested his forehead against mine and linked, *I didn't mean to. I just... I wanted to make it stop. Just for a second. The guilt, the memories. Every time I sleep, I see them. What was left of them.*

My throat thickened, and I took his hand. "You're not alone in this. We'll carry the pain together."

His breath hitched. "I don't deserve you."

"Too bad," I whispered. "You've got me anyway, and now you're stuck."

He huffed a small laugh. The kind that didn't quite make it to a smile, but our bond flooded with warmth toward me all the same. He lifted his head, and for the first time in hours, something unguarded flickered in his eyes.

"If this is what being stuck feels like," he murmured, brushing his nose against mine, "then I'm the luckiest bastard in the universe."

My lips parted on a shaky breath as love, deep and all-consuming, wafted from him like smoke wrapping around me. It was heady. Raw. Real.

I kissed him with as much passion as possible. My fingers tangled in his hair while my heart drummed against his chest. His arms wrapped around me like I was the only thing keeping him grounded.

But just as the hunger sparked between us, he pulled away.

The loss hit like a slap. My heart stuttered. "What—"

"I need a shower." He panted, forehead pressed to mine. "Give me a minute. I'll be right back."

I blinked, lips still tingling from the kiss. "Oh."

His thumb traced the edge of my jaw before he pressed a kiss there. "Don't move. I just want to rinse the blood and dirt off before I touch you the way I really want to."

Heat rushed to my cheeks. "Okay."

He made his way to the bathroom, and the water turned on a second later. I grabbed one of Ryker's shirts from the nearby dresser and then had to search to find some pants that would fit me.

Before I could even put the clothes on, the bathroom door opened.

And Ryker stood there.

Naked.

Steam curled behind him, and his golden skin glistened with moisture. His dark hair stuck to his forehead, water trailing down the muscles of his chest and stomach. His gaze raked over me like I was the only thing in the universe that mattered.

My breath caught. Heat pooled low in my belly.

He stalked across the room and reached me in two long strides. He snatched the clothes from my hand and tossed them on the wooden floor. Then his lips crashed against mine, stealing every thought from my head. His kiss wasn't gentle. It was possessive and desperate.

I melted into him as he lifted me easily and laid me on the bed.

The towel slipped away as Ryker braced himself above me, his eyes darkening with desire. Water droplets fell from his hair onto my skin, creating trails of heat wherever they landed. I reached up to trace the scar through his eyebrow, my touch reverent.

"Dammit, lil rebel. I need you," he rasped. "All of you."

I answered by pulling him down to me, our lips meeting in a desperate clash that spoke of all we couldn't say. His hands explored my body, and his fingers found me slick and ready. A groan rumbled from deep in his chest.

Spreading my legs farther apart, I made it so his fingers could easily slide between my thighs. One finger dipped inside me while his thumb found that perfect spot that made my back arch off the bed. I gasped against his mouth, my fingers digging into his shoulders.

"Ryker," I breathed, unable to form more coherent thoughts as he added a second finger and curled them in a way that made my vision blur. The pleasure built quickly, a knot forming tight in my core as he worked me with deliberate precision.

Through our bond, I could feel his own need spiraling higher. Without breaking our kiss, I reached between us and wrapped my fingers around his length. A shudder ran through his powerful body at my touch, and he nipped at my lips.

His hips jerked forward instinctively, thrusting into my palm as his fingers maintained their rhythm inside me. He pushed deep as my hand slid along his dick. Each stroke was met with a deeper thrust of his fingers, our bodies falling apart together.

"Fuck," he growled against my neck, his breath hot on my skin. "Your touch... I can't... You need to stop."

I tightened my grip slightly, twisting my wrist on the upstroke just the way I knew he liked it. His fingers curled inside me in response, sending an orgasm pulsing through me.

My body shook as he caught my wrist with his free hand, forcing me to stop stroking him. I wanted to continue, but the ecstasy crashed over me so hard that I had to concentrate just to breathe.

Before I even stopped, he removed his fingers and slid into position at my entrance. "Mine," he growled.

Yours, I linked, unable to speak, and arched up against him.

He entered me in one powerful thrust that had us both gasping. The orgasm didn't end, but instead began building all over again.

I whimpered as he filled me completely. Our bond hummed between us, amplifying every sensation until I couldn't tell where my pleasure ended and his began.

"Fate, you feel perfect," he panted against my neck, his rhythm building steadily. "Every time with you... it's like coming home."

I wrapped my legs around his waist, changing the angle, and he gasped. His eyes locked with mine, the gold flecks in them seeming to glow in the dim light. There was a vulnerability there now, a rawness he'd stopped trying to hide.

The headboard knocked against the wall as Ryker's thrusts grew more urgent. My body tightened around him as pressure continued to build even more in my belly.

"Let go for me again," he urged, sliding one hand between us to where we were joined. His thumb circled the sensitive bundle of nerves there, and I shattered. Wave after wave of pleasure crashed over me, and my body clenched around him.

The feeling of my intense release must have triggered his own. With a guttural moan, Ryker buried his face in my neck, his hips stuttering against mine as he released. I felt his pleasure echo through our bond, obliterating me with pleasure.

When we finally came down, our bodies trembled.

For a long while after, we lay tangled together, our breathing gradually slowing. Ryker's weight pressed me into the mattress, but I welcomed it, needing the grounding presence of his body on mine. His fingers traced lazy patterns on my skin, and before I could stop myself, I fell asleep.

I jolted awake. A scream came from Briar's bedroom.

I threw off the covers as Briar linked, *There's someone in here. Help!*

Is it a vampire? Ryker asked as he followed me. We were at the door and heard footsteps from Gage, Xander, and Kendric running in our direction.

Knowing I had to get there before something awful happened, I ran down the hall to her door and threw it open.

And then I froze.

Motherfucker.

CHAPTER TWENTY

I might wind up killing him after all.

Our Many-Greats-Grandfather stood in the far corner of Briar's room, arms crossed as he leaned casually against the wall, watching her with unreadable eyes.

"What the actual fuck?" I snarled.

Ryker stepped in front of me, muscles coiled. "Get away from her."

The man didn't flinch. Didn't move.

He looked at Briar like she was a painting.

My sister scrambled back against the headboard, clutching the blanket to her chest. Her face was pale, eyes wide in pure terror. "He just—he was *there* when I woke up. Just standing there. I didn't hear him come in—nothing."

A growl rose from Ryker's throat, primal and warning. "This ends now."

I took a step forward, rage surging like wildfire. "What the hell are you doing in my sister's room?"

He blinked and then disappeared. No flash. No sound. Just gone.

You're right. I want to kill him. I spun around like I could somehow call him back with anger alone.

Gage, Kendric, and Xander burst into the room, Gage running into me as all three struggled to get through the door at the same time.

I stumbled into Ryker, and Briar's hands trembled as she pulled the covers higher. "Did he cloak himself again? Like the vampires? Is he still here?"

The question made the room still.

Ryker scanned the corners, nostrils flaring as he tried to scent the air. "I don't know."

"I can't feel or see him." My voice came out tighter than I'd intended. I linked to Ryker alone, not wanting to freak anyone else out. *But that doesn't mean he won't pop back in here any second.*

"What the hell's going on?" Gage asked, gaze sweeping the room.

Briar whispered with her voice shaking. "A strange man was just... standing there. And then poof, he vanished." She pushed off the bed like it was scorched. "I want wards in my room. Now."

I nodded, fury still thrumming in my veins. "You'll have them. I swear it." However, it wouldn't help anything. He'd gotten into Blackwood territory without passing the perimeter and alerting Cassi. Whatever portal-jumping shit he could do outsmarted even witch magic.

We all stood there for a beat longer, unsure if he was really gone.

But in my gut, I knew he wasn't far away.

Um... I get this is an emergency, but Ember, do you mind putting some clothes on before Ryker calms down only to lose his shit on us? Xander linked.

My stomach dropped, and I wrapped an arm around my breasts and put the other hand in front of my cooch.

Babe, we'll find him. Don't worry. Ryker turned around to comfort me and then snarled. He tugged me into his arms with my back to the other men and placed his hands over my ass cheeks.

Kendric's gaze immediately darted to the ceiling. Xander blinked and spun around, muttering something about needing bleach for his brain. Gage barked a short laugh before clamping a hand over his mouth.

Briar's face went beet red.

Ryker snarled threateningly. "Do not fucking look at her."

My own possessiveness kicked in despite Briar being my sister. My fated mate had his naked ass in clear view. My wolf surged forward, ready to protect what was mine.

Turning toward the far wall so that her back was toward us, she made it abundantly clear that she wasn't looking at my mate.

I didn't notice anything, Ember. I swear. I was freaked out.

"Stay here with Briar," Ryker gritted through clenched teeth. "My mate and I are going to put some fucking clothes on."

The three guys hurried deeper into the room so I could walk past them without risk of running into them. We hurried down the hall, and Ryker slammed the bedroom door behind us.

"Fate," Ryker muttered, pressing his forehead against the wood. "That was not how I wanted our post-sex glow to go."

"I think I just trauma-bonded with everyone in that

house," I groaned, scrambling for the sweatpants I'd laid out earlier. "I can't unsee their expressions."

Ryker turned to grab his jeans from the floor—then stopped cold.

The air shifted. That pulse of warm, familiar energy slid against my skin.

And just like that, Many- Greats-Grandfather appeared, sitting in the same damn chair Ryker had tossed his shirt on earlier. His legs were crossed, and he wore a bored expression like we weren't standing there half-dressed. Like this wasn't the second time he'd just *appeared* in a private space without invitation.

Ryker stepped in front of me, jaw clenched. "Are you serious right now?"

Many-Greats-Grandfather tilted his head, gaze flicking between us. "I was going to wait, but I heard you all were napping, and curiosity got the best of me."

"So you broke into my sister's room while she slept?" I snapped, dragging a shirt over my head. "Again—are you *serious?*"

"I wasn't going to speak to her." He shrugged. "She wasn't supposed to wake."

"That's not the reassurance you think it is." Ryker shoved his leg into a pair of jeans. "You're creeping around this house like some nightmare who doesn't understand personal boundaries."

"Personal boundaries? We're family." He steepled his fingers. "I didn't think a formal entrance was required."

This guy was a whole level of frustration I'd never experienced before. "A formal entrance is *always* required. Why are you *here* now?"

"To talk." He glanced around like this was just another meeting room, not our damn bedroom. "I informed you that I wanted to speak to only you, but I understand your fated mate is an extension of your soul, so I will tolerate him."

Ryker crossed his arms. "I didn't realize we had to specify we were to be clothed and for you to knock before entering—especially our bedroom."

Many-Greats-Grandfather offered a tight, amused smile. "I didn't realize modesty still reigned in the shifter world. Noted."

I stalked forward a step, fists clenched at my sides. "You didn't answer the question. *Why now?* What's so urgent that you had to scare my sister and creep through our house?"

The smugness slipped from his face, replaced by something heavier. "Because something feels off in this realm. I need to understand what's going on."

Ryker's posture tensed. "What do you mean *off?*" He came to my side and took my hand in his, presenting a united front.

Many-Greats-Grandfather didn't answer immediately. He just stared like he was trying to decide how to explain it, a bit like how I looked when doing algebraic equations. "I don't know how to put it. There is something disturbing in the air, like a warning. The one time this occurred in the fae realm, a catastrophic war broke out, and our lineage was created to ensure it never happened again. If you inform me of your troubles, I may be able to help decipher the problem with the help of Fate."

I laughed bleakly, unable to hold it back. "Fate? She hates my guts."

"No, child." He shook his head and jerked back as if I'd offended him. "Our line is blessed by her. Sometimes the trials Fate decides to put you through are to make you into the person she wants you to become... a version that is worthy of her blessing."

The fae were cult members. That's what I got from that, but I didn't want to dispute what Fate was truly like. All I wanted to know was if he actually did have insight, even though I doubted it.

So we filled him in.

Everything from the witches in the cells to the cloaking spells, the vampire ambush, the little girl's magic, the witch's warning—*the royals.*

I finished with a tight breath. "The whole thing just feels... personal. Like the vampire queen isn't just trying to gain power—she's pissed. Like she's holding a grudge over something."

Many-Greats-Grandfather's mouth twitched like he found that amusing. "Of course she is. I told your grandfather from generations ago it wouldn't go over well."

I blinked. "Wait. What?"

Ryker narrowed his eyes. "What wouldn't go over well?"

The man leaned forward, elbows on his knees. "The betrayal. The vampire queen acted too calm and understanding for people who drank blood. I suspected she was biding her time."

My pulse spiked. "What betrayal?"

"You aren't aware?" He exhaled slowly. "That information should've been passed down, but maybe your father planned on telling you when he made you aware of your fae lineage."

He scowled and shook his head. "Four generations ago, the wolf king and the vampire queen fell in love despite the horrible history between the species. They agreed to complete the mate bond together and to rule both species side by side. The union was meant as a bridge to peace. Strengthen both lines."

Legs weakening, I sat down on the edge of the bed. "Clearly, that didn't happen."

"No." His tone darkened. "Because before the bond was sealed, the king found his *true* fated mate. A wolf shifter. A nobody in the eyes of vampire royalty."

I already knew where this was going. Ryker sat beside me, and I leaned my head on his shoulder as he wrapped an arm around me. Even if I had been promised to someone else after meeting Ryker, there was no way I could be with anyone but him.

"He broke the agreement." Ryker tightened his hold. "But the vampire queen must have understood why?"

"He didn't just break it. He humiliated her. Publicly. Called off the bond days before the ritual and declared this wolf as his queen." Many-Greats-Grandfather's voice was quiet now. "It shattered more than her pride. It shattered the trust between your kinds. The vampires lost face, and the queen never recovered. She pretended to understand because the fated-mate bond had already been completed, and she bided her time until she had a plan."

I'd heard the saying there was nothing worse than a woman scorned, but damn... I'd thought they'd been exaggerating.

Many-Greats-Grandfather lifted both hands. "She's not just holding a grudge, Ember. She's trying to erase a bloodline and the wolves that supported the union vocally."

My throat dried. "So... she's wounded and wants retribution against those who turned from her?"

"She was betrayed," Many-Greats-Grandfather corrected gently. "And betrayal by someone meant to be her mate—the one who was supposed to unite their kingdoms? That's not something easily forgiven."

Ryker ran a hand through his crazed hair. "But that was four generations ago. Why come after us now?"

Many-Greats-Grandfather folded his hands. "Because time works differently for those with immortality and fueled by power and pride. She waited until she determined an effective strategy and had everything in place. If she struck too soon, then she wouldn't prevail. She needed the wolf shifters to fully trust her and see her as an ally."

I frowned, piecing it together. "So she's not actually trying to wipe out wolf shifters."

"No." He shook his head. "This isn't about species. I believe this is about what she feels she's owed. She and the king agreed to rule both wolf shifters and vampires together. What's the best way to accomplish it? Kill the royals and make it appear a wolf shifter did it, and she comes in and saves the day. She's targeting the packs that supported the royals the most, which is essentially the ones that live closest to them and their protectors."

Ryker shook his head. "She's been planning this for hundreds of years."

"She has." Many-Greats-Grandfather's face tensed into a sobering expression. "And she's clearly using witch magic. Now that your fae power is stirring, you're able to see the shadows. And no one but the three of us knows why. However, you've made it clear you can see them, so now she wants to eliminate you so she can start her reign of terror at will."

Silence stretched between us, thick and heavy.

Many-Greats-Grandfather stood slowly, brushing nonexistent dust from his tunic. "I must return to my realm now. I can't stay away for long because my magic can't replenish here. The air is shifting, and I fear the worst is yet to come."

"Do you think the vampires are preparing something?" Ryker's leg bounced with anxious energy.

Many-Greats-Grandfather gave a sharp nod. "I watched them while you two slept. They're getting ready to breach the perimeter. The only reason they haven't struck yet is because they're waiting to recover. Once the cloaking spell is back in effect, they'll attack without hesitation. You need to prepare yourselves for war. There's no avoiding this. Not anymore."

I swallowed hard, my stomach twisting. "How long do we have?"

He looked toward the window as if he could read the clouds like a clock. "Not long."

"Thanks for the info, but I need you to understand something." Ryker stood, squaring his shoulders. "Hear me clearly—if you show up in this house again without warning us, without knocking or announcing your presence, I don't care who you are. I don't care if you're her ancestor or some fae relic—I'll kill you."

Many-Greats-Grandfather's lips curled into an amused smirk. "I thought over time the people of this realm wouldn't be so prudish, but each time I visit, I get proven wrong."

Neither Ryker nor I laughed.

My many-greats-grandparent stepped backward, his body starting to blur around the edges. "I will see you again someday. But you may want to keep your weapons sharp. And always watch your back."

And just like that—he vanished.

For a moment, Ryker and I just stood there, staring at the empty space where he'd been. The air still buzzed faintly with leftover magic, but it was fading, along with his scent.

"Fate," I breathed. "That was a lot."

Ryker ran a hand down his face. "Yeah. I need a fucking drink, but after what he told us, I'm not risking it."

"Ember? Ryker?" Cassi's voice rang out, edged with urgency. "Adara is awake."

Ryker and I looked at each other, and I jumped to my feet.

Once again, there was no time to breathe or rest to fully process everything we'd learned.

Ryker linked the others, *In case you didn't hear, the witch is awake.*

We reached the living room just as Kendric and Xander came bounding down the hall, Gage right behind them. Briar followed a second later, arms crossed, her face still pale but composed.

Adara—the witch—was sitting on the couch. The blanket was pooled in her lap, and she blinked slowly like the light hurt. Cassi hovered nearby, brows drawn in concern.

Something wasn't right.

This woman wasn't the one we'd brought here.

The woman we'd carried out of that prison looked nothing like the one sitting in front of us now.

She'd been middle-aged at most—maybe in her forties. A strong build, the shadows of youth still clinging to the angles of her face.

Now?

She looked eighty.

Her skin had sunken in. Wrinkles carved deeply into her face. Her eyes looked glassy, hollowed by exhaustion and something else. Time—or something like it—had stolen years from her while she slept.

"What the fuck?" Gage scoffed. "Who is that?"

Briar's eyes narrowed. "That's not the same woman."

I stepped forward slowly, feeling every stare land on me. "Adara?"

The woman blinked at me, her lips moving like she wasn't sure if she remembered how to speak. "That... is my name."

My breath caught.

Cassi shifted uncomfortably. "She's still weak, but her vitals stabilized after her last episode. I didn't notice anything wrong with her appearance until just now."

"That's convenient," Kendric said under his breath.

"We should've never trusted you," Briar spat.

But then something strange happened. Ryker stood between me and the woman like he was protecting her.

My wolf snarled as rage boiled in my body. He wasn't supposed to ever protect someone else over me. I leapt forward.

CHAPTER TWENTY-ONE

Rage surged like lightning through my veins. I didn't care how old the woman looked now. I didn't care if she was so brittle she'd snap in the wind.

She was the one who'd spelled Ryker and played games with us.

And worse—he was standing in front of her.

Protecting her.

My wolf lunged forward as my warm magic buzzed. Ryker's hand shot out and clamped on my shoulder, firm and grounding. *Lil rebel, I'm not protecting her. I'm protecting you from doing something you'll regret.*

My teeth ground together. My hands clenched into fists. "She's messing with us. We can't trust her." All I saw was red due to the way he was trying to protect that woman.

Baby, please, he linked and wrapped his arms around me, causing the jolts of electricity from our bond to help ground me. *This is what she looked like when she spelled me that day. That's what I mean by I'm protecting you, even though I love you being this damn jealous. Not gonna lie.*

I cut my eyes toward him. *Seriously, you're getting plea-*

sure out of this? Now that he'd shocked some rationale back into me, I could feel happiness floating from him. *Asshole.*

Do you still see the tether that connects the two of them? Briar asked.

I hadn't even looked, just reacted. Being more level-headed was a good idea. I took a deep breath, trying to calm my adrenaline rush.

Once I contained the anger, I pulled back and kissed Ryker's cheek before stepping from the one place that always felt like home.

My attention landed on the older lady, who'd at some point stood and taken several large steps back. Cassi stood beside her with her arms lifted, ready to defend her.

I ignored all that and located the thin, very faint thread of a shadow that connected her to Ryker.

It was exactly the same, which meant she had to be the same person. There were no other tethers that led back to him.

I took in the older woman, trying to figure out which facade was real, wondering if neither of them was.

Cassi looked between us, biting the inside of her cheek. "I understand you feel uncomfortable, but don't we at least owe her an opportunity to explain herself?"

Gage wasn't buying it. "I may not be good at school subjects, but even I know the math ain't mathing."

"This is how she looked when I first met her." Ryker lifted both hands. "When she spelled me. I didn't recognize her in the prison, but when Ember said she saw the connection between us, I didn't challenge it. I wanted answers."

I tilted my head, examining her and noticing faint wafts of shadow coming off her in waves... like she was using magic. "Well, this isn't her true appearance."

Adara's mouth dropped. "Why would you say such a thing?" Her gaze darted to Cassi in accusation.

"She didn't tell me anything." I lifted my chin, wanting her to feel my scrutiny. "I can see witch magic." I wasn't going to give her or Cassi more information. Cassi had been on her way to rebuilding the bridge she'd destroyed, but her hiding that the witch was using magic put her back at square one.

"What? That's impossible." Adara wrinkled her nose. "You're a wolf shifter."

I rolled my eyes. "Thanks for telling me. Otherwise, I would never have known."

Gage snickered, and Ryker tried hiding his smile unsuccessfully.

"Fine." Adara flipped her wrist and returned to looking like someone near her mid-thirties. Her dark hair was still matted, and dirt clung to her face. Her cobalt eyes seemed dull. "I usually hide my real appearance."

Every head snapped in her direction.

"You what?" Ryker gritted.

"I cloaked my appearance when you visited me." Her voice trembled. "I didn't want you to be able to find me again. Not after what the vampire queen had done to me."

I tensed with alertness. "Why?"

"Because when I was a young child, the vampire queen visited our coven. She asked if there was anyone who could cloak, and our high priestess said no. However, the vampires could smell the lie, so they began slaughtering us, one by one. Finally, one of my sisters broke the covenant not to share the truth about our magic and informed them that my mother was a true cloaker—one of the rarest magical abilities found."

Ryker cursed under his breath. Cassi's head jerked

toward Adara, wide-eyed. I heard a few gasps as my head spun.

Had we finally determined who the cloaker witch was?

She shook her head as her eyes glistened. "They immediately came to my mom and noticed me clinging to her leg. They asked if I was her child, and she said yes. Then they asked about my abilities, and Mom didn't respond. She didn't want the vampires to smell a lie.

"But silence spoke just as loud as if she'd offered up the truth, and the vampire queen killed our priestess in cold blood. When my mother refused to answer again, she killed the priestess's daughter—the next in line.

"When she placed a gun to the next in line's head, someone spoke up that we had seen signs that I could alter a person's emotions." She wrapped her arms around her waist and shivered. "Then she killed everyone but my mother and me and informed my mother that I should be raised healthy and to understand my magic."

Pressure built in my chest for how horrible this story already sounded.

"But you were a child." Kendric plopped onto the couch where she'd lain. "How would Ambrosia recognize you when you were older? And why didn't the coven fight back?"

"Because we were surrounded. Someone had to have betrayed us, leaking our coven location and revealing that we had a cloaker in our midst. That's why Mom and I never joined another coven." Her mouth pressed into a firm line. "There were so many weapons aimed at us; we would've all been dead if we'd tried to fight back."

She took in a ragged breath. "Unbeknownst to me, until the day my magic fully matured, the queen had kept us under observation as I grew up."

The room went still.

"My magic matured just shy of my twentieth birthday, and I saw both pride and fear in Mom's eyes. I was confused at first until she told me I had to disappear. That the only way I'd live a free life was if I ran far enough that only the goddess knew where I was. Not even Fate could follow."

My throat tightened. "But you didn't get that chance."

Adara swallowed, her jaw quivering. "The night Mom helped me pack, the vampires came. They'd been tracking us as she'd feared. With guns pointed at us, I was given two options. Help keep the vampire queen's emotions cloaked so her humanity wouldn't gain strength, and be at her beck and call for any magic she needed, or Mom would die right there in front of me."

A tear trailed down her cheek. "I have nightmares to this day about the way my coven died, and I couldn't let that happen to my mother, so I agreed. Mom yelled for me not to do it, but what kind of daughter would I be if I told the vampires no? I wouldn't have been able to live with myself."

Beside me, Ryker flinched.

"They clamped magic-absorbing chains on her wrists and dragged her away. And then the vampire queen herself stepped from the tree line."

Adara looked above our heads, her gaze far away. "The queen didn't kill me. She saw value in me." Her lips trembled. "And I agreed to stay and help her."

Briar's brows drew down, suspicion flaring again. "Why imprison you if she had your mother as leverage over you? If you were still useful?"

"Because I was tired," Adara whispered. "I couldn't keep doing awful things to people just so she could win. I understood why Mom had wanted me to say no. I understood the burden we both carried, and it wasn't something the goddess could be proud of. As I performed my tasks, I altered my appearance. Fifteen years of cloaking the queen's humanity, spying, constantly being used by the queen—I broke. I didn't want to be her weapon anymore. I wanted to be free. She didn't even allow me to see my mother in all that time. Who knows if I'll ever see her again?"

Cassi's breath hitched.

"I made it look like I'd been taken. Like someone forced me out of my home. But really, I staged everything. I was trying to disappear—to break the queen's connection to me and remove my magic from Ryker's soul." Her eyes flicked to him, guilt thick in her voice. "To stop letting him be manipulated by magic."

"You failed," Gage said coldly.

Adara nodded. "I made it as far as the forest line. The vampires were already there."

My stomach turned. "They took you to that prison."

"Where they drained me like my mother." She looked at her bruised wrists. "Of everything I had left, and Queen Ambrosia and Ryker were draining my lifeline to fuel the magic I'd cast on them."

A sour taste filled my mouth. Holy shit. The queen truly was ruthless.

Ryker's guilt ripped through the bond. Then he cleared his throat. "Can you lift the spell from me?"

Adara blinked at him, then slowly nodded. "Yes. I meant to. I just—never got the chance."

Her hands trembled slightly as she reached out. Ryker didn't flinch, but I saw the way his shoulders coiled tight. He stood perfectly still as her palms hovered over his chest, her eyes slipping closed.

My wolf surged forward, hating the thought of her

touching Ryker. However, I pushed her back and reminded her what this was for—his humanity.

Ryker grimaced, then linked, *Xander, will you go inform Bruce and Reid that the witch is awake and sharing information?*

On my way. Xander raced out the door as a quiet hum began to build in the room. Swirls of magic left her palm, flowing into his chest near his heart.

The tether between them pulsed once, and a cold sensation permeated our bond.

My heart galloped. I hadn't considered that removing the spell could affect our fated-mate bond.

I opened my mouth to ask her to stop, but the swirls shimmered and then vanished, knocking the breath out of me.

A sound like wind through brittle leaves filled the room, and then the link was gone.

Rubbing my chest, fear strangled me as I watched Ryker. His entire body jolted like a string had been cut, then slowly, a tension I didn't even realize had always been there—eased.

His hand curled into mine, and through our bond, his presence felt stronger than ever before.

Cassi placed a steadying hand on Adara's back as she sagged, her energy completely drained again.

Ryker exhaled and turned toward me, his eyes shining bright. "Thank you."

Adara didn't answer, but out of the corner of my eye, I saw her nod.

And that's when realization hit me.

I snapped my gaze to Adara. "You said you were still linked to her," I said slowly. "To Ambrosia."

"Yes, and when I replenish some of my energy, I'm

going to find a way to break the link without her being here."

"What if we don't break it?" I had to sound crazy.

Adara's head lifted.

"She's still using your mother to cloak the vampires, and you spelled her to be emotionless about everything she does," I pressed. "But if you're still tied to her..."

Ryker jerked his head back. "Then we can find her."

"I-I don't know." Adara blinked rapidly. "I'm so tired of using my magic like this."

"But can it be done?" Briar asked, stepping closer.

Adara didn't answer right away. Then slowly... she nodded. "Yes."

The word hung in the air, heavy and dangerous.

"Yes," she repeated, more firmly this time. "I'll do it. Helping you might end the connection for me and free my mother."

A shiver ran down my spine. We finally had a way to find Queen Ambrosia.

"About damn time." Gage pumped an arm. "I'm so fucking tired of waiting for them to come to us."

Just then, the door opened, and Xander returned, followed by Reid, Bruce, and Sun.

"Everyone's here," he said, breathless. "I filled them in on the way here."

Reid's expression was drawn and tired, but his eyes were alert. "Has anything else been revealed?"

"No." Briar rubbed her arms like she was cold. "She removed the spell from Ryker, and that's it."

"Well, we did just learn more information," I added, filling everyone in about the vampire queen and the king who'd betrayed her.

"She's fucking crazy." Gage's jaw dropped open.

Something still clawed at my insides, like we were missing something.

It hit me like a logging truck from *Final Destination*.

I spun to Adara again. "There's something we haven't asked."

She blinked, looking like she might collapse at any second. "What?"

I almost didn't want to press her. Asking this question could destroy any hope I had still limping in me. "You mentioned the wolf royals. What about them?"

The silence that followed was deafening.

Adara's lips parted. "They are being held in a place and situation worse than hell. Worse than what the vampires put me and the other witches through during captivity."

Gasps broke through the room like glass shattering on tile.

"They're *alive*?" Ryker's voice was razor sharp with disbelief. "But... we saw the blood. The bodies."

"You saw what you were meant to see." Adara sat on the couch next to Kendric and continued, "There was blood. The bodies were mutilated to the point that no one would be recognizable, and they ensured they left behind some pieces of the ones who remained alive to ensure you'd find that among the bodies."

Sun's eyes widened. "How do you know?"

"Because I was forced to be the distraction that lowered the royals' and the Grimstone wolf pack's guard." She shook and gagged like she might vomit. "I didn't know they'd planned to slaughter everyone, and when I realized what was going on, I didn't know how to stop it. I ran to the woods and threw up. By the time I'd pulled myself together, the vampires were putting the royal family in the back of a van. They were all unconscious. I'd waited too long to try to help them."

My heart stopped.

"You *what?*" Gage said like he couldn't trust his own ears.

Briar's hand shot to her mouth.

"Where are they now?" Ryker demanded.

"I don't know," Adara admitted, shaking her head. "But the queen was obsessed with them. She'd keep them close."

My breath caught. We needed to move. And fast. "Do you know how they made the vampires smell like wolves? That's not normal."

Her brows pinched together. "No. That wasn't me. I don't know how they did it."

A fresh wave of unease washed over the room, and Ryker's worry heightened.

"That means someone else helped her. She seems to enjoy killing people to force others into submission." Reid's arms crossed. "And they aren't even using them as food. They're killing out of malice and hate, and the queen wants everyone to know it."

He was right. Granted, vampires didn't enjoy feeding off other supernaturals. They could, but they didn't like it.

"When can you do a location spell?" Bruce's eyes glowed from where he had to be linking with others.

Adara hesitated and leaned her head back on the couch. "In a few minutes."

Briar went to the refrigerator and got the witch some water, and Ryker grabbed one of the extra blankets and draped it around her.

Closing her eyes, Adara lay on the edge of the couch, trying to get comfortable.

"No matter where she is, we all need to leave the Blackwood territory." Ryker turned his back to Adara and spoke softly. "We took Adara and freed the other witches. The vampire queen won't like looking weak."

Briar looked out the windows. "It's nearing sunset. If we're going to leave, we have to do it without raising alarms. If even one of those cloaked bastards is out there watching and sees us..."

"We're done," Gage finished grimly.

A quiet tension hummed through the room as we all stared at Adara.

Our one shot at turning the tide rested on a broken witch with barely enough energy to speak, trying to locate the most dangerous supernatural creature we'd ever faced.

"If we stay here, we're done too," Kendric answered. "If we're going to die, I'd at least like to kill some vampires on my way out."

"Well, I hope you mean that." Cassi's jaw clenched. "Because they just broke through the perimeter."

As if Fate wanted to taunt us, an agonized howl filled the air, reminding me of the night our pack was slaughtered.

And then the cold pressure slammed into me, nearly knocking me over.

CHAPTER TWENTY-TWO

The howl shattered the silence. It wasn't a warning but a cry of death.

My blood turned to ice, and Ryker's fear constricted my lungs.

"The vampires have moved." Reid headed to the front door. "And they're cloaked. We're shifting and getting ready to fight."

Sun chased after him, but I grabbed her wrist and yanked her toward me.

"No," I snapped. "Tell your people to get in the damn cars and go. Remember what happened to my pack when we did that?"

Her forehead creased. "Reid, she's right. This isn't about being cowards. It's about survival."

I blinked, completely taken aback that she'd agreed with me that easily.

"Fine. That means your ass needs to be in a vehicle *now*," he snarled.

Adara groaned, her fingers curling around the edge of the blanket like she could sense the storm rising around us.

"Xander," Ryker barked. "Get Adara to the SUV. Move."

"I've got her," he said, lifting her gently like she was made of glass.

I turned to Bruce. "You need to tell your pack to leave your territory too. I don't know if they're already attacking them or not, but if not—they will be soon."

"Fuck, this is about vengeance." Bruce's irises glowed. "I'm on it."

A crash echoed outside—glass shattering, metal groaning.

"Windows." Briar swore under her breath. "They're getting inside our house."

"I'll slow them down," Cassi offered, already lifting her hands and muttering under her breath.

"Everyone out," Ryker barked. "Follow the plan. Don't split up. Don't stop. Just drive."

Briar nodded and headed for the front with keys in hand. Kendric threw open the front door, and I caught sight of blood smeared across the porch like a warning sign.

It wasn't just a smear. It was deliberate.

A paw print dragged from the middle of the railing down. Then, a trail led down the steps.

My stomach twisted as I stepped closer.

I didn't recognize the scent at first—too much copper and fear—but the closer I got, the more it settled in my bones.

It was wolf and not foreign, belonging to one of Reid's pack members.

The vampires wanted us to know they'd broken through, killed someone who'd tried to run and left their blood like a calling card.

They were sending a message—they were here for us.

I staggered back as shadows bloomed around the porch, faint tendrils of them edging into my vision. I could feel them and smell that faint shifter scent, the pressure sliding against my skin like invisible fingers trying to push me out.

Dammit, Ember. Get your ass back in the house, Ryker linked, grabbing me from behind and tugging me back just as another window crashed upstairs.

Another tragic howl rang into the darkening skies. They had numbers and were coming in fast. *Staying here is a fucking death sentence.*

Gage cursed. Kendric spun and was headed back inside when a shadow sped toward him.

I reached for my weapon but came up empty-handed as Kendric's leg got swiped from underneath him. He fell, and a shadow dragged him to the porch steps.

Kendric's face twisted in agony as Gage held up a gun and shot. The shadow jerked back and released its hold as more jumped toward the porch.

Cold slithered across my spine, this time coming from the back of the house. We were surrounded.

They're behind us too. We have to leave now, I linked.

Hovering next to me, Ryker tensed, ready to protect me at any moment.

Kendric crawled toward us, and Briar handed me her gun.

No— I started.

You can see them, she said. *I can't. It's better for you to be armed.*

She made sense, but I hated for my sister not to have a way to protect herself.

I ran forward, gun lifted, and started firing.

Dammit, Ember. Ryker's feet pounded to catch up. *I swear you want to die and take me with you.*

A shadow launched from the dark and slammed Kendric flat on the porch. Bones cracked, and I fired. The vampire jolted off his back, but another took its place, claws dragging across Kendric's side. Blood bloomed, and his roar of pain twisted something deep inside me.

I fired again, the gunshot cracking through the night like thunder. The vampire dropped, and another came from the left, but Ryker couldn't see them.

Two are coming from the left side of the porch, I linked, pointing in their direction. *And one's coming from the right.*

Gage fired left without hesitation, and a shriek split the air as something heavy hit the ground.

Ryker's hand gripped my elbow. *How can we get you out of here?*

A black shadow blurred to my right, and I immediately knew its target. *Duck!*

Ryker dropped to his knees as I fired over his shoulder. The vampire collided with the rail of the porch, tearing through wood like paper.

I immediately aimed left and took out the two shadows that were almost on top of Kendric.

The one shadow from the right's body twisted, writhing with rage, before Kendric flipped over and unsheathed a knife then slammed it where it was clear something had landed.

It didn't stop the shadow, but it bought me the second I needed to shoot it in the head.

I spun around and heard shadows from the very back of the house. *They're coming through the house. We've got to move.*

Xander barreled toward me with Adara limp in his arms.

Kendric stood on the porch, one hand pressed to his

ribs where blood leaked through torn fabric. Cassi kept muttering spells under her breath, and a windstorm suddenly rushed the shadows that were trying to attack us.

Another window exploded, but this time in the kitchen. Gage and Briar shrieked as shards rained down. A cloaked vampire dove toward Gage from above.

I shouted, but it was too late.

The vampire landed hard. Gage went down under its weight, slamming to the floor with a grunt. His gun skittered across the tile.

"Get off him!" Briar's voice cracked. She grabbed a kitchen knife off the island and slammed it down but missed the enemy.

The shadow moved toward her, and I fired, hitting it in the chest.

It shrieked as visible blood poured to the floor, leaving Gage coughing and clutching his ribs.

"You all need to get the hell out of here before I can't hold them off any longer," Cassi shouted.

Ryker grabbed my arm again. *Where are the enemies we're going to face when running out?*

They're being pushed back, so we have a hole right in the center of the shadows if we can move now.

Briar screamed.

I whipped around in time to see a shadow latch onto her back and yank her toward the bedrooms.

My heart pounded as I fired, aiming for what I hoped was right between its eyes. Four other shadows were now in the living room behind us, and I aimed at each one. *Go down the front steps and stay right in the center of the walkway. Now.*

She hit the floor face down. The vampire screeched and

retreated, but not before it raked its claws across her back. Blood welled instantly.

Xander and Kendric took off out front, slowed from injuries and carrying an unconscious witch.

I rushed to my sister, feeling Ryker's frustration peaking. However, he knew better than to ask me to leave Briar behind. Desperate, I helped her stumble to her feet.

"You all need to *go*," Cassi grunted, sweat beading on her forehead.

I didn't argue. Ryker pushed forward, and Gage, Briar, and I sprinted for the SUV. Cassi ran behind us, and I noticed the wind was slowing.

Outside, the cold hit me like a wave.

They were everywhere. Unseen but pressing in. And we were out of time.

Three on our left, I linked, and Gage didn't hesitate. He turned midstride and fired. Since he couldn't see them, he hit only one, but the shadow thudded into the grass.

As I fired at the other two, Kendric stumbled with blood soaking his shirt. Briar ducked under his good arm and hauled him forward.

I covered their retreat, firing at a blur that surged for their backs. The bullet found its mark, causing blood to spray back on my face and chest.

Xander sprinted past me, Adara flopping against his chest. Every few steps, he dipped, making his route more unpredictable. Still, the shadows had to know what our plan was.

Cassi continued to spell the wind, though it was dying down to a trickle. When Xander and Adara caught up to Briar and Kendric at the SUV, I fired at shadows until my clip was empty.

Here, take mine. Gage handed me his rifle, and I shot at every shadow that got too close to us.

"Cassi, drop the wind. It's already almost fizzled out," Ryker ordered. "We may need your help here in a bit."

Briar threw open the back door, and Xander, Kendric, and Adara went to the very back. There were only enough seats for seven people, but we'd make eight work, even if one of us had to lie on the floorboard.

I ran out of bullets.

Get into the passenger seat now, Ryker linked to me and pushed me in through the driver's side. My hip banged against the steering wheel, but I crawled over as Briar and Cassi climbed into the back and slammed the door.

Ryker jumped into the driver's seat just as a shadow grabbed his arm. I had no bullets to use, so I threw the gun at the shadow. It made its mark but then bounced off the shadow and hit Ryker in the neck.

Pain shot through him as he shoved the shadow away and slammed the door shut. Within a second, he had the SUV running, but shadows surrounded us.

The rearview mirror went black, and my pulse spiked.

"They've boxed us in," I rasped.

Ryker threw the gearshift into reverse anyway. "Hold on."

Tires screamed as he punched the gas. The bumper smashed a body I couldn't see; bone crunched, metal dented, and the whole frame shuddered. The engine roared but refused to climb the mound caught behind the tires.

Shit. We were pinned between cloaked vamps and the woods.

Go forward! I pointed to a narrow gap between the trees. *There!* My heart hammered against my ribs as I felt Ryker's desperate determination surge through our bond.

Ryker slammed the SUV into drive and turned the steering wheel hard. The tires spun and finally found traction, lurching forward. Claws scraped against metal as we hurtled toward the tree line.

Loud *thuds* came from on top of the SUV.

"They're on the roof!" Briar shouted.

A fist punched through the ceiling, and a shadow hand came through. Gage removed his knife and squatted on his feet from his place between the mid-row captain seats. He swiped aimlessly, trying to hit something.

The vampire removed its hand, but before I could tell Gage to stop, the hand came through again, opening the hole wider as another arm went through.

It was enough for Gage to sever two of the shadow's fingers, spraying himself, Cassi, and Briar with blood.

A shadow landed on the hood, and the windshield cracked.

Take a sharp right at the tree. It was the only way I could see the shadow falling off.

Ryker floored the accelerator. The SUV lurched forward just as the shadow gouged deep furrows into the windshield. Cassi screamed as Ryker took a hard left and the shadow figure tumbled off.

Just when I thought maybe we'd gotten away from them, another crash came from above. Gage drove his knife upward just as something black covered the hole in the roof, and a high-pitched shriek pierced the air.

Briar's voice broke through the chaos. "Is that the main road ahead?"

I squinted through the fractured windshield, warmth exploding in my chest for the first time since we'd fled the house. The narrow dirt path was widening, the trees thinning, and the night sky mere minutes away.

"Almost there," Ryker confirmed, knuckles white on the steering wheel. "Two minutes, maybe less."

We barreled toward safety. My gaze darted between the road ahead and the shadows that seemed to be receding. Were they giving up? It felt too easy.

A subtle shift in the air made my skin prickle. "Ryker—"

The explosion was deafening. The SUV swerved violently as both passenger-side tires blew, sending us into a wild skid.

Metal groaned as we lurched sideways and slammed into a tree. The impact threw me against my door, pain exploding through my shoulder. Glass rained down as the windshield spiderwebbed completely.

"Everyone okay?" Ryker barked, trying to start the car again.

Moans and curses answered from the back. The engine sputtered, died, then caught as Ryker cranked the ignition. We inched forward on the rims, metal bumping over dirt.

"We can make it," he growled, determination flooding our bond.

A shadow dropped onto the hood with enough force to dent the metal. The engine made a sickening grinding noise then went silent. Ryker tried the ignition again—nothing.

"Dammit, we're going to have to run on foot," he snarled, slamming his palm against the wheel.

Cold terror swept through me as shadows converged on us from all directions, materializing out of the darkness like smoke taking form. With all the pressure on me, I couldn't breathe.

"We've gotta run while we still can," I screamed, fumbling for the door handle. "They'll be here in seconds!"

The SUV doors flew open as we scrambled into the night. Ryker dragged me out his side by my arm, his grip bruising. Cassi tumbled from the back door and hit the ground hard with a cry.

Kendric couldn't even stand. Blood pooled beneath him as Briar tried to haul him up.

"We can't outrun them like this," Gage panted, back pressed against the SUV, gaze darting around wildly. "How many are there?"

Xander held Adara's limp form, his face twisted with desperation. "Which way do we run?"

There wasn't a good answer. These fuckers were everywhere.

"They've surrounded us," I gasped, turning in a slow circle as the cold pressed in from all sides. My lungs burned, each breath harder than the last. "Ryker, there are at least twenty."

The shadows moved in perfect synchronization, tightening their circle with predatory patience. They knew we were trapped.

Kendric collapsed against the SUV, and Briar screamed, pressing her hands over the wound in his side.

"He needs stitches *now*." My sister's voice cracked, and something inside me shattered.

We weren't all going to make it out of this. The vampire queen would win after all.

CHAPTER TWENTY-THREE

Kendric's breathing hitched, and Briar pressed both palms to his side. Gage opened the trunk, searching for something. Xander placed Adara back in the trunk and stood in front of it to protect her… not that it would make a difference at this point. Cassi stood up, arms lifted, but her magic didn't work. She'd used up her supply when we ran from the house.

The circle of cold squeezed tighter.

"They're *everywhere*." I inhaled shakily, watching them slowly close in on us. They knew this was over… that they would win.

Lil rebel, Ryker linked, taking my hand and tugging me toward him. He placed his forehead to mine, and our bond cracked open, flooding me with every ounce of his love, his terror, his rage. *If this is it—*

Not without a fight, I answered, blinking back unshed tears.

He kissed me hard to the point we both tasted blood.

As I pulled back, a shadow slammed into me. I fell on

my back as Ryker snarled and kicked the spot above me. The shadow jerked to the side, but four more tackled Ryker.

"No," I shouted as fear and turmoil exploded within me.

A pressure wave rolled across my body as sharp as broken ice. It slammed into my chest, shoving air from my lungs as a shadow launched at me with its hand extended like it was going to claw me.

Briar screamed, and my blood turned ice cold.

All of a sudden, the shadows staggered, hissed, and looked up.

Wind howled out of nowhere, sending dust and dead leaves spiraling into the air. The ground trembled like a pulse. As if it might open up at any second.

I sat up, ready to continue the fight even if it was pointless. I twisted around to see what the vampires were all glaring at.

My heart stopped.

The little girl we'd saved from the vampire prison stepped from the woods, the woman with the swollen eye to her right and the tall woman with the scarred cheek to her left. More bodies filed in behind them.

Dizzy, I tried to not fall over. I blinked again, wondering if this was some sort of death dream because all the witches we'd freed were now standing in front of me. The very ones who'd sworn neutrality not even eight hours ago.

The little girl raised her hands, and white magic poured from them, striking the shadows between us. The cloaking peeled from the vampires' bodies like skin. One second, they were smears of nothing. The next, they were solid flesh, fangs, and wide, terrified eyes.

Cassi gasped. "I can *see* them!"

That was all any of us needed.

The tall witch with the scarred cheek thrust both palms outward. A slab of packed earth bucked up beneath the nearest vampire and launched it sky-high.

The swollen-eyed witch shrieked and curled her fingers into claws. Water burst from the ground in geysers. Three vampires were caught in the sudden force and then lifted off their feet and slammed into trees with bone-crushing force.

I scrambled to my feet as Ryker fought his way through the revealed vampires toward me. Blood trickled down his arms and face.

"This changes nothing," hissed a female vampire. She lunged at the scarred witch.

A fourth witch stepped forward, hair a wild halo around her face. With a flick of her wrist, the air around the vampire ignited. Flames engulfed her, and her screams pierced the night until nothing but ash drifted to the forest floor.

The vampires hesitated.

"Regroup!" a vampire snarled, his voice edged with panic. Five of them converged, forming a circle with their backs to one another as they assessed the changing battle-field. The tallest one, his black hair swept back from a pale, angular face, lunged toward Briar.

I dove forward and caught him midstride. My shoulder connected with his ribs, and we crashed to the gravel road. Pain exploded through me on impact, and pebbles cut into my skin, but adrenaline dulled the sensations to a distant throb. He hissed, fangs inches from my throat before Ryker yanked him off me and slammed him into a tree trunk.

The ground trembled once more. Through the trees, more figures approached. Seven witches stepped forward, followed by nine more. Their hands glowed with different-colored magic, illuminating the night in eerie hues of blue, green, and amber.

"The queen's worst nightmare has come," whispered the little girl, tilting her head as if the deaths she'd just witnessed hadn't impacted her.

A vampire with silver-streaked hair snarled, backing away, as three more witches emerged from the tree line. His gaze darted wildly about. "This is impossible. The queen—"

"The queen is not here," said a witch with a burn scar across her neck, her palms crackling with black tendrils of energy. "But we are."

The vampires hissed and clustered together, their movements frantic and disorganized. One lunged at Xander, who was still protecting Adara, but a witch with braided hair flicked her wrist, and the vampire froze in midair, suspended by an invisible force, before being hurled backward into his companions.

I pushed myself to my feet despite my aching body. Blood trickled down my knee, where the gravel had torn through my sweatpants. Ryker appeared at my side, his hand coming to rest on the small of my back.

More witches emerged from the darkness and added to the chaos. Streams of magic whirled in front and behind us as the witches continued their attack. The air thickened with power, making my skin feel as if sandpaper was running over it again and again.

"Impossible," breathed the silver-haired vampire, his confidence crumbling before my eyes. "You were freed from prison only to come back to be captured?"

The little girl stepped forward, her small frame commanding the entire clearing. Her eyes—too old for her child's face—found mine.

"We will protect the woman who risked her life to save

us," she said, her voice clear as a bell despite the chaos. "Fire, you and your friends can make it to the end of the road. We will protect you."

"Let's move," Ryker commanded.

I moved forward with him but looked over my shoulder for Briar. She was helping Kendric to his feet with Gage scooping up Adara from the trunk. Xander removed his gun from its holster while Cassi stumbled after us, her face pale but determined.

The witches parted, creating a corridor of safety through their ranks. The vampires even stopped trying to come forward since, each time they tried, a witch pushed them back or used magic to harm them.

As I passed the little girl, her small hand reached out. Her fingers, cool and impossibly strong, wrapped around mine. She matched my pace, her white dress fluttering around her legs like an angel's gown.

"The shadows cannot touch you anymore," she whispered, her icy blue eyes scanning the chaos around us. "But we must hurry."

The witches moved with us, continuing to use their magic when necessary. The little girl's hand remained firmly in mine, her presence oddly comforting despite the chaos around us.

"Keep moving," she murmured, her gaze fixed ahead.

A vampire with long, red hair darted from the shadows, targeting a witch at the edge of their formation—an older woman with a limp who trailed slightly behind. The vampire's fangs gleamed as he lunged for her throat. My heart lurched, expecting blood and death.

But the witch merely turned, raised a palm, and the vampire crumpled midair, his body contorting unnaturally before he fell to the ground, writhing.

A blur of motion caught my eye as a dark figure lunged from behind a thick oak trunk toward the witch with braided hair. The witch spun, palm thrust outward—but too late. The vampire had already closed the distance.

I tensed, waiting for the inevitable clash, but Ryker's grip on my arm tightened. "Keep moving," he growled, but I kept watching even as we ran.

The vampire slashed the witch's throat. Blood poured from her neck, and her hands grasped it as the witch beside her spun and launched the vampire backward until it crashed through the underbrush and disappeared into darkness.

The witch with a limp ran to the witch with braided hair and tried to help her, but the injured witch dropped to the ground. The stench of her blood was strong and fresh, and I knew the vampire had nicked an artery.

My breath caught. So many people had died because of the vampires, and these witches had come here to protect us when they hadn't wanted to. And now, one of their own had died in the process.

"We have to keep moving," the little girl whispered, and Ryker tugged on the hand he held once again, urging me forward.

The braided-hair witch's hand slackened as death crept in. Her throat had been clawed out.

My heart stuttered. That was why the vampires didn't have guns and weren't using knives and why they still smelled like wolf shifters. *The vampires still want to make it look as if wolves are fighting one another,* I linked to everyone.

Fucking bloodsuckers, Gage replied. *I'm embarrassed that I even liked them for a minute. They all deserve to die and walk around with no peace for eternity.*

Sometimes I thought Gage was melodramatic, but not this time. I agreed fullheartedly.

They wanted to eliminate the packs that were threats to them and make it look as if we attacked each other, Ryker added. His disgust and anger slammed into me, mixing with mine. *The bitch is still thinking she's going to win.*

In fairness, she might, Briar connected. *We almost died back there. Did you already forget that?*

I raised my eyebrows, and pride tightened my chest. I'd always known that Briar had spunk, but she'd also enjoyed being a pleaser. Even though I wished we hadn't had to go through all this shit, I couldn't deny that a *little* bit of good had come from it. Each one of them had been pushed to grow and develop.

Another vampire with a military-style crew cut darted in from the left, targeting a slender witch near the rear. However, the witch who'd watched her braided-hair sister die swung her arms out, causing him to fly into a tree trunk with a sickening *thwack.*

I shuddered as the vampire's body slid down the trunk, leaving a dark smear against the bark. Ryker and the little girl tugged me forward again. She was nearly as strong as Ryker, and both of them propelled me along the road, my feet kicking up gravel.

"Almost there," she whispered, scanning the tree line constantly.

The road curved ahead, revealing its end, where it met a wider paved street. My heart leapt with hope—we were almost out.

But the vampires weren't giving up. They circled, moving faster than before, their desperation making them reckless. Three more broke through the trees ahead of us, cutting off our path to the main road. Behind us, at least a dozen more closed in.

"Shit," Ryker growled, pulling me closer to his side.

The swollen-eyed witch staggered forward, her steps wavering. Blood trickled from her nose, and the dark tendrils of her magic slithered around her hands like dying flames.

"We're weakening," she rasped just loud enough for us to hear. She staggered, nearly falling before catching herself against a tree trunk. "We can't hold them off much longer."

My stomach dropped. The witches had seemed so powerful moments ago, but now I could see the toll their magic was taking on them. They'd been stuck in captivity for who knew how long. Several had bloody noses, others trembled visibly, and the chill of their magic was weakening.

"We need to get to the main road," Ryker said, scanning our surroundings. "If we can make it past those three—"

"They'll just follow us." Despair clawed at my chest. "Even if we make it to the main road, they'll still be there. I doubt they'll even care if humans see them attack."

The swollen-eyed witch stumbled toward us, her face pale and drawn. "We can't—" She cut off, swaying dangerously. "Our magic is nearly depleted. Years of captivity... drained us. We thought we had more strength, but—"

Panic clawed my throat. The vampires must have realized the witches were sputtering as a few more attacked, testing them. Several witches worked together to fend them off, but it was a closer thing.

"We need a plan." I scanned our surroundings.

Engines purred in the distance, coming quickly in our direction.

"Do you hear that?" I whispered.

Ryker's head snapped up, his golden-flecked eyes narrowing as he scanned the darkness beyond the tree line. The little girl's grip on my hand tightened.

The distant rumble grew louder, and headlights cut through the darkness at the far end of the main road. Not one pair of lights but many—a convoy, approaching fast.

"Could that be..." Cassi trailed off.

I squinted against the glare, trying to see who was in the closest vehicle barreling toward us. Could it be the Blackwood pack?

"Get ready," Ryker growled, pushing me behind him while scanning for escape routes.

There were none. The vampires had already surrounded us once more.

The vehicles skidded to a halt just a few feet away. The truck in front's door flew open before it had fully stopped. Reid leaped out in one fluid motion, gun raised. Sun emerged from the passenger side simultaneously, her weapon steady in her hands as she scanned the battlefield.

Reid's eyes glowed, no doubt giving instructions as he began firing. Three SUVs and an additional truck screeched to a halt behind him.

The Blackwood pack and Bruce and a few of his pack members poured from the vehicles—four, eight, twelve, sixteen in total—fanning out and firing at the vampires.

"Get down," Sun shouted, her eyes never leaving the vampires circling the witches.

Bullets ripped through the air, most hitting vampire targets. Vampires shrieked as their bodies jerked and convulsed before dropping to the ground. One by one, the vampires removed the guns they had hidden around their ankles and returned fire, ignoring the blood pooling under them.

"Everyone get to cover," Ryker yelled and grabbed my arm, yanking me toward the vehicles as bullets whizzed past my head.

I ducked low, heart hammering as we scrambled for cover. The little witch girl released my hand and dove behind a large oak tree, her white dress billowing like a ghost in the darkness.

Briar stumbled beside me, her face pale. Together, we crouched behind Reid's truck, the metal frame vibrating with each impact as bullets pinged against it. Cassi slid in beside us, breathing heavily, her eyes wide with panic.

Kendric limped toward us, face ashen with pain. Gage ran over, too, and threw Kendric's arm over his shoulder, helping him get to us, while Ryker stood at the end of the truck, looking for an opportunity to help. Just as he tensed to move, Xander popped out from behind a tree, firing his gun methodically to cover them.

Several more witches were taken down. I had to do *something* to help them. Casting my gaze around, I saw some large rocks a few feet away. If I got them, I could use them as a weapon.

I lunged, but suddenly a strong arm circled my waist and pulled me back against a brick wall. The jolt of the fated-mate connection sprang to life, alerting me it wasn't a wall... it was Ryker's muscular chest.

"Stay down," Ryker ordered, pushing me against a truck tire and positioning his body protectively in front of me.

I peered around Ryker's shoulder, trying to see what was happening. More Blackwood pack members had arrived, providing fresh firepower against the vampires.

A blur of movement caught my eye as a stocky wolf darted between two trees with his mouth wide open. A vampire appeared and tackled him to the ground. The wolf's whimper cut through the chaos as the vampire's teeth tore into his throat, ripping and shredding until the wolf shifter gurgled into silence.

"No," Sun shouted, emptying her clip at the vampire.

My stomach lurched as the wolf's body went limp, blood pooling beneath him. Another life taken because of a vengeful bitch. Who would've thought I'd find someone I despised more than Fate?

The swollen-eyed witch collapsed next, a bullet meant for a vampire catching her in the shoulder. She crumpled to the ground, her magic dissipating. Three more witches fell in quick succession—one with her throat torn out by a vampire, another shot through the chest, the third simply collapsing from magical exhaustion.

"They're dying because of... us." My voice broke as guilt weighed down my entire body.

The little girl now stood alone, her tiny frame trembling as a vampire stalked toward her.

Rage exploded inside me. These women—these witches who'd been imprisoned and tortured—had come to save us, and now they were dying for it. Because of me. Because I'd asked them to choose sides.

The rapid-fire gunshots that had filled the night began to taper off. Vampires retreated into the woods. Bodies— vampire, shifter, and witch—littered the ground, and the acrid scent of gunpowder and the stench of copper from blood hung in the air.

"They're pulling back," Reid called out, removing an empty magazine and reaching for another, only to find his pocket empty.

Sun's gun clicked uselessly as she tried to fire at a fleeing vampire.

Several of the Blackwood pack members checked their

weapons, shaking their heads. We'd spent everything we had, and by some miracle, it had been enough to turn the tide.

But not completely.

The vampire stalking the little girl wasn't deterred.

The little girl stood still as the vampire approached, his lips curled in a feral grin. Everyone else was either reloading or tending to the wounded. No one was watching her except me.

I moved before Ryker could stop me.

His hand grabbed for my wrist. *Ember, don't—*

But I twisted free and darted forward, keeping low. The little girl's eyes met mine across the clearing. She didn't look afraid, just... resigned.

The vampire's back was to me as he advanced on her. Twenty feet separated us.

Fifteen.

Ten.

I snatched a fallen branch from the ground just as the little girl shouted, "Fire, no!"

The vampire smirked... then turned and slammed a knife into my chest. He chuckled. "I knew you wouldn't let me hurt her."

The blade carved through me like heated steel through ice. Agony exploded in my chest, radiating outward in waves that stole my breath. The vampire's eyes gleamed with victory as he twisted the knife, sending fresh torment spiraling through my every nerve.

There was a blur of motion, then Ryker was there, face flushed with primal rage. He gripped the vampire's head with such force that his fingers left dents in the pale skin. With one savage twist, the vampire's neck snapped with a sickening crack that echoed through the clearing. The body went limp, falling away from me like discarded trash.

I couldn't feel joy. All I could feel was pain.

My knees buckled, and the ground rushed to meet me as warm wetness spread across my shirt.

Blood pulsed from the wound with each beat of my heart, soaking my shirt and pooling underneath me. The metallic scent of my own blood filled my nostrils as darkness crept into the edges of my vision.

Ryker dropped to his knees beside me, his face a mask of horror. His fear slammed into me, making my mouth taste bitter. Hands hovered over the knife still embedded in my chest, trembling slightly.

Skidding on the ground next to me, Briar sent leaves and dirt flying. Her fingers fluttered over the wound, assessing the damage. "We need to get the knife out now!"

"No." Ryker's voice was iron, though the golden flecks disappeared from his eyes, betraying his terror. "She could bleed out. The blade is keeping pressure on the vessels."

I tried to speak, but something warm bubbled from my lips instead of words. The knife pulsed with unnatural heat, sending tendrils of fire through my veins with each heartbeat.

"She's not going to survive if we keep her here." Gage ran a hand through his hair. "Our best bet is to take her to a hospital."

"If you let her rest, she'll be okay." The little girl tilted her head, examining me.

They ignored her.

Ryker's arm slid underneath me, and my body lifted.

I tried to open my mouth to tell the little girl I'd be fine, but I couldn't speak—couldn't even mind-link. My eyelids grew impossibly heavy, and the fae magic heated inside me. The argument above me faded to distant echoes as darkness rolled over my vision. Consciousness slipped away like water through cupped hands as my body lit on fire.

This had to be it. The day when all the violence and danger ended for me.

Awareness returned like a slap to the face. I gasped, lungs fighting against what felt like liquid fire. Pain crushed my chest until I couldn't breathe. This wasn't physical agony.

This was raw, primal grief, clawing through my insides like a wild animal.

"I told you not to remove the knife." Ryker's voice shattered the air, trembling with fury. "She's dying because of you."

My eyes slit open, and my vision blurred. I made out Briar's silhouette, standing tall with the little girl at her side.

"The knife had to come out." She lifted her chin in defiance. "Ashlyn agrees with me."

Ashlyn? Which witch was she?

"And you trusted a ten-year-old girl to make a call like that?" Ryker's voice cracked with disbelief, eyes flashing between Briar and the small child beside her. "Some naive kid who believes Ember will be fine?"

The little girl—Ashlyn—stepped forward, her delicate features sharply set. "I'm not naive. Fire will be fine."

Fae magic swirled through me, making me feel as if I were on fire. The wound in my chest throbbed where the heat settled.

The heat intensified, scorching through my veins like wildfire. Why had I awakened to reexperience death? My back arched, and I moaned.

"Is the damn wolf shifter here yet? I can't lose her," Ryker growled as he jumped on the bed of the truck, lifting me. "She needs help *now*."

He hadn't even noticed I was awake, but with how little I could see, I'd bet my eyes still appeared closed.

"Ryker, none of us wants her to die," Sun spat out and appeared between him and Briar. "But you're making way too much noise. We're supposed to head to the back entrance of the hospital and remain undetected."

Hospital? No. Supernaturals weren't supposed to get help from humans.

"Everyone, be quiet." Reid's face strained. His dark eyes locked on Ryker, unwavering. "I understand your mate is dying, but if you want her to live, control yourself. Let's take her in before someone comes over or calls the police."

Ryker's arms tightened around me, his heartbeat thundering against my ear. The panic radiating from him washed over me in suffocating waves. His breath came in short, ragged bursts that matched the erratic pulse of the fae magic burning through my veins.

I tried to link with Ryker to reassure him that I was awake, but the connection that had always come so naturally was now beyond my grasp. My lips moved, trying to form words, but my body refused to obey as if I were paralyzed.

The world tilted as Ryker rushed forward, carrying me across the hospital parking lot. My head lolled against his chest, each movement sending fresh waves of agony through my body.

We reached a nondescript metal door at the rear of the brick building. Before Ryker could kick it open, it swung inward, revealing a man with gray hair and tired eyes.

"This way." He ushered us through the door and down a dimly lit corridor that smelled of antiseptic.

We entered a cramped room dominated by a narrow hospital bed surrounded by blinking monitors and IV stands. The fluorescent lights buzzed overhead, casting everything in a sickly pale glow.

"On the bed," the man ordered, pulling on latex gloves. "Everyone else out. Now."

"I'm staying." Ryker still cradled me as if I might shatter.

"This isn't a democracy." The man gestured toward the door where the others lingered.

"I'm not leaving her." Ryker's voice dropped to a dangerous growl, the sound vibrating through his chest against my ear. "She's my fated mate. I can't—" His voice cracked as he carefully laid me on the bed, his hands lingering protectively. "I won't let her face this alone."

Something shifted in the doctor's expression. Recognition, or perhaps understanding. The hard lines around his eyes softened slightly.

"Fine." The man exhaled sharply. "But stay out of my way." He turned to the others crowded in the doorway. "The rest of you need to leave. I'll call when there's news. Head back to your vehicles and stay out of sight."

Reid nodded, his jaw tight. "Come on," he muttered to the others. "Let's go."

Briar hesitated, her eyes wide with worry. "I'm her sister—"

"No more exceptions." Reid's firm hand on her shoulder pulled her back. "He knows what he's doing."

With a final worried glance at me, Briar allowed herself to be led away. She linked, *I know you can't hear me, but I'm here, Ember. I love you.*

I wanted to say it back, but the fire seemed to block out anything but the agony that pulsed through my body.

The others followed reluctantly, their footsteps fading down the corridor.

The man shut and locked the door. He turned to me with clinical efficiency and ripped my shirt open along the seam. He slowly pulled it away from my injury, and then his expression became unreadable.

"What's wrong?" Ryker stepped closer, panic edging his voice. "Why are you looking at her like that?"

The doctor didn't answer immediately. His gloved

fingers hovered over the wound, lightly touching my chest. "What *is* this?"

"What?" Ryker leaned forward as his forehead lined in confusion. "What are you talking about?"

"There's no wound here." The doctor stepped back, eyes narrowing. "Just a burn mark shaped like a blade entry, but no actual penetration. The skin is intact."

Ryker's jaw dropped. "That's impossible. I saw the knife. I saw the *blood*—"

As they argued above me, something changed inside my chest. The fire that had been consuming me began to recede like waves pulling back from shore. The burning sensation that had paralyzed me started to cool, first at my fingertips, then gradually toward my core.

I gasped, drawing in a full breath for the first time since I'd awakened.

With the pain's retreat, I tried reaching for the links once again. *Ryker. Briar. I'm here.*

My thoughts pushed outward, and the familiar connections opened between us.

Relief flooded the connection from Briar's end. *Oh, thank Fate!*

Ryker froze midsentence. His shoulders stiffened, but his eyes didn't meet mine. For several heartbeats, he avoided my gaze as if afraid that meeting my eyes would shatter whatever miracle had occurred.

Ryker, look at me. Please. I couldn't take his agony anymore. I needed him to know I'd truly be okay.

Finally, he did. The gold flecks in his irises flared, and his jaw worked as his relief and joy expanded in my chest, helping make the fire dissipate faster.

Ryker tore his eyes from mine, turning to the doctor

with newfound intensity. "She just linked with me," he said, voice rough with emotion. "She's conscious. Aware."

The man's eyebrows shot up. He studied my face with renewed interest, as if I were a medical anomaly he couldn't quite categorize.

I managed to lift my hand, reaching for Ryker's. My fingers trembled but found his, squeezing with what little strength I could muster.

"She should be dead," the man murmured, more to himself than to us. "A wound like that... all that blood..." He shook his head. "I don't understand." He pulled a stethoscope from around his neck and pressed it to my chest, brow furrowed. "No magic I know of is capable of healing like this. Now there's no scar tissue. No sign of rapid healing. It's as if the wound never existed, yet I can see the blood on your clothes and her shirt."

Ryker's grip on my hand tightened. His eyes questioned me, searching for answers. But he said, "I don't care what it was. She's not dying."

It's the fae magic in me. That's the only explanation I had. *It's healing me.*

The fae magic's final pulse warmed me then settled into a gentle, steady hum beneath my skin. When I drew a deep breath, it no longer burned. I braced my palms against the thin mattress and pushed myself upright. The room tilted briefly but then steadied.

The man stumbled back a step, rubbing his eyes as if he couldn't trust what he was seeing. "This is..." His voice trailed off as he dropped his hands. "Your vitals are perfect. Heartbeat strong, breathing clear." He shook his head in disbelief. "I've treated supernaturals for twenty years, and I've never seen anything like this." His gaze darted to the door then back to us. "You need to leave. Now. If anyone discovers I've brought you in without documentation..."

Ryker nodded, already helping me swing my legs off the bed. "We're going. Thank you for your help."

"Wait." The man hurried to a cabinet and removed two clean scrub tops. "Both of you, put these on. You can't walk out covered in blood."

I took the smaller offered garment and turned my back to him to change out of my ripped shirt.

Ryker's jealousy oozed through our bond with that sludgy feel. He stood between me and the doctor as he put on his own top, making sure the man couldn't see me.

In a hurry to leave, I removed my shredded shirt and pulled the top over my head. The fabric was cool against my skin, a stark contrast to the memory of the fire that had consumed me just minutes before.

The doctor unlocked the door and peered into the hallway. "Coast is clear. Go now, and for everyone's sake, please be careful. I don't want to have to volunteer for a night shift again and not be needed."

Sudden laughter escaped my lips at his exasperated tone; then I instinctively flinched as my body braced for the pain that should have followed. Nothing came. No stabbing sensation, no burning fire. Just...normal.

"Thank you," I said, meeting the doctor's tired eyes. "I know you risked a lot bringing us in."

"Just go," he muttered, checking his watch. "And try not to get stabbed again."

Ryker's arm wrapped around my waist as we slipped into the corridor. His touch was gentle but insistent, guiding me forward with quickened steps. The bond between us hummed with his residual fear and overwhelming relief.

When we made it back outside, he paused and linked, *Can you walk on your own?*

Actually, yeah. My legs were surprisingly steady beneath me.

The night air hit my face, cool and refreshing after the sterile hospital atmosphere. Ryker's hand remained firmly at the small of my back as we emerged into the parking lot, where Reid, Sun, Briar, and Ashlyn stood outside the truck, waiting.

Briar rushed forward first, her face melting into relief as she took in my steady stance. Before she could reach me, Ashlyn darted past her with surprising speed, her small figure illuminated by the parking lot's harsh lights.

"I told them," Ashlyn exclaimed, throwing her arms around me. "I knew the fire inside you would make sure you'd be okay!" she proclaimed, beaming up at me.

I stared at her, stunned. How could this child know about the fire I'd felt coursing through my veins? Before I could form a response, the others surrounded us, their faces a mixture of disbelief and relief.

"What the hell happened in there?" Reid demanded, his blue eyes scanning me for injuries. "You were practically dead when we put you in the truck to come here."

Sun stepped closer, her gaze analytical. "No one recovers from a wound like that in minutes. Not even shifters."

"The doctor couldn't believe it either," Ryker added, running a hand through his disheveled hair. "Said it was medically impossible."

They all stared expectantly, waiting for an explanation I couldn't give. Many-Greats-Grandfather had made it clear that I wasn't supposed to share.

I shrugged, avoiding their questioning stares. I tried to

choose my words carefully so it didn't come out as a lie. I had to believe that the explanation could potentially be true if I didn't have my fae side. "Maybe the knife didn't hit anywhere serious, and it just needed to be removed so my shifter magic could kick in."

Do you not think we should tell them? Ryker linked.

Maybe, but I don't want to decide right now because, at the end of the day, it doesn't change things. I didn't want to be deceitful, but I needed to understand why Many-Greats-Grandfather didn't want me to tell anyone about my heritage.

I agree. We shouldn't rush into anything.

"We need to meet up with the others. Anyone up for riding in the bed of the truck?" Reid arched a brow.

Considering how hot my skin felt, being in the cool wind sounded amazing. "Me."

"That means me too," Ryker answered, tugging me to his side.

We all climbed in, Ryker and me jumping into the bed of the truck. I glanced at the illuminated hospital sign, the name snapping me to attention: Ridgemont Memorial.

I inhaled quickly. "We're two towns over."

Ryker tightened his hold on me as the truck rumbled to life beneath us. *We couldn't risk going to a hospital in our territory. If those vampires tracked your scent or blood trail, they'd find you.*

The truck lurched forward, and I braced myself against the metal bed. The wind whipped through my hair as we picked up speed, carrying away the lingering scent of antiseptic and blood.

Makes sense. The vampires who'd attacked us had been determined to kill me, but I didn't want to tell Ryker that.

I edged closer to him, seeking his warmth and touch.

My hand slipped on something wet beneath me. Frowning, I glanced down and froze.

A puddle of water glistened in the dimming light, diluted red around the edges. My stomach lurched, but my chest expanded.

Someone had tried to clean up my blood before I got back.

My fingers traced the damp metal, feeling the residue of what should have been my end.

Ryker's eyes followed my gaze, and his hand covered mine, pulling it away from the bloodstained water.

Briar tried to clean it while we were inside. She didn't want you to see it when you came back.

I leaned into my mate, drawing comfort from his solid presence as the truck rumbled beneath us.

He pressed a kiss to my forehead as he linked with our entire pack, *She's alive. She's going to be okay.*

Thank Fate, Xander replied.

I knew you were too stubborn to die, Gage added.

I've been so worried, Kendric connected.

Briar interjected, *After this, I'm getting quality sister time.*

You bet, I answered.

Ryker's thumb traced circles on my wrist, his touch grounding me as the truck bounced along the road. Every few seconds, he kissed me and nuzzled my neck.

Suddenly, Xander reconnected with all of us, *Cassi's recovered enough to perform the location spell on Adara. She found her, but... shit, Ryker, you're not going to believe where the queen is.*

The truck hit a pothole, jostling us. Ryker's fingers dug into my side, steadying me while the silence stretched between us and Xander.

Just fucking tell me, Ryker commanded as his frustration spiked.

She's hiding in the wolf shifter royal palace, Gage answered.

The shock hit me like ice water. The royal palace? I swung my gaze to Ryker, whose face had hardened to granite. His jaw clenched so tight I could see the muscle jump beneath his skin.

Are you sure? His rage simmered, ready to explode.

Kendric confirmed, *Cassi says there's no mistake.*

A wave of fury rolled off Ryker, so intense it made my skin prickle. His face darkened as he stared into the distance, processing this new betrayal.

That fucking palace. Right where she massacred our pack and the royals. He growled. *The vampire queen is using it as her hideout?*

Gage's voice cut through our link, bitter and hard. "It's a deliberate insult to every wolf shifter alive. It's the supernatural equivalent of giving us the middle finger."

Ryker's shoulders stiffened. *I can't wait to kill that bitch.*

She's mocking us, Briar added.

The wind whipped around us as the truck sped along the dark highway, but I barely felt it now. My mind raced with the implications of what we'd just learned.

There was only one thing we could do. *We need to move tonight while we have the element of surprise.*

Ryker's head whipped toward me, his eyes widening. *Fuck no. Absolutely not. I almost lost you already once tonight.*

That was the thing. I wasn't asking his permission. I straightened my shoulders, ready to fight.

CHAPTER TWENTY-FIVE

That's exactly why we should attack now. I pulled out of his grip, letting the night air separate us. *Think about it. They think I'm dead. They know the prison witches are drained from the fighting. They know several of us are injured, which means they won't expect us to strike back now.*

No. Ryker shook his head and growled. *We need time to regroup and plan. We need—*

We need to seize this opportunity. The fire that had healed me was still burning in my veins. *They've taken the wolf shifter royal palace. They've killed our kind. And now we have a chance to end this before they recover. We did damage to them back there. And the last time Ashlyn revealed their true forms, the vampires couldn't cloak for at least a few hours.*

Ryker gritted his teeth. *You nearly died tonight, Ember. I held you while you bled out in my arms. I'm not about to watch you rush toward another death. I barely survived this time. The only thing that kept me going was your beating heart. But living through that again... I can't handle it.*

I agree with Ember, Kendric interjected. *She's right, and that's coming from me, who is injured. They won't expect us tonight. The element of surprise could be our greatest advantage.*

We need to end this, Gage added. *I'm tired of being hunted.*

It'll be sweet vengeance to kill her where she killed our pack and royals, Xander linked.

Ryker's jaw clenched so tight I could hear his teeth grinding. The truck hit another pothole, and he steadied me automatically, his touch gentle despite the fury radiating from him.

This isn't a democratic vote, he snapped.

I scooted closer to him, lowering my voice so no one in the cab could hear us. "This isn't about democracy, Ryker. It's about survival."

His irises glowed brighter in the darkness. "And rushing in half-cocked isn't survival. It's suicide."

"It's not half-cocked. Look at me." I placed my hand on his chest, feeling his heartbeat thunder beneath my palm. I continued, "Really look. I'm healed. My fae magic made me stronger."

The truck swerved around a sharp bend, sending us sliding. Ryker's arm shot out, steadying me against him. For a moment, we were pressed together, the electric shocks of the bond jolting between us.

"I can't lose you again," he whispered with raw vulnerability in his voice.

I cupped his face with both hands, my thumbs tracing the sharp angles of his cheekbones. "Listen to me. I'm not going anywhere." I leaned in, pressing my forehead against his. "I feel even healthier than I did this morning."

His hands found my waist, fingers digging in as if to anchor me to this world, to him.

"We have to strike while they're weakened and not expecting us," I continued. "Every hour we wait gives them time to regroup, to strengthen. To prepare for us."

Something flickered across his expression—a moment of clarity breaking through his fear.

"I need you with me on this." I kissed his lips since the next part was going to sting, though I truly didn't want it to. But as Dad always said, intent didn't matter if it upset someone. "I'm not asking for your permission, Ryker. I'm asking you to step up and be the alpha I know you are."

His face crumbled. "Lil rebel, please. Don't ask this of me. I don't give a fuck about anyone else. I just need you safe!"

But I had to. He didn't want to hear the truth because then he'd have to agree. "Your pack is ready to fight. They're willing to risk everything because they believe in this cause—in ending the threat before it grows stronger. Waiting doesn't just put everyone else at risk; it puts me right there with them."

He closed his eyes and rasped, "Fine, but we do this my way. No going rogue on me. I won't budge unless you promise me that." His eyes opened once more, staring straight into my soul.

That decision was easy. I'd follow him anywhere. "I promise."

He reopened the pack link. *We attack tonight.*

About damn time, Gage replied. *I left you alone because I was hoping she'd talk some sense into you.*

A flash of irritation flowed into me via the bond, making me slightly edgy.

Kendric connected, *The longer we wait, the more time*

they have to recover from our attack and from Ashlyn weakening the witch who's cloaking them.

The truck slowed, turning into a section of Blue Ridge National Park.

We're almost there, Ryker interjected. *Let me think for a minute, and we can discuss when we get there.*

I lay my head on his shoulder, enjoying the last few minutes we'd have of solitude until after the war. I could only hope that we would win.

Don't worry. Ryker tightened his hold on my waist. *This time, I won't let anything happen to you. I'm sorry that I didn't protect you like I should've earlier.*

The guilt oozed through our connection, weighing it down like an anchor.

Don't you dare. I turned toward him and pointed at his face. *Me getting hurt was not your fault. I ran out of your hold. You tried to stop me. That was on me. Not you.*

He hung his head, casting his gaze downward. *Protecting you is the most important responsibility I have.*

"Hey." I hooked my finger under his chin, forcing him to meet my eyes. "That logic works both ways. If you're responsible for my safety, then I'm responsible for yours. We're partners, Ryker. If either of us gets hurt, it's not a failure of the other."

His face twisted. "It's different."

"How?" I challenged, dropping my hand to his chest where his heart thundered. "Because you're the alpha? Because you're male? Tell me exactly why your life matters less than mine."

The truck hit another bump, but neither of us moved.

"I can't breathe without you," he whispered, voice rough. "Because the thought of you not existing in this world makes everything meaningless."

My heart clenched. "And you think I feel any different? When you were injured, when I thought I'd lost you? Was that my fault too?"

"Fate no." He grasped my hands. "That was out of your control."

"Then how was tonight any different? Because if you feel guilty about tonight, then I need to feel guilty for each time you got hurt and I couldn't protect you."

The truck lurched to the right, and we drove past a weathered wooden sign that stated Blue Ridge Campground - Site 7 with an arrow pointing down a narrow gravel path.

A storm of emotions brewed on his face, but before he could respond, the truck crested a small hill, and my breath caught.

The clearing stretched before us, bathed in moonlight. This wasn't a campground, this was a staging area. Dozens of vehicles—trucks and SUVs—were parked in a loose semicircle.

Wolf shifters and witches mingled all together. They all looked tired, but there was an edge of eagerness to them. Each one stared at our truck as Reid pulled up and parked.

The moment the engine died, Ryker captured my face between his palms. The love and affection he felt for me exploded into my chest.

You're right about all of it. His thumb traced my cheekbone. *I'm sorry. It's just— Loving you this much feels like carrying my heart outside my body.*

Before I could respond, Gage's face appeared, and he smiled as he lowered the gate of the truck. "You're really okay!" He jumped into the truck bed and pulled me away from Ryker, giving me a bone-crushing hug.

Ryker snarled and jumped to his feet, smacking Gage in

the back of the head. He snarled, "She almost died not even an hour ago. Let her go."

Gage released me with a sheepish grin, raising his hands in surrender. "Just making sure she's real."

The truck doors opened and shut, and soon Reid, Sun, Briar, and Ashlyn joined us.

I scanned the clearing, noticing I couldn't locate the two remaining members of our small pack. "Where are Xander and Kendric?"

"In the SUV at the end," Gage answered, nodding toward a black vehicle parked at the edge of the clearing. "Kendric's not doing well, and Xander is trying to help slow the bleeding."

My stomach twisted. I'd been so caught up in my own recovery and the argument with Ryker that I'd forgotten how badly Kendric had been injured.

I stilled as a thought came to me. If I could heal myself, could I heal others? My memory went back to when Ryker was near death, and the warm magic that I now knew was fae had flared in me and pulsed out of my hands into him. If I'd helped Ryker, maybe I could help Kendric.

I jumped down from the truck bed. Many-Greats-Grandfather's warnings echoed in my mind—I needed to keep my fae lineage secret. But Kendric's life hung in the balance.

Where are you going? Ryker asked and caught my arm.

I met his gaze steadily. *I think I can help Kendric.*

How? he linked.

I explained to him my hypothesis

Okay, you should try, but we keep it a secret outside of our pack. Only the six of us know. He released my arm with a reluctant nod.

Deal. I didn't like keeping things from our pack members. Doing so had caused a lot of problems after all.

I hurried across the clearing, my heart hammering against my ribs. The black SUV loomed ahead, its back door hanging open. Inside, Kendric lay across the back seat, his face ashen beneath his tan. Xander knelt beside him, pressing a blood-soaked washcloth against the jagged claw marks in Kendric's chest. The metallic scent of blood filled the confined space.

"I think I can help him, so can I take your place?" I lifted a brow.

Xander's brows furrowed, but he moved out of the vehicle. *I can't believe you're standing here. I thought we'd lost you.*

Well, you're stuck with me for at least a little longer. I took Xander's spot and moved between the captain row seats next to Kendric.

His seat was leaned all the way back, and I placed one of my hands on the warm, soaked towel.

Kendric's breathing was shallow, each inhale rattling in his lungs. The wound was worse than I'd realized—deep gouges that exposed muscle and bone.

Still, Kendric opened his dark eyes and gave a small smile. *It's good to see you unharmed, but I don't understand how it's possible. Either way, I'm glad I kicked some ass before I completely go out.*

You're not going out, I replied, placing my other hand beside the first on his chest. *Not if I have anything to say about it.*

Briar appeared at the SUV door, her light copper hair gleaming under the moonlight. Her eyes widened at the sight of Kendric's wounds. She linked to just me, *Oh Fates. He looks worse than I remembered.*

I'm going to try something. Don't worry.

"What do you mean?" Briar climbed into the vehicle beside me, her forehead lined with confusion.

I didn't answer. There wasn't time for explanations. I closed my eyes, concentrating on the strange heat that had saved me. It wasn't as intense now, more like embers than flames, but still much warmer than it had been before I'd nearly died.

I reached inside myself, tugging at the fire that had saved me earlier. For a terrifying moment, it didn't respond.

Then it flared like it had when I was healing and spread like wildfire through my veins. My hands grew hot—almost unbearably so—as energy surged through them.

The washcloth sizzled beneath my touch, causing me to startle. I yanked it away, revealing the raw, torn flesh beneath. Without hesitation, I pressed my bare palms to the wound.

Kendric's back arched, and he gasped, his eyes flying wide open. "What the hell?" he moaned.

"What's happening?" Briar cried, reaching for my arm. "Are you hurting him?"

"Don't." Ryker's voice cut through the night as he appeared behind her. "Don't move her."

The heat from my palms intensified, pulsing with a rhythm that matched Kendric's heartbeat. Sweat beaded across his forehead and trickled down his temples as his body shuddered beneath my touch. His eyes rolled back, revealing the whites.

"Ember," Briar whispered, her voice trembling. "What's happening to him?"

I couldn't answer. Every ounce of my concentration was focused on the energy flowing from my core, through my arms, and into Kendric's mangled flesh. Beneath my fingers,

I felt his skin knitting back together. The sensation was both exhilarating and terrifying.

Ryker moved behind Briar, placing his hands on her shoulders and gently pulling her back. "Give them space," he murmured, his eyes locked on Kendric's face.

Kendric flushed as his body jerked and trembled beneath my hands.

Enough, Ryker commanded. *That's enough.*

I couldn't stop. The energy continued to flow, my hands locked to Kendric's chest as though fused there. His wounds were closed.

Ryker's hand clasped my shoulder and tugged me back. *Ember, stop. You're draining yourself.*

He was right. I could feel the magic leaving my body and depleting me. With a gasp, I finally broke the connection and fell back against the other seat. My vision swam, darkness creeping in at the edges. Kendric lay still, his chest rising and falling in deep, even breaths.

Where moments ago there had been gaping wounds, now only fresh pink skin stretched across Kendric's torso, crisscrossed with silvery scars.

Xander leaned in the open door, his face pale. *How is this possible? He was bleeding out less than two minutes ago.*

Briar's face had also gone ghostly white, and her gaze darted from Kendric's healed chest to my exhausted form. *Wolves can't heal others like that.*

I leaned against the seat behind me, fatigue washing over me in waves. I linked with just Ryker, *Can you tell them?*

Of course. He sat next to me, his own face tense, but he didn't hesitate. He added everyone to the link just as Gage appeared on the other side of Xander.

How's our guy... Gage trailed off, taking in what I'd just done.

Ryker connected, and the thrum of his alpha will laced his words. *What you just witnessed...*" Ryker paused, taking a deep breath. *"What I'm about to tell you cannot leave this pack. Not a word to the witches, not to Reid's wolves, not to anyone."*

You don't have to alpha-will us for that. Gage rolled his eyes.

We have to be safe. Ryker then informed the others about Briar's and my heritage.

Briar gasped, one hand flying to her mouth. *Fae? We're part fae? I didn't even know they truly existed.* She wrung her hands. *Mom and Dad would have told us.*

They didn't tell me either. But the man that was in your bedroom—he's like our great-great-great-great... I trailed off. *Fuck, I don't know how many greats to put in before grandfather, but that was him.*

The creepy guy in my bedroom? Her head jerked back. *Ew. And why didn't you tell me?*

I just found out today, and everything has been going to hell since then. My head spun. *And I wasn't sure if I believed him.*

Briar's expression shifted, the shock of the revelation giving way to determination. "We'll talk about this later. Right now, we have vampires to kill."

I nodded, relief washing through me at her understanding.

Kendric's hand suddenly dropped from his chest and touched my knee. His fingers trembled slightly, but his grip was surprisingly strong.

"Thank you," he whispered, voice raw with emotion. His eyes, clear and alert, held mine with an intensity that made my breath catch. "I was dying. I felt it. And then... fire. Your fire pulled me back."

Before I could respond, shouts erupted outside the SUV.

"Ryker! Ember!" several voices called in unison, their tones urgent. "Reid, Sun, Bruce, and Cassi want to talk to you. We need to move."

"Stay here. Keep an eye on him." I glanced at Kendric. "He needs rest."

Briar pursed her lips and leaned her head back. "Go. We'll handle things here."

Ryker helped me out of the SUV, his hand at my elbow steadying me as my legs trembled. The energy drain from healing Kendric had left me weaker than I wanted to admit.

You should rest too, he linked, the skin around his eyes tightening.

I shook my head. *Not a chance. I'm not sitting this out.*

He inhaled deeply, but he didn't argue as we made our way toward Reid's truck. Reid, Sun, Bruce, and Cassi were huddled around a map spread across the hood.

Reid tapped his fingers on the map. "We need to move fast. Ashlyn says the cloaking spell will start regenerating in about two hours."

"What can you tell us about the palace?" Sun rocked back on her heels. "You know it better than any of us."

Ryker leaned over the map, studying it for a moment before placing his finger on a spot near the center. "Here. The royal palace sits in the heart of the Grimstone pack's territory since we were their protectors." His finger traced a circle around the building. "It's fortified, designed to withstand attacks from all sides, but there are hidden tunnels."

Bruce frowned. "Entry points?"

Ryker nodded.

"This approach is solid," Zoya stretched out her fingers. "But if these tunnels have been there for centuries, could the vampires know about them too?"

"They're known only to the Grimstone pack's inner circle. Even most of the royals didn't know they existed." Ryker rolled his neck.

I leaned my head on his arm. "Then we split into two teams."

"We'll need a mix of our packs and witches," Reid replied. "Bruce, do you have any men who could meet us there?"

Bruce cleared his throat. "Yes, I'm mobilizing them now. Since the place is four towns over, we'll be getting there right when the witch could be strong enough to cloak them again. We need to move quickly before they recover, but we can't leave our injured unprotected. There are about forty of them."

With her amber eyes flashing, Zoya stepped forward. "Ashlyn's unveiling spell can be performed again. She's stronger than any witch I've ever seen, and she's only ten." She gestured to the little girl, who was huddled near a circle of stones, watching us.

"That little girl is amazing." Despite my exhaustion, hope spread in my chest.

Ryker's hand slid to the small of my back as he addressed Bruce. "The injured can stay here. This is a campground, and they should be safe this far away."

Sun clapped her hands together with a sharp, decisive sound that cut through our discussion. "Sounds like we have a plan. Let's load everyone up and go. If we're going to hit them while they're weak, every minute counts."

Around us, shifters and witches began moving with

renewed purpose, their earlier exhaustion replaced by the electric energy of impending retribution.

Ryker squeezed my hand. "Are you sure you're strong enough for this? Healing Kendric took a lot out of you."

I straightened my spine, ignoring the lingering weakness in my limbs. "I'll rest on the way there." I linked with our pack, *It's time to roll.*

Worry lined his forehead, but Ryker knew there was no point in arguing.

We split into the vehicles, and I couldn't help but notice that only a few parents and children were staying behind. Even the injured wanted to fight against the woman who'd tried to steal everything from us.

Pointing at a vehicle, Reid led our group to an SUV so we could all ride together. I sat in the front passenger seat and leaned it back while Ryker drove. I needed to regain some strength before we got there. Within seconds, sleep had taken me.

My heart raced as Ryker and I stood by the three fallen oak trees. We'd need to climb over the huge trunks to find the hidden entrance. We'd run into no issues getting here, and my skin was crawling because of it.

I checked my weapons to make sure I'd secured the gun and dagger each of us had been given. A late Grimstone pack member's junkyard still had a locked safe where backup weapons were stored, and we'd stopped there on the way. With our total number of one hundred, we had enough weapons to arm everyone, even the witches.

Briar, Ashlyn, Zoya, Bruce and fifteen of his pack, forty of Reid's people, and fifteen more witches stood behind us. I wasn't surprised when Adara demanded to be in our group. She was still hiding her true face, but she was eager to get in there and see her mom.

Are you sure you're strong enough? Ryker's troubled face twisted in concern.

I promise I'm fine. The short nap was all I'd needed to recharge, but he didn't seem to believe me.

Kendric, Xander, and Gage had gone with the other half of our army so that we could effectively communicate. We were all dodging questions about why both Kendric and I seemed fine. We'd gone with stating it was clearly a blessing. That it had seemed like we were worse off than we truly were, which wasn't untrue. If I hadn't been blessed with healing power, neither of us would be here.

Ryker looked over his shoulder, noting everyone was ready. "Okay, let's—"

But then gunshots fired.

CHAPTER TWENTY-SIX

I spun around, searching for shadows or vampires. We were close to the two-hour mark Ashlyn had predicted, though it was an estimate at best.

Nothing was near, but then another shot cracked in the distance.

We stumbled upon some vampires on patrol, Kendric linked. *We're all disbursing, and I'm taking Sun, Cassi, Xander, and one of the Grimstone pack members with me into the secret tunnel.*

What about Gage? A lump formed in my throat.

I'm staying with the others since I know my way around and can link back to you all, Gage replied. *But thanks for worrying about me.*

Be careful, all of you, Ryker replied evenly, but his face was taut. *Keep us posted on what's going on with everyone.*

The wind kicked up, and a branch snapped somewhere in the darkness. Some of our group members flinched, heads whipping toward the sound.

Ryker's jaw tightened as he assessed their fear. With a sharp jerk of his chin, he motioned for them to continue forward. "Stay close to us," he commanded, voice barely audible. "We can't afford to separate."

The weight of what we were about to do pressed on my chest. We climbed over tree trunks to find bigger oak trees blotting out any view of civilization. The dense branches and leaves offered protection since some leaves still hadn't fallen.

Ryker followed a twisted path through dense underbrush, gradually sloping downward. He pushed aside a curtain of hanging moss to reveal a narrow gap between two massive boulders. His shoulders barely fit through the opening as he slipped inside. *Watch your step.*

I followed right on his heels, the stone cold against my palms as I squeezed through. The passage opened into a small clearing where a depression in the ground marked our destination. Ryker knelt and brushed away fallen leaves to expose a metal handle embedded in what looked like solid earth.

He gripped the handle with both hands, and his muscles flexed beneath his shirt as he pulled upward. The door budged an inch, and his face contorted with effort as a low growl rumbled in his chest.

I dropped to my knees beside him and wrapped my fingers under the edge he'd managed to lift. Together, we heaved, and the door finally gave way with a groan of rusted hinges.

A cloud of dust and what looked like fur particles erupted from the opening, making us both recoil.

Stale air hit my face. Ryker went first, disappearing into the blackness. I followed, each step cautious on the metal rungs of the ladder. The others filed in behind me, the last one pulling the door closed above us with a dull thud that seemed to echo forever.

We moved forward in near-total darkness, our eyes adjusting to reveal a low-ceilinged tunnel. I traced my fingers along the rough stone walls for balance, feeling cold wet liquid there. The passageway was eerily silent—no skittering of tiny feet, no distant drips of water, nothing living seeming to have been here in what felt like decades.

Something crunched under my boot. I froze, heart pounding, and squinted, trying to make out what I'd stepped on.

Bones.

Small animal bones, picked clean and scattered across the floor. But they were old, crumbling to dust under pressure.

There are no live rats or mice down here. My stomach churned uncomfortably.

Ryker paused, his broad shoulders tensing. He crouched down, examining the ground with heightened senses. "You're right. No fresh droppings, no nest materials."

A chill crawled up my spine that had nothing to do with the damp air. *It seems likely that a strong witch or several witches live here to make the animals leave like that.*

Ryker frowned. *We need to keep moving.*

After another hundred yards, the tunnel began to slope upward, and the air gradually became less stale. My wolf stirred restlessly beneath my skin, sensing we were approaching our destination. Muffled sounds filtered down from above—voices.

Ryker stopped.

The distinct murmur of multiple people talking drifted through the tunnel. Their words were unintelligible, but the cadence suggested a meeting of some kind.

They're in the royal meeting chambers. Ryker began moving forward again at a steady pace.

The voices grew clearer, and then I recognized a voice that had me stopping in my tracks.

Felix.

The vampire queen's son, who'd been punished for turning a human who'd attacked me.

His entitled ass was discussing security breaches and patrol adjustments. My pulse quickened. We reached the end of the tunnel, where a small grate next to a wooden door allowed us to peer into the chamber.

Through the thin slats, I could see a massive oak table surrounded by vampires in formal attire. Maps were spread across the surface and weighted down with ornate daggers. Felix stood at the head, his pale fingers tracing lines across territories, while officers nodded solemnly. There were about fifteen vampires with him, and my stomach revolted when I saw Lucinda, Bella, Martin, and even Simon among them.

Ryker signaled silently, directing our group to get ready and to use daggers, not guns, so we wouldn't alert more vampires. Each of us mimicked his movements to ensure that everyone knew what was about to happen.

We were going to attack.

We're ready, Briar replied from the very end of the group.

Ryker's muscles bunched, and he braced against the door. One powerful kick and the wood shattered inward with a deafening crash. He was through the opening before the vampires could process what was happening, a blur of lethal movement.

Adrenaline made everything clearer as I jumped onto the middle of the table. The room erupted into chaos, chairs scraping the wooden floor and the vampires shouting for help.

"Wolf shifters," Felix spat as his face contorted with fury and shock. "Why are you shouting for help? Handle them!"

Lucinda, Bella, and Martin brandished their weapons and attacked.

I launched myself off the table, knocking Lucinda backward. Her head cracked against the wooden floor as I rolled to my feet, already facing the next threat. Ryker lunged forward with his dagger out, slicing through Martin's throat, while Bella turned and ran out the regular door.

Around me, the witches used their daggers to attack in ways that proved they'd trained with a blade. The wolf shifters held their own, taking down a few vampires with their daggers.

Ryker pinned Felix to the wall with his forearm pressed against the vampire prince's throat. Felix hissed as Ryker leaned in close, his voice dropping to a deadly whisper.

"You thought you could hurt her and live?" Ryker got in his face, not seeming worried Felix might try to bite him. "This is for trying to kill my mate."

"I'd do it all over again if given the chance," Felix said and spat in his face.

Ryker's hand plunged into his chest with a sickening crunch. Blood spurted across the wall. The vampire prince's scream died in his throat as Ryker yanked his hand back, clutching Felix's still-beating heart.

I couldn't look away as Ryker crushed the organ in his fist, blood oozing between his fingers. Felix's body crumpled to the floor.

I turned from the grisly scene, but all I saw were twelve other vampire bodies bleeding to death. My stomach churned as Ryker's love and anger swirled through our bond. The human part of me recoiled at the brutal execution, but my wolf—she panted with savage satisfaction.

Ryker had shown everyone that he would tear apart anyone who threatened what was his. What was ours.

My wolf's approval radiated through my body and our bond like liquid heat.

Three vampires had gotten away, so when approaching footsteps echoed in the corridor, I wasn't surprised. I wiped blood spatter from my cheek with the back of my hand.

A few witches seemed alarmed by what Ryker had done, but they tore their gazes from Felix's body and removed their daggers while the wolf shifters unholstered their guns.

New vampires came into view. And, of course, at the back was Raven.

The betrayal stung like acid in my mouth. Raven stood with our enemies like she'd always done, having played us for fools until now.

"No one hurt Raven. She's mine," Briar snarled, her voice barely human.

My sister slammed into Raven and pinned her to the wall, and the others reacted instantly. Daggers whistled through the air, and one by one, the vampires dropped.

Briar's sense of betrayal etched deep lines into her face. She pressed her dagger to Raven's throat.

My lungs stopped working. I didn't want Briar to do something she'd regret.

"Before you kill me," Raven started as her eyes filled with tears, "Let me tell you that the wolf shifter royals are in the basement. There are two witches down there that you'll have to address. Most of the guards are running through the woods right now, attacking whoever is out there and searching for the rest of your group."

Ryker laughed bitterly as we positioned ourselves behind Briar. His voice was cold, mocking. "And why exactly would we believe a single word from your mouth?"

"You'd smell the lie if I were lying." Raven lifted both hands. "I'm trying to help you to make up for what I did."

My heart wanted to believe her. The very thing that got us all in this situation now. "If a witch can make you smell like wolf shifters, then she can hide the smell of a lie."

"No one's doing that," Raven said, but Briar pressed harder on her neck, and her last few words were just a whisper. "Ambrosia didn't kill the royals. She has them in the basement, draining them of their blood so vampires can drink it. She figured out that if we drink several ounces of wolf shifter blood daily, vampires can lose our scent completely."

Her words were like a punch to my gut. Many-Greats-Grandfather hadn't been kidding when he'd stated that he suspected the vampire queen had been plotting this for centuries. She had every detail mapped out.

If what Raven said was true, that put the last piece of the puzzle in place—why the vampires smelled faintly of wolf shifters and why they killed primarily with claws and ripping out necks. It was the best way to pin it on us and turn our kind against each other.

"Why would we trust you? If a witch spelled you, we wouldn't know it," I demanded, stepping closer. As I spoke, I searched for any sign of a shadow to indicate magic on her. "You've been playing both sides this entire time."

Raven's eyes flickered from Briar to me, then to Ryker. Her shoulders slumped, but her gaze remained steady.

"You shouldn't trust me," she admitted. "I haven't given

you reason to. But I'd been searching for a way out from under the queen's control before I had to betray you." Her fingers trembled against the wall. "She suspected that my loyalty had begun to change and left me out of plans."

That could explain why some of her actions had seemed genuine.

I don't see signs of magic, I linked, unsure what to do with this information now.

We don't have time for this, Ryker linked, taking the spot next to Briar. *Let me handle her. We can't risk her betraying us again.*

Briar's bottom lip quivered, and I loved that Ryker understood her. She was angry, but if she killed Raven, she'd wind up living with huge regret. She had such a big heart, and I hoped the world never robbed her of that as long as I was around to keep her out of trouble.

Ryker squeezed Briar's shoulder gently. *Let me.*

My sister hesitated, her dagger still pressed to Raven's throat. I saw conflict in my sister's eyes, the need for justice battling with her compassion.

"She betrayed us all," Ryker said, his voice steady. "This isn't something you need to carry."

A tear trailed down Briar's cheek as her grip loosened. She stepped back, allowing Ryker to take her place, and I moved to her side and wrapped an arm around her shoulders.

"I'm sor—" she began, but her plea was cut short.

Ryker plunged his dagger into Raven's chest. Her face didn't change at all, and she didn't even try to fight Ryker. Blood bloomed across her cream dress.

I expected Ryker to do more because I felt his sense of betrayal and need for revenge, but then something drifted into me that I hadn't expected. Heartbreak and remorse. He still cared about Raven.

Instead of twisting the knife like the vampires had done to me, Ryker released his dagger and stepped back, and she slid down the wall and to the floor. *She's incapacitated and won't harm more of us now. I'll leave her life in Fate's hands.*

We're in, Xander linked. *There aren't any guards.*

I shuddered, realizing that part of what Raven had just told us was true.

Raven said most of the guards are outside. Ryker watched as blood trickled from the corners of Raven's mouth. *So let's get down there. Gage, they're outside, targeting you all and searching for the rest of us.*

Fuck yeah, they were, but I heard a walkie-talkie go off. They were just informed that the palace had been breached and they were heading back inside.

We had to move fast.

Ryker tore his gaze from Raven's slumped form, guilt and doubt settling uncomfortably in our bond. Yet he squared his shoulders and moved with purpose.

"The vampire guards are coming back. We need to move fast," he barked.

Briar's silent tears streamed down her dirt-smudged face as she stared at Raven. Her shoulders shook with each suppressed sob, but she didn't make a sound. I squeezed her arm gently, pulling her away from the blood pooling on the floor.

The rest of the group was eager to move.

Ryker led our group through the corridor, following Raven's directions despite what he'd just done. The irony wasn't lost on me, but it wasn't something I'd say. We were trusting the information of someone we couldn't afford to question now. But keeping the royals in the basement made sense.

Everyone's sadness ebbed, and our anxiety strengthened. Two sets of stairs led to the basement.

The air grew colder with each step, and the unmistakable coppery scent of blood made my stomach lurch. The metallic tang overpowered even the musty dampness of the underground space.

Ryker paused at the bottom of the stairs, his body tensing. His face hardened into stone.

The fact that we'd made it down to this level without issue had the hair on my neck rising.

A narrow hall stretched before us, and the pressure of magic around me made me feel as if I couldn't breathe. Still, I moved forward, knowing that we had to end this now. We rounded a corner, and the passage widened into a cavernous basement.

My breath caught in my throat.

In the center of the room stood a witch. Black, inky energy swirled around her body like a living storm, and her eyes appeared soulless.

The twenty-three royal wolf shifters lay arranged in a perfect circle around her, their bodies unnaturally still. Tubes ran from their arms, necks, and legs and connected to ornate glass containers that pulsed with dark-red liquid. Their faces were ashen, drained of life. A strand of the witch's magic connected to each of them.

We found the royals, Briar linked, and I heard the gasps of the wolf shifters behind us.

My eyes were drawn to movement in the corner of the room.

There stood Ambrosia. Even surrounded by death, her beauty was timeless. Her maroon lace dress seemed to show off the cruelty in her eyes. Her long chestnut hair waved over her shoulders, accentuating her curves.

Beside her stood another witch—one who looked like an older version of the real Adara. No magic swirled from her, indicating the vampires weren't cloaked again... at least, not yet.

The vampire queen scowled, the hate in her eyes somehow shining even brighter. "Impossible. You're dead."

Her words rang in the air as my mind raced. How many times had she assumed we were dead, only to be disappointed? I'd lost count.

Vampires are returning to the mansion in groups, Kendric linked. *We're delaying them as long as we can, but you need to hurry.*

Panic and rage emanated from Ryker, stealing the little breath I had left. Just when we'd thought we had an edge, the vampires changed their strategy to compensate.

"Handle this now," Queen Ambrosia hissed at Adara's mother, her voice cutting through the basement like a blade. "Cloak the vampires again. I don't care if it drains every last drop of your power."

The older witch's face paled, but she nodded and raised her trembling hands. The air around her began to shimmer, and my skin crawled as the pressure of magic increased.

I fell to my knees.

The rest of our group surged forward as one. There was no time for strategy or careful planning—if that witch completed her spell, we'd lose our advantage completely.

"Stop her!" I shouted, unable to move at all.

CHAPTER TWENTY-SEVEN

My wolf surged forward, and my fae magic blazed inside me, but the pressure from the witches' vile magic wouldn't let me move faster. I raised my gun and tried to fire at Ambrosia, but our group got in the way.

Multiple footsteps stomping down the stairs had me glancing over my shoulder just as twenty vampires flooded in, guns raised, fangs bared.

"Vampires," I yelled, but it wasn't soon enough because they opened fire.

My ears rang as bullets tore through flesh and bone, and several of our people dropped. Blood pooled beneath their bodies, the metallic scent making the stench of blood stronger and mixing with gunpowder.

Adara's mother tried to call her magic, but all I could see were faint wisps pulsing from her body before they faded once again.

Fear poured from Ryker, but I couldn't see him. All I could see were vampires rushing past me as if I weren't even there and my people falling.

I'm coming, Ember, he vowed, panic urging him to locate me.

Pay attention and fight, I replied, not wanting him to be careless and be harmed.

Three wolf shifters dropped to all fours, bones cracking and reforming as they shifted. Their clothes shredded as massive wolf forms emerged, and they snarled and lunged at the nearest vampires.

The rest of the wolf shifters opened fire. The witches tried to use their magic, but it wasn't nearly as strong as earlier. They hadn't had time to recharge.

A silver flash caught my attention. Ryker leapt over a fallen body, his dagger slicing through a vampire's throat. Blood sprayed across the concrete as a witch with auburn hair moved with deadly precision toward the witch casting the spell on the royals.

A vampire took aim at her back, and I screamed, "Watch out!" But with all the noise, I couldn't even hear my own words.

The distraction cost me. Cold fingers wrapped around my throat and yanked me backward with inhuman strength. The world blurred, and suddenly, Queen Ambrosia's face was inches from mine, her perfect features twisted with rage.

"You've been quite the thorn in my side," she hissed, her breath like winter frost against my skin. Her grip tightened, cutting off my air. "I've been trying to kill you ever since I realized you could see our hidden vampires."

This close, I could see how dark her soul had become. The humanity-cloaking magic blocked out her true eye color with black tendrils that covered her irises and smoked outward.

Black spots danced at the edges of my vision as I clawed

at her fingers. My wolf thrashed beneath my skin, desperate to break free, and my magic burned as hot as a blue flame.

The magic from the witch spelling the royals continued to weigh on me like iron chains, pressing on my chest even as Ambrosia's fingers dug into my throat. My lungs burned, desperate for air that wouldn't come. I thrashed in her grip, my fingers scrabbling uselessly against her marble skin.

"You should have died *months* ago," Ambrosia snarled, her fangs gleaming. "My shadows should have taken care of you. But at least I can watch your life fade in front of my eyes and know that you're dead."

I summoned every ounce of my strength and drove my knee upward. It connected with her stomach, but all she did was flinch. Panic clawed at me as the edges of my vision darkened further.

My wolf howled inside me, the sound echoing through my mind even as my physical voice was silenced. The fae magic within me surged, crackling beneath my skin.

Ambrosia's claws sliced into my throat. My fingers tingled with numbness as I wrenched my arm upward, my hand aiming for Ambrosia's eyes.

She jerked her head back, but my nails scraped her perfect cheek, drawing four crimson lines. The vampire queen hissed, her grip faltering for a split second.

I gasped a shallow breath, not enough, but it was something. The chaos around us blurred—gunfire, snarls, screams—and I focused everything I had on survival.

"You're stronger than I thought," Ambrosia whispered, her tone almost admiring. "Too bad you're not willing to be on the right side." She moved so that one of her knees kept my arm down and her free hand bound the other.

Something had to give, or I'd die.

Ember, Briar linked. *No!*

A blur slammed into Ambrosia from the side, and her grip on my throat vanished as she was knocked sideways. Her body crashed into the concrete wall with enough force to crack the surface.

Ryker stood between us, a savage snarl twisting his features. Blood matted his hair and streaked his face, but his eyes burned with primal fury. He crouched low, and daggers gleamed in both hands.

"Touch her again, and I'll rip you limb from limb."

I dragged in desperate gulps of air. My hand touched my bruised throat, and I felt the trickle of blood running down my chest. The witch's magic still pressed on me like a physical weight, making each movement feel like pushing through mud.

Ambrosia laughed, the sound musical. She straightened and smoothed her lace dress as if we were at a garden party rather than a battlefield.

"I've killed alphas centuries older than you, pup." Ambrosia beamed. "Your little daggers won't even slow me down."

Ryker lunged forward and slashed at her throat. She evaded with barely a shift of her head, her expression bored. His second blade carved through empty air where her heart should have been.

"Too slow," she taunted from behind him.

Ryker spun, but her fist connected with his jaw. The crack echoed through the chamber as he staggered back. Blood trickled from his mouth, but he regained his footing.

I struggled to my knees, still fighting the witch's magical pressure. I couldn't stay down. Not now.

The room spun as I forced myself upright, my vision clearing enough to take in the death and fighting around me. Bodies littered the floor—at least half our people lay motionless, blood pooling beneath them. The survivors fought with desperate ferocity, but the vampires were gaining an edge.

My gaze went to the far corner where Briar huddled, her face pale with shock. Blood soaked one of her sleeves. She pressed her hand against the wound, crimson seeping between her fingers.

Ambrosia's laughter rang out as she dodged another of Ryker's attacks. "Your sister will join you soon enough in death."

Something inside me snapped. The witch's magic still pressed against me, but my focus on Briar broke something loose inside me. If I didn't do *something*, she'd die. And I also had to save Ryker.

My power surged, rage and desperation fueling it beyond the magical restraints. My fingers found the dagger at my hip, and I charged at the vampire targeting my sister.

My dagger sliced through the air. He was fast, but desperation made me faster. The blade sank deep into his neck, hitting the spot where spine met skull. His body went rigid, mouth frozen in a silent scream as I twisted the blade and yanked it out.

Blood spurted from him as he crumpled to the floor.

Ryker's fear spiked, and I spun, dagger still dripping with blood, only to freeze at the sight before me.

Standing with an arm wrapped around Ryker's throat, Ambrosia's other hand tangled in his hair, she wrenched his head to expose his neck.

"No!" I screamed, abandoning my position near Briar.

I sprinted toward them, moving purely on instinct. The dagger in my hand felt like an extension of my arm as I hurled it with all my strength. The blade spun and sliced across Ambrosia's forearm. Her grip on Ryker faltered just enough for him to wrench free.

Ember, stay back, he yelled.

Like hell I would, but even if I wanted to, it was too late.

Her head snapped toward me, and she bared her teeth. "That's fine. I'll let him watch you die first." She moved with blinding speed, crossing the distance between us before I could blink. Her hand clamped around my throat again, lifting me off my feet. She then slammed me against the wall in front of the staircase.

The impact forced the air from my lungs.

"Here, no one can intervene as easily." She smirked. "I'm going to take my time killing you and then make sure your mate suffers pain ten times worse when it's his turn."

I clawed at her hand, desperate for air. My vision wavered, darkening at the edges as Ambrosia's lips curled into a victorious smile.

Still, I'd take it if it meant Ryker would survive. *Run now!*

Like hell. Ryker struggled to his feet, his eyes wide with horror. Blood streamed from a gash on his forehead as he lunged forward, but his legs buckled. He crashed to his knees, still too far away.

"Any last words?" Ambrosia threw her head back and laughed like she'd just told the funniest joke in the world. "No? Okay." She raised her free hand, allowing her nails to lengthen into razor-sharp points. Then she moved to slash at my exposed throat.

A deafening crack split the air, and a millisecond before her claws could connect with skin, her body jerked violently. She dropped me.

My knees hit the concrete and pain erupted on impact, but I looked toward the staircase.

I inhaled sharply, my lungs filling once more as I took in Raven. She lay belly down on the concrete stairs. One of her arms was crooked beneath her while the other stretched out, holding a gun.

A slick ribbon of blood marked her crawl from the upper landing to here. She whispered, "I'm so sorry. I should've done that a long time ago." Then the gun slipped from her fingers and clattered down the steps. Her eyes rolled back, and she went still.

"Raven?" The name rasped from my shredded throat.

No answer—only the slow spreading pool beneath her.

Behind me, Ryker pushed himself upright, disbelief pouring through our bond.

The moment Ambrosia's body hit the floor, a strange hush rippled through the basement, followed by a series of dull thuds.

A few gasps came from the open area where the royal wolves lay, and the battle continued.

Five of the ten remaining guards crumpled where they stood, their guns clattering to the floor.

My stomach flipped. They must have been sired by Ambrosia. And she'd pretended it was illegal to do that. I couldn't help but wonder if anything she'd ever said was true.

Raven just killed the vampire queen, I linked.

There was a pause before Kendric replied, *Raven?*

The surviving vamps broke ranks, some snarling, some bolting for exits. The wolf shifters, who were in animal form, tore into the panicked stragglers.

The witch conducting the spell over our royals still chanted.

Adara's mother stepped to the witch's flank. "I will protect you," she vowed, looking at me but lifting trembling palms as though to shield the ritual.

The witches moved in synch, preparing to attack, but

Ashlyn stepped between them and Adara's mother. The little girl said, "I will not allow you to harm her."

My heart shattered. Out of everyone, I'd truly believed Ashlyn was on our side.

Adara's mother dipped to one knee and snatched a dagger from a dead coven sister at her feet.

Time hinged on a breath.

A wolf shifter lunged, but Ashlyn batted him down.

Adara's mom whipped around and drove her blade into the dangerous witch's back.

The witch gasped and spun around as the magic that seemed to explode from her began to lessen. She swayed on her feet, blood already trickling from her lips. "You betrayed me."

"No, you betrayed us. I only did what I had to do to protect my daughter." Adara's mom grasped the front of her black dress right where her heart was. "I will never forgive myself for what I've done, but I can stop it from happening in the future." She then yanked out the dagger, and the other witch crumpled.

Ashlyn had read her intentions and hadn't betrayed us.

The crushing magical weight evaporated, and air rushed into my lungs. My head spun, and suddenly Ryker was there beside me. He pulled me into his arms, and the buzz of our connection sizzled between us.

Wolves finished off the remaining monsters in seconds. Then—silence.

Uh... Gage connected. *About a quarter of the vampires dropped dead for no reason, and half the others just ran away.*

Same, Xander replied. *We're heading to the basement.*

Our survivors rushed to the royal wolf shifters as panic took over once more.

My mind went to Raven.

Could I save her? She'd ended the war.

I pulled away from Ryker, who tensed.

What are you doing? His eyebrows rose, causing blood to run down his nose from his injury.

I want to try to heal Raven.

I ran up the stairs and dropped beside her.

Her eyes were half-lidded, lips already a waxy blue. Her heartbeat was faint and growing weaker.

"Stay with me," I begged as I slipped my hands into the top of her dress so I could place them over the wound.

Yanking hard, my fae magic spread like wildfire through my veins like it had for Kendric and myself.

Please don't let me be too late.

Ryker slid in beside me, and Briar knelt on my other side, silent, eyes shining. None of us spoke.

The heat exploded through my fingers, but it hit the resistance of what I realized was Raven's vampire essence. The two forces bucked against each other, canceling each other out until nothing but a faint spark remained.

I tried again and again and again until I wound up leaning against the wall in exhaustion. Still, I kept trying. Ryker's arms braced my back, supporting me.

I could feel his worry, and I knew what it meant. He was afraid of what would happen if I couldn't save her but also knew he wouldn't be able to stop me from continuing to try.

"No, no, no—" My tears blurred Raven's face. I poured out everything—my strength, my heartbeat, my hope—until my vision tunneled.

Raven's pulse continued to slip away under my hands.

A sob ripped free. I bowed my head, shoulders shaking, hot tears splattering her blood-slick skin.

Hurried footsteps came down the stairs, and Kendric arrived with Xander on his heels.

Raven's chest hitched.

A ragged gasp scraped past her lips. Her eyes fluttered open, focusing on me, then toward the footsteps.

"Kendric..."

Something shattered in his expression, and he dropped down hard beside us.

"I'm here." His voice cracked.

Raven's fingers twitched. Kendric laced his fingers with hers as his lips pressed into a hard line.

I'm sorry. I sniffled. *I can't save her. I tried.* My head swayed as exhaustion closed in on me once more.

"I was wrong," she whispered. "I thought loyalty mattered more than... than what I felt." She coughed, crimson flecking her mouth. "You made me see her lies." Her gaze moved to Ryker and me. "And neither of you did anything wrong. You shouldn't have trusted me after what I did. Don't carry the guilt."

"Do *not* say goodbye." Kendric shook his head, tears streaking the grime on his cheeks. "We'll see if a witch—"

"It's too late. But listen." Her bottom lip quivered as she took in a rattled breath. "I did love you. That part was real."

A sob tore from him. "And I love you. I'm sorry I didn't listen."

A faint smile curved her lips. "Worth it." Her fingers slipped from his. The last breath left her in a soft exhale. Stillness settled.

Something inside me caved. The fae fire that had been keeping me upright flickered, drained by the failed healing. I lay my head on my mate's chest.

"Ember." Ryker's hold tightened.

The world rocked, and I pressed into his chest as Briar's

cool hand touched my cheek, distant voices echoing.

"I—I tried," I mumbled, eyelids too heavy to lift. "I'm sorry." The guilt crashed over me, even though Raven had told me not to let it.

You did more than enough, Briar linked, kissing my cheek. "Rest, sis."

Through the bond, Ryker's fear bled into relief as he cradled me. *Rest, lil rebel. I've got you.*

More footsteps raced down the stairs, yet I couldn't make out who it was. But then I heard Adara scream, "Mom!"

Darkness swept in—quiet, painless. The last thing I felt was Ryker's heartbeat thundering against my ear and Kendric's broken cry carrying Raven's name into the silence.

***

One week later

The setting sun blossomed in beautiful colors—pinks, purples, and oranges, cast over the royal graveyard at the very edge of the Grimstone pack territory.

Fresh earth stretched in tidy rows, and Kendric laid the first white rose on Raven's granite stone. It was one of many denoting the true warriors who'd fallen in the war. For the first time ever, people outside of the royal family had been buried among them.

The recovering wolf shifter King Harry had decided that those who'd fought the night that he and his daughter had been saved would be buried alongside the twenty royal family members who hadn't survived, including the witches and Raven.

Kendric stood, squaring his shoulders, but the pain and

regret haunted him so much that his skin seemed to sag from his bones. He didn't speak; he didn't have to because every single one of us knew what he felt.

Briar followed with a sprig of lavender and placed it on the tombstone of King Harry's brother.

King Harry and Princess Liv laid an intricate floral collage over the queen's stone.

More survivors moved forward to show their respect to the dead, including the witches.

Ryker's hand slid into mine. Guilt still sat heavy under my ribs, but it had begun to shape itself into something useful. Every morning since the battle, Ryker and I had shifted and run the Grimstone perimeter twice, determining how we could best support the king and bring true peace between shifters and the remaining vampires.

Our pack and the witches who'd fought with us had remained at the palace, including Ashlyn. Reid and Sun had gone home to take care of their pack after losing half of them. The fact that Ryker, Sun, Reid, and I had managed to forge a new alliance between us would make things go so much easier.

Similarly, Bruce had gone home to his own pack to ease the turmoil there.

Life was slowly settling into this new normal, but we still had to define it.

When the last shovel tamped the soil, Kendric cleared his throat.

"She saved more lives than she took," he said, voice steady. "That's the story I'll tell. And I loved her."

"And we will always be grateful." King Harry limped up to Kendric and patted his arm. "She helped us truly turn the tide."

The king then spoke of the rest of the dead and broke

down at the end when he had to say goodbye to his wife—his fated mate. The other half of his soul.

The strange warm tingle that always happened when Many-Greats-Grandfather was watching me raised the hair on my neck. But I didn't bother looking for him. I now understood I'd only see him if he wanted me to, and when he did, he would always appear in front of me.

When the ceremony was over, Ryker led me back to our new home, Briar on my other side.

Kendric, Gage, and Xander stayed behind with King Harry and his daughter, seeing them back home to the palace.

The Grimstones' reputation had been restored and, per the king, had always and would always be the protectors of the royal family. The declaration had meant the world to Ryker, and I felt him start to believe he was worthy. And I loved being part of his story and watching him lead like he was meant to.

I say we do some baking when we get back. Briar took my hand. *The family favorite. I think it's time to share it with our new pack.*

I smiled as both sadness and joy competed inside me. Sadness that Mom and Dad couldn't be here with us, but joyful to share this special dessert with our new pack.

Sounds like a great time, I replied, knowing that Briar would be with me, helping me make it.

I remembered Raven's words from that night in the SUV when she'd been driving while I'd tried to save a dying Ryker. The meaning finally clicked. We did need to enjoy the time we had and relish the moments that made us smile. Life was too short, even if we were immortal. And I would spend the rest of my life appreciating them, with the people I loved by my side.

ABOUT THE AUTHOR

Jen L. Grey is a *USA Today* Bestselling Author who writes Paranormal Romance, Urban Fantasy, and Fantasy genres.

Jen lives in Tennessee with her husband, two daughters, and three miniature Australian Shepherds. Before she began writing, she was an avid reader and enjoyed being involved in the indie community. Her love for books eventually led her to writing. For more information, please visit her website and sign up for her newsletter.

Check out her future projects and book signing events at her website.
www.jenlgrey.com

Fated To Darkness

The King of Frost and Shadows

The Court of Thorns and Wings

The Kingdom of Flames and Ash

Rejected Fate Trilogy

Betrayed Mate

Cursed Magic

Wicked Fate

Fated To Darkness

The King of Frost and Shadows

The Court of Thorns and Wings

The Kingdom of Flames and Ash

The Forbidden Mate Trilogy

Wolf Mate

Wolf Bitten

Wolf Touched

Standalone Romantasy

Of Shadows and Fae

Twisted Fate Trilogy

Destined Mate

Eclipsed Heart

Chosen Destiny

The Marked Dragon Prince Trilogy

Ruthless Mate

Marked Dragon

Hidden Fate

Shadow City: Silver Wolf Trilogy

Broken Mate

Rising Darkness

Silver Moon

Shadow City: Royal Vampire Trilogy

Cursed Mate

Shadow Bitten

Demon Blood

Shadow City: Demon Wolf Trilogy

Ruined Mate

Shattered Curse

Fated Souls

Shadow City: Dark Angel Trilogy

Fallen Mate

Demon Marked

Dark Prince

Fatal Secrets

Shadow City: Silver Mate

Shattered Wolf

Fated Hearts

Ruthless Moon

The Wolf Born Trilogy

Hidden Mate

Blood Secrets

Awakened Magic

The Hidden King Trilogy

Dragon Mate

Dragon Heir

Dragon Queen

The Marked Wolf Trilogy

Moon Kissed

Chosen Wolf

Broken Curse

Wolf Moon Academy Trilogy

Shadow Mate

Blood Legacy

Rising Fate

The Royal Heir Trilogy

Dawning Ascent

Enlightened Ascent

Reigning Ascent

Stand Alones

Death's Angel

Rising Alpha

9 798888 531890